NEVER
LET
GO

NEVER LET GO

Lori Duffy Foster

LEVEL
BEST BOOKS

For Angie, my sister and best friend

Praise for Never Let Go

"A dark and suspenseful page-turner about obsession and betrayal, from a veteran storyteller. I couldn't put it down. Highly recommended."—William Landay, bestselling author of *All That Is Mine I Carry With Me*

"How far would you go, what would you be willing to do, to find your stolen baby? Never Let Go is a compulsively readable tale of old feuds, secret jealousies, and a long-ago murder. Author Lori Duffy Foster takes us on an exciting journey of high stakes and high suspense. Unforgettable!"—Gayle Lynds, *New York Times* bestselling author of *The Assassins*

"Once I started reading, I could not put this well-written and fast-paced drama down. ... There were so many plot twists that kept me in the game and when I thought I was on firm grounds with where the narrative was going, the author changed the direction all to keep me emotionally invested as the drama unfolded to its conclusion."—Dru Ann Love of *Dru's Book Musing*, Raven Award winner and two-time Anthony Award Nominee

Chapter One

She had filled the tub as high as she dared, yet her naked belly broke the surface, a pale and soft island in the stillness of the water. Her fingers trembled as she ran them along the exposed skin. Friends had warned her that it would take months for her abdomen to tighten again, but she hadn't believed them. Six months after giving birth to Christopher, and she still had a bit of dough. Now she was glad for it. It reminded her he was out there. Her baby was real, and he was alive. If she died, he would still live. But as soon as his image came to mind, the ceiling and the walls began closing in around her. The air grew thin and hot. Christopher crying. Christopher hungry. Christopher cold and alone. She gripped the edges of the tub and jerked her body into a sitting position, gasping for air.

"What do you think you're doing?"

The accusation echoed off the concrete walls that caged her in the small, rectangular room. The water had been so soothing she'd nearly forgotten where she was. How could she do that? How could she forget for even one second that she was trapped here, sealed in this room with no windows and only a small vent for air? Her breath came rapidly now, and she struggled to slow it down, counting a new rhythm in her head. Was she losing her mind already? She could not let that happen. She grabbed for the towel she had set on the toilet cover and stood quickly, fumbling with the rough terry cloth as she wrapped it around her body, unsure where to look as she spoke.

"It's just...I just...my muscles hurt, my chest hurt, everything. I thought it might help."

Her voice quivered, and she hoped it wasn't obvious. She didn't want to

1

show her fear. Or maybe she should. Maybe that was what Rachel wanted. Maybe Rachel needed to witness her desperation. It hurt so badly, this intense need to hold her baby, to caress his soft skin, and breathe in his newness. The pain exhausted her, overwhelmed her. She was certain she would break inside under the force of it all and collapse within herself. His six-month birthday was yesterday. She pulled the towel more tightly around her body and stared at the stained and cracked floor, fighting to regain control of her emotions, fighting off the claustrophobia and the panic that came with it.

"Did you have a good soak?"

The faceless voice that boomed from a speaker mounted high in a corner was once welcome and familiar to Carla. It was a whisper of conspiracy in the dark when they were ten years old and sneaking downstairs late at night for ice cream. It was a call from a cafeteria table, giving her direction and a sense of belonging on the first day of junior high. It was the harmony as they sang with their playlists on the drive to the movie theater on a Saturday night. But this voice had changed. This voice was thick with confidence, control, and loathing. It was terrifying. Carla didn't know *this* Rachel.

"Remember that spa we went to for your sixteenth birthday?" Rachel said, a little more kindly now. "Just you and me? Your mom dropped us off with a boatload of money for the whole day. That was nice, relaxing in those massage chairs with cucumbers on our eyes and mud on our faces. We went out to dinner after the spa, and the waiter brought you a piece of cake with a candle in it. Remember that, Carla? Your mom loved me. She liked having me around. That's why she sent me with you, because she loved me like a daughter. It was like she was giving me a present, too."

Carla closed her eyes and took deep, slow breaths. She focused on steadying her voice despite the weakness in her legs and the tremors in her hands. This was a good memory, a connection. Rachel had to be insane. Why else would she do this? Maybe she had ghosts in her childhood Carla didn't know about. Was Rachel's mother abusive in some way? She couldn't remember. They spent most of their time at Carla's house as kids because Carla was an only child and Rachel shared a bedroom with her older sister, but it never occurred to Carla there might be another reason. If she was abused, the fact that Carla became a mother recently might have stirred something awful, some horrible memories she had never shared, never spoken about. Maybe not to anyone. Carla's mother was always good to Rachel. Maybe that was the key, the way out of this dungeon.

"You and my mom, you got along well. She's probably worried sick, Rachel. Did you tell her I'm okay?" Carla focused on the camera, which was mounted under a clear Plexiglas dome in the center of the ceiling. "Did you tell her where I am? You don't want to hurt her, do you? You need to let me go."

Carla kept her eyes trained on the camera as she stepped out of the tub, her legs still shaky. She wasn't sure why she had filled the tub and climbed into it. She'd done it without thinking. Once it was full, she was drawn into the water with visions of turning it red, of slitting her wrists and ending the nightmare in its warmth. It would all be over. No more pain. No more panic. No more fear. But there were three problems with her plan: The tiny room was void of anything sharp, a camera followed her every move, and she didn't really want to die. As long as she remained alive, so did the chance she would get out of this place and hold Christopher in her arms once more.

"Your mom?" Rachel laughed. "She deserves to suffer a little. She's a bitch, Carla. You know that. She never cared about you. You were a clumsy introvert with your nose always stuck in a book. You were an embarrassment to her. Having me around? That's what made you bearable to her. Think, Carla. I'm the only one who ever cared about you. Not even Nick cares, really. He'll forget about you as soon as someone else spreads her legs for him, but don't worry. I won't let him hook up with just anyone. I'll make sure it's me. It was always me he wanted. You seduced Nick and confused him, and now we have to fix this. It'll work out, and we'll all be happier, even you. I'm doing this because I love you. You're scared now, and you don't understand, but you'll see."

Carla breathed longer and deeper, keeping the tears at bay. She'd read about this after one of those famous kidnappings, about how kidnappers like to make their victims feel emotionally and physically isolated. They degrade them and destroy them to make them submissive and dependent.

3

That's what Rachel was trying to do by saying her mother didn't love her and by telling her, Nick didn't care about her either. Rachel had already succeeded in making her physically isolated and dependent, and now she was working on the emotional part. She would not let her win. Carla sank down onto the twin mattress on the floor, just a few feet from the tub, and covered her face with her free hand. What did Rachel want? Did she want to see her cry? Did she want her to get angry? Did she want her to agree? She could do those things. She could fake it. She would do anything to get out of there. But she didn't know what to do or say, and she was tired of trying to figure it out, so very tired.

"I was going to send you in some breakfast," Rachel said, "but I've changed my mind. You have to learn to respect me, or we'll never get anywhere. I don't think you realize how much I do for you. This whole thing wasn't easy. But maybe after you've gone hungry long enough, you'll understand you need my permission to take a bath. I have to get to work now, and I've got to go see that husband of yours. He's pretty distraught, you know, since his wife took off with their baby. He needs me right now."

Carla flew up from the mattress.

"No, no! Don't leave me again." She pleaded with the camera, hoping Rachel would meet her eyes and see her, really see her. Her heart quickened and her chest, already aching, felt like it might break. She couldn't breathe. What if she ran out of air? Out of water? There was no way out. It was a concrete grave. She didn't care how desperate she looked. She'd do anything, anything at all, to keep Rachel there. She couldn't bear to be left alone again.

"Talk to me. That's all. I'll be good. I need to hear your voice. Please, Rachel. You are my friend, too. If it's Nick you want, you can have him. I'll divorce him. I'll never speak to him again. Please, just don't leave me alone. I'm scared. I won't tell anybody. I'll say I ran away, that I had a breakdown or something. You won't get in any trouble. I promise."

"That's not going to work, Carla. I've been thinking about this a long time. You need to trust me. I know what I'm doing. You weren't happy. You said it yourself. You gave up your dreams for Nick. You settled here in this lousy little town when all you ever wanted was a studio in Manhattan. Maybe you could have been a famous editor by now. Maybe you still can be. But I like this little town, and I love Nick."

"No. That was a long time ago. Rachel. Come back here, Rachel!"

Carla stared at the speaker and willed Rachel's voice to flow through it, but she heard nothing. Rachel was gone, and Carla was alone and helpless. The door was sealed. There were no windows to pry open. The room itself was no bigger than a generous walk-in closet. She had no TV, radio, or phone. No way to communicate with anyone. Rachel could forget about her, or get in a car accident, or have a heart attack, or anything, and no one would know Carla was here. She would die, here alone in this room, of starvation. There had to be a way out.

Carla let the towel drop from her frame and rushed for the door, slamming her body against it. She had to get out. Now. Her breath came hard and heavy, and her palms were wet with sweat. There was no handle, and she could see no hinges. Just the outline of the door itself. The thin cracks were sealed with a rubbery substance or silicone, probably from the outside. Rachel wouldn't have had much time to seal Carla in before the drugs wore off, so quick-drying silicone was probably her only choice. She had bragged that police had searched the basement and found nothing, so she couldn't have covered the door with concrete block and fresh mortar. It would have been too obvious, still wet. So maybe that was it. Maybe it was nothing more than a silicone-sealed door that kept her in, possibly with heavy shelving or furniture in front of it. But she had nothing to dig at it with, and her nails were useless. She had already worn them down so much that her fingers bled. She pounded and pounded, praying someone would hear her, but Rachel had already assured her that was impossible. The room was soundproofed.

Carla turned and looked around the room. She knew she was in Rachel's basement. Rachel had told her that much. She built the room herself as soon as she found out Carla was pregnant, sneaking concrete blocks and insulation into the house a little at a time so she wouldn't arouse suspicion. She learned how to soundproof it on the internet. She left the original walls concrete block but had painted them white. The toilet, sink, and tub were already here, a gift from the last owner. The former owner had started to frame the bathroom in, but those boards were gone now, removed to create seamless, rectangular living space. Carla could get from the mattress to the toilet in nine steps if not for the battered armchair that filled the space between them. Rachel had talked about finishing the basement, creating the female equivalent of a man cave, but this wasn't at all what Carla had imagined.

From the location of the toilet, Carla could imagine where the room was located in relation to the rest of the house. She knew the sealed door led to the remainder of the basement and that the rest of the walls in her room were exterior walls with no extra reinforcement or soundproofing. That was no consolation, though, since this part of the basement was fully underground. She would have to break concrete and dig through several yards of soil to escape, and Rachel would see that from the camera. There were no windows in here, but the other half of the basement was not entirely underground. There was one small window on each side of the stairs, which rose up to the foyer. If Carla could open this door and push through whatever soundproofing covered it on the other side, she could probably slip through one of those windows or escape up the stairs. Maybe not, though. They were quarter windows, and the openings might be too small, and then Rachel might come downstairs and kill her. Would she kill her? Would she go that far? Was Rachel capable of killing? Carla would never get past this door anyway.

On a flat, LED screen mounted on the exterior wall, an older man in a polo shirt and khaki shorts walked a terrier of some kind. Carla was tempted to call out to him, but she had to remind herself he wasn't really there. He had walked his dog past Rachel's house at this time one year ago. The constantly rolling video was a source of pride for Rachel. When she came up with this plan, just days after Carla told her she was pregnant, she started recording the view through her living room window night and day. By the time she kidnapped Carla, she had recorded a full year's worth. So, she set the time and day to match exactly the time and day this year and kept it running nonstop. It was just like looking out a window, she bragged, except everything Carla saw was from the prior year. Rachel said it would give her a sense of time and of the seasons because she might be locked up for a long time, and Rachel knew Carla would need something to occupy her mind. A year. That was how much she had recorded, just in case. So, she was prepared to lock Carla up for a year.

Each day, she saw Rachel come and go on the video, always at different times—sometimes when the sun was strong, other times when it was low in the sky—and each time, she wondered: Did I meet her for coffee that day? Did we talk on the phone, exchange text messages? Did I stop by her office? Is she leaving now to meet with me, or is she returning from dinner together or from a meet-up at the gym? Rachel had been planning this since the day Carla told her she was pregnant, and Carla never knew, never even suspected.

Carla wanted to break the screen, to throw something at it, if only because Rachel was so proud of what she'd done. But she had to admit she needed it. It had been only four days, and already she was going out of her mind. Rachel had also left her a jigsaw puzzle, but she couldn't bring herself to touch it. It was hard enough just to make her body move. She passed some of the time with sit-ups and push-ups, figuring she'd better keep up her strength in case she got the opportunity to escape. But she spent most of each day sitting in that dingy old armchair, staring at that screen, biding her time until she could lie on the mattress and try once again to sleep. Who knew four days could be so long? She found herself staring now as she let her body slide against the door and fall to the ground. Her leg rubbed against the narrow opening at the bottom of the door that Rachel slid her meals through. Carla had tried reaching through that, too, but Rachel pushed the trays through with some kind of stick or device. The opening was about a foot wide and only about three inches high, and after she served her, Rachel blocked it again with something that wouldn't budge.

She tried saving the squat cup or the plastic tray, thinking they might prove useful, but Rachel always demanded them back before she would give her more. She never gave her any tableware, forcing her to eat with her fingers, and the cups were made of paper and held only a few ounces of water. Carla had barely touched the food over the past four days, but now she wished she had. What if Rachel decided never to feed her again? What if she let her starve? She had to find a way out, but how? Thanks to that camera, she was always on display and, as tempted as she was to disable it somehow, she knew that would likely get her killed. She'd like to think Rachel wouldn't do that, that she wasn't capable of anything so horrendous, but Carla didn't know this Rachel. She didn't dare assume anything.

Carla drew her knees to her chest, in part for the psychological comfort of the position, but also because her breasts were sore and had started leaking again, and the pressure of her knees on them felt good. They weren't hard like they had been for the first two days, and they were far less painful, but they still leaked, sometimes heavily, several times a day. Her body was so confused. She wasn't ready to stop nursing Christopher. She just wasn't. She buried her head in her knees and remained there, naked and curled up against the door, until the lights started to dim, indicating it was bedtime. She didn't want to break another rule. She was already getting so hungry it hurt. So she uncurled her body, grabbed the t-shirt, underwear, and sweatpants she had left on the floor when she bathed, dressed, and threw herself down on the bed. This time, even though she fought it, she slept, waking only to scream for her baby.

Chapter Two

The lawn needed mowing, and the garden needed weeding. The natural pine porch needed a coating of sealant. They'd neglected their outdoor duties this summer in favor of time with their baby. They were "those" parents, comparing his milestones to average babies and relishing the fact that he'd beaten them all. They knew all his expressions, all his cries, all his giggles. He was an Einstein. He was an artist. He would be the country's next president. He would fall in love and be happy, like they were. He was perfect.

Nick sat in the driveway with the car running and his foot on the brake, waiting for the heavy, wooden garage door to open. For this instant, he could pretend Carla's Subaru would be there in the other bay with the rear-facing car seat in the back, the one they'd bought when she was seven months pregnant. He could pretend she was in the house, cradling the baby in one arm while she worked on dinner—some new recipe she'd found on a health blog. Her laptop would be open on the desk in the corner of the family room, where she would have spent part of her day working on a freelance piece even though she always said she didn't have time. She would eventually sell the piece for just a few dollars or in exchange for copies of the journal, but that would help her keep a foot in the door in case she ever decided to return to the magazine.

Nick swallowed hard. Carla was like that, always doing too many things at once, never slowing down, afraid she'd miss something if she did. She'd been lost since she left work to stay home with the baby, and she'd started talking about going back part time. But she couldn't figure out a way to do it. Her full-time job as an editor and staff writer had required frequent trips to New York City and, even though her managing editor had said she could work from home after the baby was born, she knew he would expect her to travel again eventually. She couldn't leave Christopher overnight like that, at least not yet. Carla went over and over the scenarios during breakfast, at the dinner table, in the middle of the night when she couldn't sleep, ways she might be able to make it work, but she just couldn't do it.

She was unhappy about her job, but she had options, and she chose to be home with Christopher. Nick had made it clear that he supported her, regardless of her choice, hadn't he? What good would it do to take off? What would she have gained? If she wanted to work full time again, she could find a job here. There were a couple regional magazines and plenty of freelance opportunities. It wasn't like she made a bundle in her old job anyway. Nick didn't tell the police how she felt about work. It would have given them more reason to believe she'd simply run away. They didn't know her like he did. Nick closed his eyes and listened to the creaking and shuddering of the garage door as it lifted. Then he opened them again. Her side of the garage was empty. No wife. No baby. The moment was gone.

The century-old cape they'd bought together four months before they married felt dark and cold, despite the warm June sun. He threw his keys on the kitchen counter and sat on a barstool, resting his elbows on the granite and his head in his hands. Their wedding picture hung on the wall across the room, and he couldn't help studying it. They were so young then. Long reddish-blond tendrils framed Carla's freckled face as she looked up at him like no one else mattered. In her hands was a bouquet of orchids, her favorite flowers. His own six-foot-three frame still had that boyish, boney look. He was grinning right back at her with his arm snuggly around her shoulders. They had changed physically over the years. Their bodies had softened slightly. Their skin had grown a little more weathered. His hair was thinning. But she was still gorgeous and funny and kind. And she still looked at him that way sometimes, the way she did on their wedding day.

For three days, he'd tried to convince the police something was wrong, that Carla would never leave him. For three days, they insisted she was having a post-partum crisis of some sort and that she would come home eventually. But she didn't and, last night, when a junkyard owner found her Subaru on the fringe of his lot, they finally listened. They listened while Nick sat across the table in a bare-walled room with nothing to eat or drink for six hours, answering their questions. They watched while he took a polygraph test. They lectured, telling him the tests were unreliable and that they would be watching him closely until his wife and baby were found. And then, out of nowhere, they released him.

The "good" cop in this whole routine handed him a business card and assured him this was all normal, that they had to rule him out as a suspect, or they wouldn't be doing their jobs. He promised he'd call if he heard anything new and that he'd do his best to get a plea for information in the news. The infant seat was missing from the car, but the base remained. No diaper bag was left behind. No purse either. That gave Nick a little comfort. Wherever she was, she and Christopher were together, and she'd had time to take what she needed. He could not think about the worst. Not yet. They were alive. He needed to believe that, and the missing diaper bag and purse were evidence in his favor. The police were not convinced of foul play, but at least they were considering it now. They agreed with Nick that it would be unusual for someone who ran away to ditch her car less than ten miles from home.

"We'll use the photo of her with the baby," the investigator said. "It's better than separate photos. Everybody loves babies."

So, Nick knew he wouldn't see Carla's Subaru when the garage opened moments ago. He knew he would not find Carla inside cooking dinner. He knew baby Christopher would not be in her arms. He knew, but he couldn't help hoping.

He lifted his head and looked around the room. All he wanted was sleep, but he couldn't bring himself to try. Not now. Not when the state police finally had a reason to look for them. He reached for the remote and turned on the small television that looked down on him from a swivel mount where the breakfast bar met the wall. He didn't want to miss the news. He thought about calling his own parents with an update, but he couldn't convince his hand to pick up the phone. He didn't really want to talk to anyone anyway. He'd already put flyers up all over town and the surrounding communities. It was a tight-knit area. Everybody knew everybody in this part of New York State just south of the Finger Lakes. People were born here, and they died here. The only exceptions were the few outsiders who were attracted to the quaintness of Maplewood Falls with its Victorian homes and well-kept downtown and brought their dreams for unique cafes, antique shops, and used books stores with them. If anyone local had seen her or Christopher, they would have called, and he needed to stay just in case she called or walked through the door.

He could check his email. He'd posted on all the social networking sites he could think of, and his pleas had spread like crazy. Unfortunately, they had only attracted sympathizers and crazies so far. A guy in England said Carla was working as a stripper in a club in his neighborhood. A woman from Detroit claimed she was her long-lost daughter. A couple of people accused him of driving her away with too much sex, too little sex, or by having affairs while she was pregnant. A few others accused him of abuse. Two women offered to marry him if she didn't come back. He couldn't weed through all that now. He just couldn't deal with the disappointment he knew he would feel when he saw that nothing of value was there, nothing at all, despite all those messages and all the people who had shared his post.

He brought up the guide on the television. No news for another hour. Coffee. That was what he needed. He moved through the kitchen without thinking, without feeling, and poured the old coffee from the pot into the sink. Then he refilled the reservoir and reached for a new filter. Empty. Of course. Everyone who had come by in the past few days had made a fresh pot of coffee. It made them feel useful. He didn't want it then, but he did now, and the filters were gone. He was arranging a paper towel in the filter's place, relieved to have a task, when the doorbell rang. For a moment, he let himself think it. He imagined her walking in, swinging the infant carrier, laughing, and telling a story about some crazy mix-up that took her on a four-day journey with no means of communication. But then he remembered she wouldn't ring the doorbell. Carla would simply walk in. This was her home.

Nick sucked in a long, deep breath and opened the door.

"You look positively awful."

Rachel pushed past Nick holding a tray with two coffees in one hand and a paper bag in the other. Her leather purse had slipped from her shoulder to the crook of her arm, and she shut the door behind her with her foot. With a tilt of her head, she shook her hair, dyed the deepest black and cut into a smooth shoulder-length bob, from her face and handed the tray to Nick. She looked tired as well, pale despite her red lipstick and thick mascara. She was perfectly dressed, though, as always, wearing a sleeveless top that was tailored to her body and capris that tapered mid-calf. He could never understand how they were friends—Carla and Rachel. Carla was nothing like that. She preferred comfortable clothes—jeans and a sweater in the winter, shorts and a t-shirt in the summer—and only the slightest trace of make-up on her skin. Carla was quiet and contained while Rachel was loud and brash. Carla savored her pregnancy while Rachel had seemed appalled by Carla's growing belly.

"I'd have brought beer or wine, but it's a bit early for that," Rachel said, setting the bag on the breakfast bar and reaching inside. She pulled out a cranberry-orange scone, tucked a napkin underneath it, and handed it to him.

Nick sat at the stool he had vacated only moments before and took the scone while Rachel freed a coffee from the tray and placed it in front of him. Rachel had come by every day since Carla disappeared, always anticipating his needs. She could be draining, but he had to admit she'd been a great help. She was also the last person to see Carla, which gave Nick a little extra tolerance for her. She and Carla had lunch together the day Carla disappeared. Carla was excited about it. She told Nick that Rachel had suggested take-out at her house because she wanted Carla to be comfortable and not worry about possibly leaving a restaurant if the baby acted up. That was a huge step for Rachel, who had always expressed frustration over babies in public places and had never even held Christopher. The old Rachel would have suggested hiring a sitter or going out for drinks when Nick was home to take Christopher off her hands, forgetting that Carla was nursing.

Nick's last conversation with Carla was still fresh in his mind. It was seven in the morning. She was standing in this very kitchen in baggy pajamas pants, a white tank top, and bare feet, looking sexier than ever. He wanted her right then and there, but the days of that kind of spontaneity were over, at least for a while. The baby was hungry, and he had to get to work. Still, that image of her had distracted him all morning and afternoon. He left work early, hoping to find her at home.

Carla had already been up with Christopher for two hours that morning, yet she seemed full of energy. She floated around the kitchen, grabbing a plastic bowl with a rubber suction cup on the bottom and a rubber-coated spoon, stopping only for a quick sip of decaffeinated coffee. He watched as she filled the bowl with baby cereal and poured warm breast milk over it, mixing the two together gently and then taking it to Christopher, who reached out from his highchair in anticipation. As she fed Christopher, Carla insisted Rachel was warming up to the baby, that she had been asking about him more and was interested in hearing about his milestones. She had even brought over an outfit a few days before. But Nick was skeptical. People shouldn't have to "warm up" to their best friend's babies, he said. He figured Rachel invited Carla to her house because she didn't want to be seen in a restaurant with a baby, not because it was more convenient for Carla.

"Oh, come on," Carla had said without taking her eyes off Christopher. While Carla scooped the sticky paste with the tiny spoon, Christopher dipped his hands into the bowl, squeezing cereal between his fingers with a squeal. Nick reached over with a napkin to remove a chunk from Carla's waves, which were falling in her face. It was a gesture he'd been replaying in his mind ever since.

"Give her a break. She's trying," she'd said.

Nick sighed.

"You are a much better person than I am," he said.

Then he kissed her on her cheek and kissed Christopher on the top of his warm head and went out the door like he had on every other day. That was it. His last conversation with his wife, but Rachel was with her later that day. She told the police she picked up Chinese food from their favorite place and

14

arrived home at noon to find Carla and the baby already waiting on the front stoop. The baby was in his car seat, and he was fussy. Carla was sitting on the top stair with him beside her, rocking him, when Rachel approached. Carla seemed distracted while they ate, hardly touching her food, Rachel said. She checked her cell phone every few minutes and ignored the baby when he cried, which was unlike her. Then Carla took off with him in a hurry after lunch, saying she needed to get to a dentist appointment. A neighbor also saw her leave and agreed that she seemed rushed. Nick checked with their dentist, and so did the police. There was no dentist appointment. She'd just had a cleaning a month before, and there were no issues.

Rachel gestured to the scone, which Nick had barely acknowledged.

"Eat. You need it. You don't want to be all weak and broken down when she comes home, do you? You don't know what you might have to deal with." She pulled a scone out for herself and took a small bite. "She can't hide forever, especially with the baby. They'll find her. Eventually, she'll have to take out some money or use a credit card, and when she does, they'll have a better idea where she might be."

Rachel covered her mouth with her hand.

"I'm sorry," she said. "I know she wouldn't leave you, but I would rather believe that she did. It's easier, you know, to think that she needed a break and will come back any minute with Christopher in tow, feeling refreshed and ready to deal with the world again. It's a good thought, a positive one."

Rachel didn't know about the car, Nick thought. She would soon. The police would have to question her again. He should tell her. She'd be angry when she found out he knew this morning and said nothing. But he couldn't. He was too worn out, and he didn't have the energy to explain. It was going to take all he had left to call the store and let Malcolm know he'd be out for at least another few days. He'd have to give him a bonus when all this was over. Nick was lucky to have a manager like Malcolm, someone he could trust to run the place in his absence. Malcolm was just fifteen and a bagger when Nick inherited the store all those years ago, but he learned fast, and he was good with people. He wasn't so good with inventory, but Nick could stop by and take care of that when the store was closed. He didn't want to see anybody now, especially not his employees. He just wanted to see his wife and baby.

"You weren't here when I came by last night." Rachel had almost finished her scone, which she washed down with coffee. "I was worried."

Nick curled both hands around the thick paper coffee cup, drawing from its warmth. He didn't want to lie. He hated to lie, but he needed Rachel to leave, and she would have all kinds of questions if he told her. He wanted to be alone. Soon, he would have to face reality again, but he wasn't ready for it just yet.

"I had stuff to take care of. I can't live like this forever, doing nothing. Look," he said, gesturing toward the coffee maker. "I'm running out of everything. I don't even have filters for coffee. If you hadn't come by, I'd be drinking paper towel fibers right now."

Rachel placed a hand on his shoulder and rubbed it gently. Something about her touch made Nick uneasy. It was too familiar. She was Carla's friend, but he'd always felt uncomfortable around her. He wasn't sure why. She'd had a crush on him in high school, but that was nearly two decades ago when they were freshmen. She'd gotten over that long before he started dating Carla. Maybe because it was always just Rachel, or Rachel with some new guy, while all their other friends were halves of couples. He'd never known Rachel to have a long-term boyfriend, but then again, he'd never paid much attention. He usually tuned her out and let Carla do the talking and the listening. Mostly listening.

"Poor guy. You look tired. You need some rest. I hate to take my coffee and run, but I'll come back tonight with a few groceries and some dinner, okay?" Rachel stood with her coffee and grabbed her purse. "You have my cell number. Call me if you hear anything at all. I mean that. I'm here for you."

"Rachel, I'd rather you didn't. You're doing too much, and I'll be fine."

She leaned over and gave him a peck on his cheek, and for a moment, he thought he caught a whiff of his wife's perfume. But it was just his mind playing tricks on him. He wanted her back so badly he was imagining her scent. He heard the front door shut and immediately, the house was empty again. As Rachel's car engine started, Nick was distracted by another sound, the introduction to the morning news. Hers was the fourth story, and the investigator was right about the choice of photo. The picture of Carla with the baby was perfect. Nick dropped his head into his hands and cried.

Chapter Three

The air was warm, the sun was bright, and the weekend was about to begin. Sawyer Hamill parked his patrol car in a vacant lot off Main Street and waited. It wouldn't be long before somebody towing a motorboat flew through town at sixty miles an hour, too impatient to slow down for the two-mile stretch. He had no regrets about leaving the Syracuse police force four years ago to become chief in Maplewood Falls, but if he could negotiate his terms again, he'd find a way to get out of issuing traffic tickets. Between the obnoxious drivers and the paperwork, it was the task he dreaded most.

He yawned and stretched, draping one arm over the open driver-side window. The early summer air felt good. Sitting in his car watching traffic wasn't helping him stay awake. He'd been up all night, listening and watching behind a two-way mirror as state police questioned his former classmate in the disappearance of his baby and his wife, who was another classmate. He hadn't planned to stay so long, but he couldn't bring himself to leave. As an eight-person force, the Maplewood Falls police department had to turn more complicated investigations over to the state police. His department didn't have the resources for something like this. But it was still his case in a way, in his hometown, involving two of his friends. How could he not stay?

Until they found the car, state police investigators had been working under the theory that Carla Murphy had run off with the baby. She had no known enemies and no stalkers that anyone knew of. She didn't do drugs, and she had made no other obvious lifestyle choices that would have put her in jeopardy. If she had simply run off, their disappearance would be a civil case since Carla and Nick were not divorced and had equal rights to their child. Police would get involved only if they felt she was a danger to herself or the baby. But the car changed things. Someone had ditched it in that junkyard, hoping it wouldn't be found. Carla could be that someone. Maybe she was afraid they'd issue Amber Alerts and that she might get pulled over, so she got rid of it and found another way out of town. But it had been four days, and she still hadn't used her cell phone or any debit or credit cards. She had not even hinted to anyone that she might take off and the only one who noticed any odd behavior was Rachel, who was odd to begin with.

Then there was Nick. He held up well during the questioning, but state police let him believe he didn't. Polygraph tests aren't entirely reliable. Some people are just good liars, so they wanted to keep him on edge. Just a bit. The tactic could work either way. Some people mess up when they think they are safe. They get cocky and careless. Others are motivated to make mistakes by fear. They work harder to cover things up and lead police right to the evidence. The investigators sensed that if Nick was involved in their disappearance, he was the second type. But Sawyer knew Nick, and he knew Carla. Something was wrong here. The state investigators were missing a bigger piece of the puzzle. He doubted he would get much sleep at all until he figured it out.

Sawyer's eyes drifted from the road to the half-eaten bag of butterscotch candies on the seat beside him. He had promised himself he would cut back on sugar. Heather had said he was setting a poor example for the kids. She was right, but he needed it today. Just one candy to help him stay awake. He unwrapped a piece and was about to pop it into his mouth when a tiny voice intervened.

"Daddy, we brought you lunch."

There, outside his patrol car window, was Andy, just tall enough to rest his chin on the window frame, holding up a brown paper bag with his six-year-old fingers. His seven-year-old sister Sophie was right behind him. Bryce, who was a month shy of four, pulled his hand from Heather's and ran toward the patrol car. Sawyer slipped the candy back into the bag and reached for the lunch. The summer sun was always good to Heather. It was only June, and already, her skin had bronzed, and her brown waves had taken on a coppery hue. She wore a tank top and shorts, but he could see the strings of her bikini tied around her neck. Three kids later and she still turned heads when she walked on a beach.

"It's like a drive-through, dad," Sophie said with a grin. "You get lunch through your window."

The kids smelled of sunscreen and wore water shoes on their feet. They must have come from Chapin Park, where Heather had planned to take them hunting in the pond for turtles, frogs, and minnows. That was one thing he loved about this town. It was surrounded by patches of state- and county-owned property and vineyards. Lots of vineyards, which occupied the valleys outside of town in the spaces between the Finger Lakes. Maplewood Falls would never lose its lushness—the maples, oaks, balsams, and pines that covered the rolling hills and lined the streets—and it would never lose its rural flavor. Even though the village had its own schools, grocery store, banks, and gas stations, it could never grow much beyond its current boundaries. The nearest large city, Rochester, was too far away to be any threat.

"Thanks, guys," Sawyer said. "Step back a bit and let me get out and get some hugs."

Young arms encircled his legs and waist as soon as he stood. He made his way to Heather and gave her a kiss. Bryce had already lost interest in hugs and lunches and had climbed into the front seat of the patrol car. Thankfully, Sawyer had thought to shut off the engine and take the keys. Heather amazed him, the way she juggled all three kids with ease, always knowing what each needed or wanted while also taking online courses toward her master's degree. She managed their finances with equal expertise, developing a plan that would allow them to pay off their house in nine more years and retire comfortably in their early sixties. She had it all figured out. From December through April each year, Heather worked for a local accounting firm, preparing W-2s for client companies and doing taxes for individuals and LLCs. Her hope was to become a CPA by the time all three kids were in school full time and to eventually become a partner in the firm.

"We made a picnic lunch for ourselves, so we figured we'd make one for you, too. Sophie made the PB and J and Andy packed it up. Bryce thought you might like the Mario Bros napkin." She tousled Andy's hair as she spoke.

"Yup. I gave you an apple and two Oreo cookies," Andy said.

"And I can't wait to eat them," Sawyer said.

"Look, Mom." Bryce slid out of the patrol car, holding the bag of butterscotch candies. "Look what I found. Can I have them?"

Sawyer was saved from Heather's wrath by the buzzing of his cell phone.

"Come on, kids. We have to let daddy get back to work. One candy each, and that's it. Then give them to me." She shot Sawyer a look that told him they would have a conversation about this later. "Let's head down to the playground and have our lunch."

Sawyer watched as the kids trailed Heather down the street toward the park on the other end of downtown, wishing he could join them. The voice on the cell phone was Izzy Rodriguez, a former restaurant manager who was opening his own place in town. Sawyer got back in the car and waved to Heather and the kids, who had all turned around for one last look, all except Bryce, who had grabbed his mother's hand again and was yanking her forward, urging her to walk faster. The urgency in Izzy's voice finally pulled his attention away.

"Sawyer, we have a problem. I didn't want to call nine-one-one and get this all over everybody's scanners. You know how it goes. People would swarm the place, and we've got work to do. We're already a month behind schedule."

"What's up, Izzy? You finally catch somebody on camera?"

Izzy was converting the old warehouse, which was located on a service road that ran behind Main Street, into an ale house. It was a great location with lots of parking, and he'd have plenty of signage on the main road to lure diners and beer connoisseurs when the place opened. But the warehouse had always attracted kids looking to party and drunks who needed a safe place to sleep it off, and that hadn't changed with the start of construction. Izzy had said he was planning to install video surveillance, especially after someone made off with a few tools two weeks ago.

"Bones. That's what's up. And they look like they're human. No, they are human because they still have clothes on them," Izzy said. "The guys were digging for a new septic line when they found them. We can only see the foot and leg bones right now. We didn't want to dig any further and ruin it for you. There's a sneaker, and it looks like the person was wearing black jeans."

"Shit," Sawyer said. "Don't let anyone near it, and don't touch anything. I'll be right over."

As he drove across town, Sawyer was careful not to exceed the speed limit. Cops didn't need flashing lights in a town this size to attract attention. If someone saw him driving fast, the guessing game would begin. Was it a domestic? A suicide? Another break-in at the antique shop on Bolivar Road? Sawyer wouldn't have raced to the antique shop, though. If the Steubers insisted on leaving their barn full of valuables unlocked, they deserved to get burglarized. He hoped this would turn out to be a natural death, someone who had disappeared unnoticed or from another town and made his way here. But he knew that was unlikely. People don't bury themselves.

Chapter Four

Carla's rings slipped easily off her finger, the result of more than two days without food. Rachel was punishing her for the bath, and she had decided one missed breakfast wasn't enough. Carla needed to experience the pain of hunger, the uncertainty of when or whether she would get food again, so she would remember that feeling if ever she chose to disrespect her again, she said. Now Rachel was demanding her rings, a sacrifice that would prove she'd learned her lesson. Carla held the rings in the palm of her hand and stared, and then closed her eyes, trying to remember the precise way the diamonds sparkled in the light, the exact curvature of the letters that formed the engraving, the promises she and Nick made to each other as he slid each ring onto her finger. They are just rings, she told herself. Nothing more.

"Why do you want them?" she asked, directing her voice toward the slot at the bottom of the door where an empty, brown, plastic tray, the kind used in food courts and school cafeterias, awaited them. Rachel had promised to send food through immediately if she shoved the tray through the opening with the rings on board. A warm sausage and egg sandwich she had made herself, along with a bit of orange juice.

"Why won't you ever speak to me through the opening? Is it too much? Are you afraid it'll be too personal, that you'll remember I'm real and human, not just some freaky show on your computer screen? Dammit, Rachel! Speak to me."

She clenched her fingers around the rings and held them to her chest, not quite ready to let them go. The tray disappeared. Carla stretched across the floor toward the opening and reached inside to grab it, but Rachel was faster. She had already sealed it off. Carla had missed her chance. There would be no food. She was hungry and a little weak, but she didn't panic. A stronger feeling overwhelmed her. For some reason, Rachel needed those rings, but she couldn't get into this prison without creating an opening, so she couldn't just take them. Carla knew she would likely give in the next time Rachel demanded them. She was hungry, and she refused to die in defense of diamonds and gold. But this feeling, this feeling of power, made it worth the wait. It was comforting to know she had some control, even though it was so little.

Carla slipped the rings back onto her finger and waited for Rachel's voice to come through the speaker, but it didn't. She was angry—Carla could figure that out—and she was probably punishing her further with silence. She would come back, though, and Carla would give her the rings, and Rachel would feed her. Carla knew that, and it calmed her nerves as much as it was possible to calm them. Rachel made mistakes. She made a mistake by not leaving herself some way to enter the room without freeing Carla. She must have made other mistakes. She was only one person, and she wasn't an apprenticed carpenter. Before this, she probably couldn't have even changed out a doorknob. So, there must be a weakness. Something.

Despite the silent treatment, Carla knew it was always possible Rachel was watching her. So, she couldn't be obvious as she examined the walls, the ceiling, the floor, the bathtub, and the sink for flaws, any flaws that might be keys to escaping. She stretched out on the mattress and tried to appear as if she was simply staring at the ceiling, but every now and then, she glanced around the room, held that picture in her mind, and studied it.

The room was small, barely as wide as the mattress's length. Maybe eight feet. It was longer than it was wide. Next to the mattress sat the chair, and only a few feet from that was the sink, which was set into an old, yellowed countertop supported by an empty, white cabinet. The toilet and bathtub were on the wall opposite the mattress with the toilet nearest the sink. That was it. Rachel had been kind enough to put a rug on the little bit of empty floor space in the room. It was odd that she insisted on such touches—the rug, the video screen, two pillows instead of one, Carla's favorite brand of shampoo and conditioner. Did those things make Rachel feel better about what she was doing? Was she telling herself that it was okay that she had sealed Carla in the basement because she gave her conditioner that left her hair silky and smooth, but didn't weigh it down?

The first thing Carla studied was the air vent, which had been cut into the ceiling near the middle of the wall that divided the room from the rest of the basement, the wall with the sealed door in it. The ceiling was low, but the vent was just a small round opening, no bigger than a dinner plate. It was nothing she could fit through. Even so, it had to bring air in from somewhere—from outside, from another insulated room of the house, from the rest of the basement. If she screamed long and hard, maybe someone would hear her. Her heart quickened with excitement until she thought about what Rachel might do if she caught her. What if she plugged the vent? What if she just sealed her in here tight, and she died slowly from suffocation, like the victim in that horrid story she read in high school that haunted her for weeks, "The Cask of Amontillado?" She shook off the thought and forced herself to look elsewhere.

She had already tried standing on the toilet and pushing on the ceiling. It was not concrete like the walls, but it appeared to be made of two-by-six boards nailed to the floor joists with insulation in between. It wouldn't budge. Rachel had caught her and had mocked her for it. She insisted the room was "escape-proof," but she warned Carla never to try anything like that again. So, Carla had to get smarter. No more exploring with her hands. Eyes only. The plumbing ran along the back wall and up through the ceiling, probably under the floorboards of the kitchen, to a water heater and pump on the other side of the basement. She could shake the pipes back and forth and try to widen the opening while Rachel was at work. She wasn't sure what that would accomplish, though maybe she could shout through it, or it would ensure her some air if Rachel ever plugged the vent. But she had no way of shutting off the water. The place might flood too quickly, and Rachel would catch her on the camera if she failed. She focused on the door again. Whatever sealant Rachel had used was rubbery like glue. It had been sprayed in from the other side, and some chunks oozed all the way through the crack to Carla's side. It would have to be quick drying because she only had so much time before Carla regained consciousness and started pounding on it. She had gotten some of it out with her fingernails, but it probably ran a good two inches deep, about the thickness of a door, she figured. She would need something long, thin, and durable. Preferably metal.

Even if she did find or make a tool, there was Rachel to think about. She would have to work when she knew Rachel was gone, and only then, and she would have to find somewhere to hide the debris. Like with every other plan, there was also the risk that Rachel would catch her on camera again. She didn't know whether Rachel reviewed footage when she got home each day or watched from a link on her work computer, laptop, or cellphone. That would be quite a risk though, to check the footage from somewhere else if people were looking for Carla and Christopher. Someone could look over her shoulder. Rachel was smarter than that. Still, she was not in her right mind. It was hard to know what risks she might take.

Of all the plans though, this one would likely have the least consequences. Rachel would demand the tool if she caught her and probably punish her somehow—deny her food or water for a few days—but the room wouldn't flood, and Rachel wouldn't have to plug air vents to stop her. She would just need to fortify the door area more to ensure that Carla did not escape, a thought that immediately made Carla nauseous. But it could take months to dig all that sealant out, even if everything else fell into place. Even if she succeeded, she had no idea what barriers awaited her on the other side.

Carla drew in a long breath. This time, when she stared at the ceiling, she pictured Christopher with his wisps of strawberry blonde hair much like her own, looking at her with her husband's eyes, the color of dark tea with a touch of honey. His skin was like Nick's too, pale and smooth, but not starkly pale like her own. Creamy. She smelled his sweet baby breath and tried to feel his warmth against her body. The last time she saw her son, he was in the car seat near her feet by Rachel's dining room table, and he seemed startled that she had rested him there. Carla had been holding him, but she'd felt dizzy and had asked Rachel to take him. Rachel just smiled from across the table. She didn't move, so Carla put him in the seat. The next thing Carla knew, she was on this mattress in sweatpants, and a tee-shirt Rachel had put her in. And Christopher was gone.

Losing Christopher was hard enough on Carla, but what about Nick? What was going through his head? Carla knew Rachel had sold their son to people who were desperate for a child and who didn't care where he came from. She'd arranged the deal through some crime ring that specialized in this kind of thing, buying and selling babies. Several times already, Rachel had taunted Carla with the story, telling her how she met her contact in a McDonald's parking lot with all kinds of witnesses around. She had worn a wig and driven Carla's car so she would match her description and had exchanged Christopher for fifteen thousand dollars in cash in a wrinkled McDonald's take-out bag that smelled like fries.

"That's what your little boy was worth," she said. "Fifteen thousand dollars in a stinky bag. It's not much, but this luxury condo of yours put a dent in my savings account when I built it. Thanks to your little boy, I can start building it back up. It broke my heart when you told me you were pregnant, Carla. You were never going to have children. How many times did you say that before you left for college? You were never going to have kids, and you were never going to come back here. You used that baby to keep Nick, but Christopher needed two parents who loved him, not one, and now he has that. He will be fine, and Nick and I will have our own baby someday. Nick is sad now about Christopher, but he'll get over it."

Rachel had been her maid of honor, but who was she really? Who was this person Carla had confided in most of her life? It was true. She had not wanted kids when she was eighteen years old, but she was just a kid herself then. How could she have known what she really wanted? Some girls dreamed of being mothers. In her own dreams, Carla was at the helm of some huge, New York City magazine, setting the trends her staff wrote about. Kids didn't figure into that scenario. Maplewood Falls didn't figure in that scenario. But Christopher was planned. She wanted a baby. She loved him, more than she thought possible.

And it was true that she felt betrayed when Nick decided to operate his uncle's store. He'd worked there since he was twelve, stocking shelves and bagging groceries. He'd always said he hated it, that he wanted to study engineering, but he never applied to engineering schools. Instead, he got his associate's in business at the community college and his bachelor's at Alfred State, where he could commute from home. When his uncle died, he took over the store, and he proposed. Carla was living in New York City at the time, one year into her first full-time job as a staff writer at *Healthy Woman* magazine. It didn't pay much, but it was enough to cover the rent in the Queens apartment she shared with three other women. The distance was hard on their relationship, and she knew she couldn't earn enough to support them both in New York City while also helping pay for a wedding and waiting for the store to sell. Her move back home was supposed to be temporary, at least in her mind. He was supposed to sell that store. He promised her. The money would have helped him get back on track and figure out what he wanted to do with his life. That was their plan.

She worked out an agreement with her editor that she would commute to the city every other week, and that worked well for a while. When she left *Healthy Woman* for the writer/editor job at *Glamorous*, she negotiated a deal that allowed her to work even fewer days each month in the city. Nick tried to hold up his end of the bargain, or at least he seemed like he did. He let a few people know he might sell, but he told Carla that he needed to bring revenues up first. Higher revenues would mean a higher sale price. He came up with new promotions, new inventory, new renovation plans—all designed to draw more customers and boost the bottom line. When two years passed and he still had not listed the store, he argued that buyers wanted to see consistency. A year or two of solid sales wasn't enough, he said, and she believed him. So she waited, and while she waited, they bought a house, and then they had a baby. By the time Christopher came along, it no longer seemed practical to move. It all just kind of happened, and she complied. She never pushed the issue with Nick and by the time she realized she had signed away her dreams with her vows, it was too late. She confessed those thoughts to Rachel once, over several Malibu Rum and Cokes during one of their monthly girls' night outs.

But dreams change, don't they? She regretted her confession the next morning, and she told Rachel that. She loved her job at the magazine, and she would work there again when Christopher was old enough. She wasn't living in Manhattan, but so what? She still traveled to the city frequently. She had her favorite restaurants, her regular jogging routes, the museum with the sculptures she liked so much. Carla sighed. Maybe this was all her fault. Maybe she really was lying to herself, and maybe the pregnancy was part of some role she was playing. But even if that were true, she loved Christopher, and she loved Nick. Her love was real, and that was all that mattered. Wasn't it?

Though her heart ached for Christopher, she at least found some comfort in the idea that he was with a family, people who would take good care of him. He was safe. But Nick knew nothing. He didn't know whether she'd run off with the baby, was kidnapped, or was in some terrible car wreck off a rural road where their bodies were waiting to be found. He knew nothing about his wife or son. If he believed Rachel's story—that she had run off with Christopher—then he would believe she was unstable, and that Christopher was in danger because a mental breakdown would be the only explanation for her departure. She loved Nick, and she loved their life. She missed her job, but she enjoyed freelancing, and she knew she would find something satisfying eventually. She had no reason to leave him, but that wouldn't stop others from believing it.

Carla turned her attention to the video screen on the wall. The neighbor was walking his dog again, the same time he walked him every day. The sky was cloudy, threatening rain, and Carla had to remind herself again that the video was a year old. It could be bright and sunny outside this prison or cold and dreary. She had no way of knowing. Earlier, she'd seen an older mother pushing a stroller while a toddler straggled behind, stopping to observe bugs on the sidewalk. The mother turned back, squatted next to him, and watched with him, letting go of the stroller for a few moments to get a closer look. The scene should have filled Carla with warmth, but her only thought was for the baby in the stroller.

"Watch him," she warned the mother aloud. "Watch him or someone might just take him." Carla couldn't tear her eyes off the screen until the mother stood up, grabbed the stroller handle with one hand, and guided her toddler with the other, moving along. When she got Christopher back, she thought, she would never let go. Not ever.

Chapter Five

Sawyer remained at the construction site well after sundown. He had to call in the state police with its forensic team before he could touch anything. He took his own photos while they captured the burial site and the skeleton from every angle. They measured, they dusted, they observed, and took notes. He enjoyed working with the state police. They were professional, and they were never condescending. They recognized his value and let him take the lead in the initial evaluation and questioning. He wouldn't want to be one of them, though. Too many troopers died young, often right after retirement. It was the stress, getting a call about a domestic in progress when they are forty miles away in a county with no sheriff's patrol, knowing that the speed of their arrival could make the difference between life and death. That kind of thing. It took a toll on a person. They spent more time in their cars than Sawyer did as well, and the nature of the job often meant they had to hit drive-throughs for breakfast, lunch, and dinner. The small-town thing looked good in comparison.

It didn't take long to figure out who was buried near the warehouse. Sawyer knew as soon as his bones were fully exposed. He was wearing that same t-shirt, the t-shirt he wore most every day of the week, the one with "Led Zeppelin" written across the chest. The shirt had degraded, and it fell apart as technicians removed and bagged his remains, but the design was clear. That was enough for Sawyer, but dental records left no doubt about his identity. His teeth were a mess, loaded with fillings from the three times he'd visited a dentist in his short lifetime. The skeleton belonged to Leland Boise, a local teenager who disappeared with his grandmother's cash fifteen years ago when Sawyer was a senior in high school.

Leland was a freshman at the time, but he was sixteen. School wasn't his thing. Sawyer had silently cheered for him when he went missing. The kid had lost both his parents to drugs, and his grandmother wasn't all that stable herself. She hid her money because she didn't trust banks and spent what she didn't hoard on cheap crafts, magazine subscriptions, and lottery tickets. She wore bright, red rouge in perfect circles on her cheeks with lipstick to match. Her hair colored changed with her moods—from deep black, to cheap blonde to an orange-red that clashed with her lips. Most days, she walked up and down Main Street for hours, mumbling to herself and smiling brightly at people who passed by. Meanwhile, Leland alternated between the same two pairs of jeans and a couple of graphic t-shirts each day. He was skinny, pale, and quiet, and he kept to himself. He never caused any trouble.

Leland had no close friends as far as Sawyer knew, and the police report of the investigation into his disappearance confirmed that. The investigation was half-hearted. The file only was about a quarter-inch thick, and there was no evidence in the storage shed. The officer took a statement from the grandmother, who died just a few years later of a stroke, and talked to a couple kids at school who had seen him earlier that day. It seemed Sawyer wasn't alone in hoping Leland had fled with the cash to New York City or North Carolina or Florida to start a new life. State police were contacted, but they didn't get involved. That was back in the day when the village police department was larger, and more cases were investigated on the local level. Tax cuts changed things. The total amount of missing cash was twenty-one thousand dollars, and the case remained carelessly open with no warrants for his arrest or contact information for any missing persons database. The files were eventually tucked away with the cold cases. But it was clear now that Leland never left Maplewood Falls. He never used that money. He never had a chance.

Sawyer stared at the photos of Leland's skull, bashed repeatedly with a blunt instrument. Maybe a baseball bat. Maybe a rock or a pipe. Whoever killed him kept going long after he was dead, breaking him open like an egg, and then smashing the yolk after it spilled out. Robbery was not the motive.

State police investigators found money in his shallow grave, scattered on top of him. It didn't make sense. Why would anyone kill him, and then throw the money on his body? There was evidence. Not much, but it was something. After all these years, his jeans remained somewhat intact, and so did the note in his pocket. It was written on a small rectangle of college-ruled notebook paper in moisture-smeared blue ink with neat, uniform curves: "Change in plans. Something came up. Meet me at midnight by the warehouse. Bring the money in a lunch bag. I promise everything will be okay. I love you."

The handwriting was feminine, most likely that of a woman or a girl. But why? Who would do something like this to Leland, of all people? He had no friends or a girlfriend that anyone knew of, but he also had no obvious enemies. Someone needed that money and convinced Leland to steal it, but then left it. A drug addict? A former acquaintance of his parents? Was Leland into drugs? Did the killer get scared and drop the money? Maybe Leland and this girl or woman had planned to run away together, and someone killed them both. Maybe she promised him sex in exchange for money. A sixteen-year-old virgin could be bought. But it comes back to the abandoned cash. Why leave it? The note specifically asked him to bring the money. The troopers brought in dogs, but they'd turned up nothing so far. No evidence of another body. But there were other possibilities. The killer might have kidnapped the note-writer and killed her elsewhere, possibly motivated by anger at having caught her with Leland. Maybe it was her father or an ex-boyfriend. She might have witnessed the murder from behind a tree, or from within the warehouse and kept quiet out of fear, or she might have been involved. She might have set Leland up by telling this lonely and alienated kid that she loved him and participated in the killing or even killed him herself. The killer might have done it for kicks, out of anger, for revenge, jealousy. Maybe the lover was a man. Maybe Leland was gay, and his boyfriend didn't want their relationship known. So he lured him here with promises of running away. Maybe the cash didn't matter.

And then there was the timing. Carla disappeared just days before Leland's body was found. Everyone knew about the construction at the site and the restaurant. It was big news in town. Did she fear this was going to happen?

33

Did she run away because she was involved in his death or knew something about it, something that put her in danger, too? Did someone abduct her out of fear that she would reveal the killer? The note was not hers. He had seen plenty of her writing during the search of her house. She was a sloppy writer, her writing almost unreadable at times. But it was still a possibility that couldn't be ignored.

Sawyer leaned back in his chair and closed his eyes, trying to picture Leland in the school hallways, in the gym, in the bathrooms. The building housed grades seven through twelve, so they must have passed each other in the halls, maybe even brushed shoulders or elbows. There had been a fight once. It was somewhere deep in Sawyer's memory. His sophomore or junior year of high school. He couldn't remember. It was in the parking lot near the track, far from the main building. It must have been junior year because Sawyer remembered now that he was walking to his car, his parents' old Dodge, when he saw it happen. Leland was with a group of guys, which caught Sawyer's attention because these were not people who would normally associate with someone like him. The guys were mostly younger than Sawyer. They were the kind who smoked pot in the woods before school, who sneaked vodka into the dining hall in water bottles, who drove lifted cars and trucks that were sanded and repainted where the rust had eaten away at them and bore bumper stickers intended to offend drivers behind them. They were not Leland's friends.

In his memory, hands shoved Leland, not once, but three times until Leland was pinned between the group and the passenger side of a car. Sawyer heard a teacher shout as he watched Leland push back, a move that seemed to surprise his attackers. One of the attackers raised a fist, but Leland blocked it and threw a punch in return. Sawyer saw blood as the teacher entered the fray and pulled them apart. A custodian provided backup for the teacher, but that was all Sawyer remembered. He'd taken note of the fight and filed it somewhere in his brain, but it wasn't important to him at the time because Leland wasn't important to him. He wondered now who those guys were, whether they might know anything about his death. It didn't fit, not with the note in Leland's pocket and with the money left in his grave, but the way his skull was beaten in, that was done by someone who was angry. Maybe by someone who wanted revenge.

A knock on his office door startled Sawyer. Through the glass, he saw state police investigator Roland Zittle, who was working on Carla's disappearance. He tossed the photo onto his desk. Then he leaned back in his chair and motioned him in. Zittle grabbed a chair, turned it around, and straddled it, resting his arms on its back. He was a big guy—tall and beefy—unlike Sawyer, whose thin frame often drew comments from the motherly types who wanted to fatten him up. Sawyer's build made him look taller than his six feet, and his hair—a mop of thick, brown curls—added to the illusion.

"We're seeing a lot of each other these days, aren't we?" Zittle said. "First, a woman disappears with her baby. Then a teenager who went missing more than a decade ago turns up dead. All in the same week. Going to need your help on all this, especially since you seem to know all the players."

"So, you got Leland's case, too, huh? Can't get it out of my head. I was thinking about borrowing a few yearbooks and seeing whether I can match that handwriting. There are a lot of possibilities. A kid like that probably craved love and attention. Anyone could have lured him in—a fellow student, a teacher. But the yearbooks seem like the best place to start. The timing sucks, though. The kid could have waited until we found Carla and the baby before he made his reappearance."

"About that." Zittle furrowed his brow and seemed lost in thought for a moment. "Forensics found strands of what appears to be synthetic hair, likely from a wig, on the headrest of the driver's seat in Carla's car. Now, at first, I thought Carla disguised herself to get out of town unrecognized. You know, ditched the car for a ride with someone else or for a second vehicle she'd stashed at the junkyard and changed her appearance. But here's the problem: The wig hair matches her color and the length is about the same as hers. So, what do you make of that? Why would she cover her hair with a wig that matches her hair?"

Sawyer swallowed hard. This was not what he wanted to hear. He knew what Zittle was getting at. It had been lurking in the back of his own mind from the very beginning. Christopher was a chubby-cheeked baby who always seemed content, the kind of baby old ladies couldn't keep their hands away from, the kind that made women like his wife want another even though they'd agreed long ago they were done, the kind that might make someone who was lonely and mentally unbalanced snatch him for themselves, eliminating obstacles without remorse. A baby like that could bring in a lot of money.

"We need to get an Amber Alert out on that baby. Just the baby. Every photo out there right now is of Carla with Christopher in her arms, but if…if they are not together…if someone stole the baby." Sawyer rubbed his face hard with the palms of his hands. "Jesus. How am I going to tell Nick?"

Chapter Six

Carla must have fallen asleep on the mattress. She hated when that happened because it was harder to keep track of the hours. She was fighting to wake up, and Rachel wasn't helping. Her voice, loud and firm, filled the room and pounded inside Carla's head. She wanted the rings, and if she didn't get them now, she would shut the water off.

"You can live three weeks without food," she said. "But you'd be lucky to make it three days without water. Then, when you're dead, I can just come in and take the rings off your finger. I'll seal the place back up again and let you rot. No one will ever find your body."

No. Please, no. Carla's throat tightened, and she struggled to swallow or breathe. Sweat formed on her skin, fluid she couldn't afford to lose, not if Rachel took her water away. Her eyes flittered from one corner to the next, searching for openings that didn't exist, willing the walls to crumble or simply dissolve. The thought of being trapped in here or dying in here…she couldn't think it. She had to block it. She had to slow her breathing and regain control. If Rachel had wanted to kill her, she'd have done it by now. She needed Carla.

How did she not see this coming? She and Rachel had been best friends all through grade school. The boys loved her even then. They gave her their lunch cookies, let her sit in the back of the bus, and gave up their homework answers for her, all while Carla watched from the sidelines in awe. That didn't change in high school. She had a continuous flow of boyfriends, though she avoided the jocks and never kept any single boyfriend long: They bored her; they nagged her; they hovered, she'd said. Later, when sex became part of the game, there were new complaints: They came too fast; they took too long; they were too rough; they were too gentle. She always had a valid reason for ditching them, but she was never without a date when she wanted one.

She had a successful career in real estate, too, and she had other friends, other people she hung out with apart from Carla. Their friendship had survived Carla's stint in New York City. Rachel visited at least once a month, sometimes when Nick was there, too. Nick never led her on, never flirted with her, as far as Carla knew, and Rachel seemed genuinely excited for her when they got engaged. She even helped her find the venue for the reception, screen bands, and select a wedding dress. Yes, Carla had been less available since Christopher was born, but wasn't that the natural order of things? Couldn't best friends remain best friends even as they moved forward with their lives? How had she missed the signs that Rachel was going over the edge? She just couldn't remember seeing any. Rachel was always the center of attention, the life of the party, even if it was just the two of them. That hadn't changed. She needed to wake that Rachel up, to bring her back to reality.

"Rachel, I love you. You've been my friend forever. I'll give you the rings if that's what you need, but I want to help you. We can get through this. I know you're not well. I won't press any charges, and we'll get Christopher back. Just let me out of here so we can talk. I need to see your face. You need to see mine."

Rachel laughed.

"See you? I've always seen you, always watched you. I watched you holding hands with the guy I was in love with, kissing him in the school hallways, marrying him, having a baby with him. I really thought you'd both get it after a while, that he'd realize you weren't right for him, and you'd break up or divorce, and then we'd be the way we should be. Nick and I would finally get married and start a family. But then you got pregnant, and I knew I had to do something. This is for the best, Carla, you'll see. With you out of the picture, he'll finally be able to admit his mistake and love me the way he's meant to. He just couldn't see it anymore with you there, but I felt it. I saw the way he looked at me, the way he craved me. He sees me when he kisses you. I know it. I let it go too far. You were a greater distraction than I had predicted. I should have gotten you out of his way a long time ago."

She's gone crazy, Carla thought. What if she has a breakdown and ends up in some mental institution for months or years and never tells anyone Carla is here? She couldn't let that happen. Nick didn't even like Rachel all that much. She was full of herself, he'd said. He put up with her because she was Carla's friend. How could Rachel have misinterpreted any of that? What would Rachel do if Nick pushed her aside? Had she already made an advance? Would she kill herself? Kill him? Oh, God, no. If only Carla could get to Nick. Send him a message somehow. She'd have to convince Rachel she was on her side, little by little. Not too quickly, or she wouldn't buy it. Rachel was smart. She'd graduated salutatorian and sailed through college. She'd sense it if Carla wasn't careful, but Carla needed to know how Nick was treating her. She needed to make sure he didn't upset her. She needed to help Nick and Rachel get along to buy time.

"Why didn't you tell me you were in love with him? You never told me. How could I know? If I had known, Rachel, I wouldn't have dated him at all. You're my friend. Friends go deeper than that. But you never told me. You never gave me a chance."

"A chance?" she hissed. "You told me to shut up, remember? Back in ninth grade, when I first laid eyes on him. You said I was obsessing over him and driving you crazy. You said I was creeping you out, and you called me a stalker. You laughed, but you meant it. So, I shut up, just like you asked, because that, Carla, is what friends do. I dated other people. Lots of other people. But I never stopped loving him. Not once. And he never stopped loving me. He dated you to get close to me, but then you trapped him. Good friends don't do that to each other. You need to learn how to be a friend, and you will stay here until you do."

"But what if – what if he doesn't love you? What if he chooses someone else?"

Carla waited for a response, but there was no sound. She had pushed the limits. She shouldn't have gone there. Rachel would turn off the water, and that would be it. A part of her, a small part, thought that would be okay. She could just curl up on the mattress and die. Either she would simply cease to exist and feel nothing in her death, or she would discover an afterlife and leave all this pain behind. This feeling, this justified claustrophobia, was too much. Sometimes, the panic and the fear made her want to claw and dig at the walls until she'd ripped all the skin off her bones and filed her bones into dust. But then she'd remember Christopher and Nick, and she'd focus on them, on their images and the memories, and that would give her strength. It was getting harder, though.

Finally, Rachel's voice broke into her thoughts.

"Let me explain," Rachel said. "This is a love triangle, Carla. Each side, each angle, depends on and compliments the other. If one side collapses, we all collapse. In other words, we all die. If Nick chooses someone else, it's that simple. We all die because I can't live without him anymore, and I can't bear the thought of him with another woman. But he won't choose someone else because he loves me. I'm coming to get the rings now. Put them on the tray, and I will send a tray of food in after, just like I promised. I still keep my promises. I'm a good person. It's just that things went wrong, and I have to make them right."

Though Carla had reminded herself over and over that the rings were just material goods, it didn't help. She felt barren and empty after she put them on the tray, like she'd just sacrificed a part of herself. She'd so rarely taken them off—to paint, to work with ground meat or knead dough, to have them cleaned at the mall while she shopped—and she'd never had them off for more than an hour or so. She knew she'd feel differently if she'd lost one or had to give it up for other reasons. It was the circumstances that hurt so much. Rachel wouldn't tell her why she needed them, but Carla could guess. It was more than a fetish. She would use them to prove Carla was dead, or she would mail them to Nick as proof she had run off and didn't love him anymore. Rachel was trying to void her relationship with Nick, void the existence of Christopher. That was what made the pain so much more intense.

She knew something else, too. She knew Nick would never love Rachel in return. She had to find a way out of this place. She had to warn Nick and stop Rachel. The love triangle would collapse because it never existed. And then what? Nick would have no idea how dangerous it would be to swat Rachel away right now, and if Rachel pushed him, he would do just that. Until she got out, Carla would have to coach Rachel, tell her what made him happy and what annoyed him. She would have to make Rachel tolerable. It was the only way she could think of to keep him alive.

A set of fresh clothes came through the slot the next evening, and Carla knew the drill. Change into the new clothes, put the dirty clothes on the tray, neatly folded, and push the tray through the slot. When Rachel received the old clothes, she would send in dinner. The outfit was the usual attire: baggy, gray sweatpants, white underwear, white ankle socks, and a large, white men's t-shirt. Never a bra. She supposed she didn't have much use for one in here anyway.

She had wanted to ask Rachel about taking a bath again, but she wasn't sure how to ask or what it would cost. Everything cost her something, usually a meal or two. So, she had to decide what was more important: food or hygiene. She'd been waiting until Rachel was gone each morning to pee and brush her teeth. If she saw her do either, it might give her an idea. Rachel might decide Carla needed permission for those two things as well.

She had become so used to the routine that she pulled her hand back when she felt something hard underneath the t-shirt. That was not normal, not the new normal. It could be something dangerous. She backed away and scooted into a corner.

"Oh, come on. I told you I won't hurt you," Rachel said over the speaker. "For Christ's sake, put the t-shirt on. I don't need to see your boobs."

Another not-normal thing. Rachel usually waited outside the slot for the old clothes. Why was she watching her now? Had she run back to her computer, or was she just outside the room, watching on her phone? Slowly, Carla crossed over to the tray with one arm over her naked breasts. She grabbed the t-shirt and slipped it on, revealing a book with the word "Journal" on the cover, three pencils, and a child's pencil sharpener.

"It's a gift," Rachel said. "It must be killing you to not write all this time. I want to make this stay comfortable for you. I know this is hard, but you are still my best friend."

The softness in Rachel's voice stunned her. Rachel had kidnapped her and sealed her in a basement. She sold her baby and was trying to seduce her husband, and now she was concerned that Carla might be itching to write? Her first instinct was to rip up the journal and break the pencils. How dare she? What was wrong with her? But then she remembered. Everything was wrong with her. Rejecting the gift would be a bad idea.

She took the journal into her hands and caressed the cover. It was nice, she had to admit that. The cover was made of deep brown leather with rustic lettering. The pages were of high-quality cream paper, more like stationary. She brought the journal to her face and took in its smell. It smelled like a new book. She missed books. The pencils were basic, yellow Ticonderoga number twos. The plastic sharpener was simple and blue. In any other situation, it would have been the perfect gift.

Carla forced out the words.

"Thank you."

"You're welcome. I will be down in a minute with your dinner."

This was the old Rachel, giving her a gift like this. Was she beginning to emerge again? They'd had so many good memories together. How could things change like this? How could anyone change so dramatically and abruptly without anyone even noticing? Of course, that probably is not the way it happened. This Rachel was likely there all along. And if that was the case, the journal did not come without strings attached. Rachel must want something or plan to use the journal against her somehow. Carla would have to think carefully about what to write. Rachel could request the journal at any time, and she would have to comply. Rachel had the power. She could turn off the water again or refuse her food. She was in control.

Dinner was another surprise: two piping hot slices of pepperoni pizza and a salad with Italian dressing. It was the only hot food Rachel had ever given her. For the first time since she woke up in this prison, Carla allowed herself to believe there might be hope. Maybe Rachel's mental disturbance had peaked and crashed. Maybe she was becoming aware of what terrible things she had done and would release her soon. Carla made a decision. She would write only about the good things in her journal, about the good times she'd had with Rachel. Maybe this was a way to reach that old Rachel and pull them all out of this nightmare.

The first memory that pulled at her was when they were nine or maybe ten years old. It must have been spring because Carla was wearing her purple windbreaker and the water in the creek behind her parents' house flowed high. The creek was a favorite spot of theirs. It always offered some form of breath-taking adventure, from catching salamanders to the consequences of truth or dare—skinny dipping in the small pools that were icy in the spring and refreshing in the summer. On this day, the grass had begun to green, and wildflowers sprouted from among their blades. Tiny crayfish scattered when they lifted rocks from the creek bed. The sun was warm in the fields, but the trees had started forming their seasonal canopy in the forest that owned the creek, making it just cool enough to require a jacket or sweatshirt.

Carla's fingers were cold from playing in the water, and she had planned to suggest they go inside for a snack when Rachel squealed and then covered her own mouth. Carla tripped over wet rocks and soaked her right foot in the cold, rushing water in her struggle to join Rachel a few yards upstream. As she approached, Rachel stretched out a hand with her palm facing Carla, indicating she should slow down and tread quietly. There, on the bank, were two baby foxes, so tiny they seemed unreal. Red fur framed their faces and colored their legs, while darker, almost black fur covered their backs. They tumbled over each other, nipping and swiping at one another with their paws. The sounds they emitted were like nothing Carla had ever heard. If she hadn't seen them, she would have sworn they were human babies who had learned to whimper and cackle. They stood mesmerized, fighting the urge to join them in play. The babies seemed not to notice Carla and Rachel, but their mother did. She crested the bank and bumped them with her nose, calling out orders with a soft whimper of her own.

Carla and Rachel did not run after them. They stood as they were until they heard Carla's mother call from the house. Carla reached for Rachel's hands, and the two friends jumped up and down in excitement before they rushed up the hill, where Kool-Aid and peanut butter and jelly sandwiches awaited. Carla and Rachel never talked about that day again. It was one of those moments that remains within, growing more precious, more valuable, with age.

So, it almost seemed like a violation, a sin, to put it on paper, but Carla forced herself to write. These were the kinds of memories that might bring Rachel back. She closed the journal and tucked it under her pillow. In her dream that night, the mama fox taught the babies to hunt. Carla was one kit, and Rachel was the other. They crouched behind an old log, waiting for mice to scoot past. When Carla spied one, she pounced just as she'd been taught, but her teeth would not pierce the mouse's fur. It wriggled from her grasp and escaped. With a huff of disgust, the kit that was Rachel leaped through the air from behind Carla and landed with the mouse between her paws. Before the mouse could recover from the shock of her presence, she pierced it with her teeth and took it inside her mouth, swallowing it whole.

When she awoke, Rachel had a new demand. She wanted her to tear a piece of paper out of the journal and write Nick a note. Rachel told her generally what to write, but wanted Carla to put it in her own words. "Write like your life depends on it," she said. "No breakfast or lunch today. I will give you dinner if I am satisfied with the note."

Chapter Seven

L eland was reported missing in the Fall. Maybe that was part of the reason Sawyer had felt optimistic about his disappearance. It was his senior year, and he rushed into it headlong, fueled by anticipation and excitement. He and Heather had been dating only a month, but there was something about her—a quiet but mischievous strength, a coyness—that made her different from his past girlfriends. She wasn't his type. He'd always dated blondes or bottled blondes whose primary interests included cheerleading, prom, and makeup. Heather was a soccer and basketball player who had moved up to varsity freshman year. Her hair was brown, not blonde, and so were her eyes, but she was far from ordinary. Her waves—silky and long—took on a reddish hue in the sun, and her eyes were a deep, dark, brown flecked with amber, like nothing he'd ever seen. She always had this look like she was on fire.

And there was soccer. Sawyer had already scored at least once in each game, three times in the last game. Homecoming was a week away, and he felt invincible. They would win, and he would score the goal that made it possible. He felt it in his bones. It was a good time to be alive, and he just assumed everyone felt the same way. He was enjoying the moment and looking forward, taking the SATs, meeting with the guidance counselor, reading up on different colleges and the programs they offered.

Sawyer had always known he wanted to be a police officer, but he was torn between getting a college degree first or applying directly to the police academy after high school. The guidance counselor was pushing for the academy. There were a few that accepted eighteen-year-old cadets, and

Sawyer's grades were not the best. Their guidance counselor was one of those who believed college was overrated and should be reserved for the elite, the top five or ten percent of the class. It was Heather who steadied him that Fall, who took him through the pros and cons and convinced him to spend four years at a state university. That degree gave him the advantage when he was up for promotions in Syracuse and when he applied for this job. It was a good decision, and, thanks to Heather, he was confident enough to stand his ground when his counselor told him he was making a mistake.

So, when he heard Leland was missing and that the money had disappeared with him, he couldn't help but think the best. All was right in his own world. How could it possibly be wrong in someone else's? He wanted to believe in Leland's story, a story of flight and freedom, and so did the community. It was a good story, a comforting one. He never thought to question it because, honestly, Leland didn't matter to him, and he wasn't willing to surrender this euphoria to any other possibility. Maplewood Falls is a small community. The misfortune of one affects all. Like the rest, Sawyer was selfish. He made up a happy ending for Leland because it suited his own needs. But what else was going on then? What had he been blind to?

The sounding of a horn behind him brought Sawyer back to the YMCA parking lot where he had just dropped off his two oldest kids for day camp. He moved his car forward to let the next parent pull up to the curb, where a volunteer with a clipboard was waiting. A small line had formed behind him. The other parents had probably recognized his car and given him a little space before letting their impatience show. He was glad he was not in a patrol car. How long might they have waited then?

Heather usually took the kids to camp, where they swam, did crafts, and played games three summer days a week, but she wasn't feeling well that morning. He offered to take their youngest to a sitter for the day, but she refused, saying it would pass. She looked so tired. He worried she had a fever, but she said her temperature was normal. Sawyer pulled out of the YMCA parking lot and headed toward the town building. He needed coffee. A new café had opened on Main Street, and he'd been meaning to introduce himself to the owners, so he parked at the station and walked the downtown stretch, smiling and waving at shop owners and employees who were just opening their doors or preparing for the day ahead. Maplewood Falls was not a full-fledged tourist town. It wasn't a destination. It was a pleasant place to stop along the way. Main Street reflected its status. Most of the eateries catered to the lunch and breakfast crowds. They were nestled among antique shops and art studios, the kind of places that tempt people to take a break from driving. But locals filled the outdoor tables at this hour in the morning, and the drug store drummed up the most business. In the evening, the liquor store would become the most popular shop with locals and tourists alike.

Sawyer was almost to the café when a voice called out to him.

"Hey, Chief! Come sit with us."

The voice came from a table of five men who ranged in age from their thirties through their seventies, sitting outside DJ's Diner. These men considered themselves the political force of the town. Good people from good families, so they believed. They tolerated women in their working worlds, but not in this social one and not in any political realms. Definitely not here at the table. They saw themselves as the good 'ole boys, and everyone let them, even though they really had no power at all. Charlie, the man who had called him over, had been trying to convince Sawyer to join them for two years, ever since Sawyer issued tickets to a teenager who ran a stop sign and hit Charlie's tow truck. Sawyer was just doing his job, but Charlie seemed to view it as a favor.

"Have a cup, Chief," Charlie said, motioning to an empty chair beside him. "Take a load off."

Sawyer paused a moment to be polite and return the welcoming nods from the rest of table. At least two of the men would have to get to work soon. They usually started off as a larger bunch, between seven and ten men, but those who weren't retired or disabled drifted off well before nine. They rarely bought more than a cup of coffee, but they tipped well, from what Sawyer had heard. A form of rent, he supposed.

"Thanks for the invitation, but I have to get back to the station soon. I just wanted to make a quick stop at the new place to introduce myself to the owners."

"They've got you running ragged, don't they? What's going on with Nick's wife and kid? Any word yet?" The inquiry came from Liam Walsh, a realtor who had given most of his business over to his kids, but still closed a few deals now and then, especially if the money was big. There had been rumors about Liam's business practices, about false insurance claims. But he lived outside of the village, out of Sawyer's jurisdiction.

"It's not really my case. State police are handling it," Sawyer said. "I couldn't talk about it anyway."

"What about that dead kid?" Liam pressed. "My grandson knew him. Went to school with him. Said he was a strange one. I can't see wasting taxpayer money on that investigation. That kid's family was trouble. His grandmother was crazy. He was just going to be a burden anyway. Another one in jail or on the Welfare rolls."

Sawyer felt the heat rise in his cheeks.

"Murder is murder, Liam, no matter what you think of the victim. Someone out there took his life. You have no right to weigh the value of his existence, and neither do I. We will investigate his death just as aggressively as we would any other."

"You mean state police, don't you?" Liam said. "You're never going to get a bigger force with that attitude. It's time you started handling your own cases, don't you think? It's nobody else's business what goes on in this town."

Charlie nodded in agreement.

"Whoa." Dean Mills, a retired doctor from the next town over, stood and raised a palm in Liam's direction. "No need to get personal here." He pulled a couple of dollar bills from his wallet and set them on the table under his cup. "The district attorney made the decision to pass on the big investigations because you folks pushed for tax cuts that reduced the size of the force. Don't go pinning it on the chief here. Everything comes at a price. Come on, Chief. I'll walk you a bit. My car is parked down the block."

Sawyer took Dean up on his offer and motioned a farewell to the table. He was right. The tax cut cost him two and a half positions, making the force just small enough that the district attorney worried about the lack of resources and how that would affect his cases. He didn't want cases falling apart because Maplewood Falls didn't have enough time to investigate properly or enough training. People like Liam didn't want more police. More police meant it might be a stranger who pulled him over for driving erratically at night instead of a nephew who bought his story that he was just tired and then failed to administer a breathalyzer. That oversight earned Liam's nephew desk duty for the next two months and ensured that Sawyer will never promote him, but that didn't bother Liam. Liam got what he wanted. Sawyer shook his head at the thought. The new café was just a few yards away and across the street. He could see the owner outside, setting up an easel with a blackboard that advertised the day's lunch specials. He would walk back to the station on the other side of the street.

"Sorry about Liam's behavior there," Dean said. "He's a good guy, but a little opinionated. Likes to hear himself talk, you know?"

"No worries," Sawyer said. "Keeping my cool is part of my job. Thanks for providing the distraction."

Sawyer turned to cross the street, but Dean grabbed a hold of his arm.

"Liam talks lots of nonsense, but he's right on this one," Dean said, his voice low and serious. "Not about the kid, but about the investigation. It's a waste. When someone has been dead that long, sometimes it's best to leave it alone. There is no one left to mourn, and the flesh has already rotted away. Why stir things up?"

Sawyer shrugged off his hand.

"What's the deal, Dean? Are you all about the money, too? I thought you were above that. The kid is dead, and someone killed him. A killer is out there somewhere. Maybe we'll never know who did it, but we have to try."

"Just think about it," Dean said. "I practiced medicine in these parts more than forty years. You get to know people. There are things you can't talk about, and there are things I can't reveal, either. Patient confidentiality and all that. But I can tell you that nothing good will come of this. Leave it alone."

Sawyer stepped forward, closing the space between them.

"If you know something, if someone came to you with injuries related to the killing or confessed their involvement, you have an obligation to report that. This is a murder. Confidentiality doesn't apply. Tell me now."

49

Dean put his hands in his pockets, sighed, and rocked back on his heels. "No one confessed to me, and I didn't treat any related injuries. I can't help you there. But when you spend enough time listening to people's problems, you figure things out. You develop an instinct. I'm telling you to leave it alone. It's better that way."

Sawyer began to speak, but Dean cut him off.

"That's all I have to say, Sawyer. I have nothing to give you but advice. Do what you have to do, but be careful." He sighed long and deep, turned, and walked away, leaving Sawyer alone on the curb.

Chapter Eight

Maplewood Falls was a small town, and the weekly shopper was its only newspaper. But missing babies are big news, and the Amber Alert had stirred interest among media all over the state. Nick had been answering calls and the door all day, doing exactly what he was told. He talked to them. He gave them a story. He knew what they were all thinking and what some were brazen enough to ask. If the baby had been kidnapped, Carla was dead. But he couldn't believe that. Her purse was missing. The car was traceable to her. Why not leave her purse in the car or just take the money out of it? Why take the purse? It didn't make sense. He could not allow himself to believe she was dead. He would not.

Carla's mother had gotten a few calls, too, and she cooperated as Nick had requested. They needed to make Carla seem real to the public. People needed to know that she wasn't just the mother of a missing baby, but that she was someone's child, too. He had hoped some TV reporters would go out and interview Carla's mother, but none did. The house Carla grew up in was off a series of dirt roads on partially wooded farmland about ten miles out of town. Too far for a story that was already on the periphery of their coverage areas. It was a shame. Carla's mother looked so much like her. Maybe they would have understood his desperation a little better if they'd met her. No one had contacted Nick's parents, who had retired to Florida three years ago, or Carla's father, who had flown in immediately, but returned to Alaska after a few days. Nothing to do here but twiddle his thumbs and wait, her father had said.

The more coverage, the better, Zittle said. Nick only wished they had realized how many journalists would show up at his house, so they could have done a press conference instead and gotten it over with. He'd done three television interviews and sat down with two newspaper reporters for nearly half an hour each. He was grateful, but between the in-person visits and the phone interviews, he was exhausted, so exhausted he didn't hear the car pull into the driveway.

Rachel had something tucked under her arm when she burst through the door this time, a brown wooden box. He was appreciative of her efforts at first, but she was wearing on him with her constant presence, and he had planned to ask her to leave if she showed up. She wanted to come along yesterday when he drove around the rural area where Carla's car was found, showing the photo of her with Christopher to everyone he saw and asking questions, but he managed to avoid her. He didn't want her company then or now. He didn't want any company. He needed to stop thinking, stop thinking about the fact that the Amber Alert focused on Christopher and only on Christopher.

Nick had gotten nowhere with his own search, and he was depleted. He had no energy left to eat, sleep or talk, and he was glad for that. He'd already changed into his cotton shorts and a tee-shirt, ready to spend another night in the living room recliner, wishing for sleep but unwilling to close his eyes in case Carla came to the door or the phone rang. He didn't dare sleep in the bedroom. Christopher haunted him there with his cries in the middle of the night. Nick would wake up in a sweat and rush to the nursery, where he would find it just as empty as before. Every time. Nick started to speak, intending to send Rachel home, but then he recognized the box. It was a mancala board.

"Carla told me once you liked to play when you were frustrated with work. I'm new to the game, but I thought it might help. It might take your mind off things a little, maybe." Rachel flipped the case open on the kitchen table. Then she reached into her oversized purse and pulled out a bottle of Maker's Mark whiskey.

"I'm pretty sure this is your favorite, too."

Nick picked up one of the stone playing pieces. It felt good in his fingers, smooth and soothing. Like a worry rock. He never had to ask Carla. She'd sense his mood and pull the board out, and they'd play all evening. They'd laugh, and they'd tease each other, getting more competitive with each round. By the time he pulled her into bed, his worries would be forgotten. And in the morning, when his worries returned, they would seem trivial. Small and harmless. Who would have thought mancala could become foreplay? He smiled at the thought. They hadn't played since the baby was born, but that was because they were both tired. Christopher was still waking once or twice a night, and Carla was the one who got up with him most of the time. She was nursing and didn't want to introduce a bottle just yet. They made love, but it was planned, not spontaneous. He always asked first, out of respect for her exhaustion, but the sex was still good.

It seemed wrong in some ways, the thought of playing a game, especially this game, when his wife and son were missing, but that piece felt good in his fingers. Something about the ritual of it felt right. Maybe it would help him think. There had to be something she did or said that would give him a clue. If someone was after her, wouldn't he know it? Wouldn't she have told him? Or was this some random thing? It wasn't a carjacking. That was his first thought. They'd found the car. A carjacker wouldn't have ditched the car so carefully, would he? Carjackers usually want to get somewhere fast, or they want to sell the car as is or for parts. If they ditch cars, it's usually after they reach their destinations, and can run away without anyone noticing. They choose parking lots or on-street parking in busy downtown areas, not junkyards in the middle of nowhere. And Carla did not run off. She wouldn't do that.

It was hard to tell what the police were thinking, but he knew they still weren't taking the disappearance seriously enough, despite the Amber Alert. The discovery of the car had changed things, but not for long. They found no evidence of foul play inside, they said. No blood, no damage, nothing to indicate she'd put up a fight. And that one detective kept pushing him to go to civil court to get an order forcing her to bring the baby back. He clearly believed she'd left him. Everyone seemed focused on Christopher as the sole victim. The only person who seemed intent on finding Carla was Detective

Zittle, one of the two who had questioned him the other night. Nick still couldn't tell whether Zittle considered him a suspect, but that was okay. As long as he believed it was a crime, he would keep looking for evidence.

"Hey." Rachel said. "You going to play or just stand there, hogging the pieces?"

Rachel stood before him, holding two low-ball glasses of whiskey on the rocks. She set them on the table and then took a seat, motioning for him to do the same. Her smile was soft and slow, unlike her usual quick flash of teeth, and he noticed for the first time that her eyes were hazel, a light shade that could almost be mistaken for blue. It was good of her to do this. He needed to remember that as much as he wanted to push her away, she was suffering herself. Carla was a good friend of Rachel's, and now Carla was gone. Yet here was Rachel, putting her own needs aside for his sake. He had to admit it was a relief to lean on someone a little instead of trying to keep everyone else from falling apart. Carla's mother was a wreck, and her father had grated on his ex-wife's nerves the entire time he was here. Nick's, too. He was useless, too self-involved to be of any help. Nick's own parents were trying, but any conversations always ended with his mother in tears and Nick comforting her. This was his wife and baby, damn it, and they all wanted him to make it better. Where the hell were they? Where were their other friends? The people they watched the Super Bowl with every year, rotating houses, so Carla and Nick hosted only once every four years? Where were the friends they met for dinner before Christopher was born or went on hikes with as recently as a few weeks ago with Christopher in a backpack carrier? He knew some had tried, but that he had probably pushed them away with his sullenness. Rachel ignored his moods and inserted herself anyway. Maybe he needed that. Nick dropped into a chair at the kitchen table, where Rachel was already distributing the stones.

"You don't have to do this, Rachel. You must have better things to do." Nick swallowed half the whiskey in one gulp. It felt good, the burn in his throat, the instant warmth that spread through the rest of his body. He'd made a point of avoiding alcohol since Carla and Christopher disappeared, fearing he'd give into it and lose them forever. But this felt good. Just for tonight, he thought. A little bit tonight, and then no more.

Rachel set up the board, referring to her cell phone for directions.

"I want to be here, Nick." She reached across the table and placed her hand on his. Her skin was surprisingly soft, and her fingernails were perfectly shaped and painted. He fixated on her nails, the color of cranberries, unable to pull his eyes away. Carla used to paint her nails before Christopher came along, but now she worried he would swallow chips from the polish if he sucked on her fingers. She had a pedicure once, about two months after his birth. He'd given her a gift certificate and forced her to go, agreeing to come along and hold the baby. He felt his hand begin to tremble. Rachel pulled her own back and apologized.

"I didn't mean to upset you. I just—I just want to help. Tell me how I can help."

The trembling had moved through his body now and threatened to overwhelm him. This kind of thing had happened a lot lately, and it usually began with no warning. It was the emotions taking over him mentally and physically. He had to bring it under control. He had to learn to be stronger. He drank the rest of the whiskey and set the glass down hard, startling Rachel. Nick leaned across the table and looked into her eyes, not caring whether he was scaring her. Not caring about much at all.

"I want to know she's safe, Rachel. I want to know our baby is safe. That's all I want. I want the nightmares to stop because they happen night and day. Can you even imagine how I feel? What it's like to suddenly lose the two people in the world who mean the most to you, who are a part of you, with no explanation, nothing at all? I need something, anything at all. I can't go on like this. I just can't."

Rachel broke from his stare and played with her glass on the table, watching the ice as she slowly swirled it around. She had not yet touched her whiskey. She looked comfortable. That was the only word Nick could think of to describe her. She was calm and relaxed, like it was any other day. Like Carla was in the nursery changing the baby and would be right back. How could she be that way? How could anyone be that way when his whole world was in constant motion, constant chaos?

"What if that something isn't what you're looking for? I find it hard to believe Carla would have run off. I'm her friend. She would have told me if she was unhappy. I mean, I know she wasn't entirely satisfied, but who is? Life wasn't perfect. She sometimes talked about New York City, about wanting to go back there, and about the fact that she never imagined herself settling here in Maplewood Falls. But I'm sure you know about the sacrifices she made to be with you. Or, I should say, the compromises. She never described them as sacrifices. She could have told you if she wanted to move. She didn't have to run away."

Nick couldn't believe what he was hearing. Was she really suggesting Carla wasn't happy, that he somehow forced her into a life she didn't want? That he was so selfish and intimidating that Carla couldn't express herself? What had Carla told her? Why was this the first time he was hearing of it? Carla wanted to settle here with him. She wanted a baby. He never gave her ultimatums or threatened her. She was the one who proposed moving back home when they got engaged. It made financial sense, she said. She never asked him to move to New York or anywhere else. He could feel the heat rising from his chest and into his cheeks, but Rachel wasn't done.

"So, it's hard for me to believe, too. But then again, she behaved so oddly that day. She was distracted, like she wanted to tell me something, but couldn't. And we hadn't been all that close lately, not with the baby and everything. I was a jerk. A little jealous, maybe. I'm single and in my thirties. I suppose my biological clock is ticking. I wasn't there for her like I should have been. Maybe she wasn't comfortable talking to me. What if you get information and it's not what you want, not what either of us want? What then, Nick?"

Nick said nothing for a moment. He was struggling to compose himself. She was just saying what everyone was thinking, but he had stupidly thought she was different. He had let her into his house night and day, let her take care of him. He had let his guard down around her, this woman he didn't even like. What was he doing? His stomach turned. It felt like a betrayal, allowing her in here, drinking whiskey, playing games. He stood without thinking and shut the hinged, box-like board, spilling most of the stones onto the table.

"Rachel, please take your board and that bottle and get out."

He did not raise his voice. He didn't have the energy for an angry show. He just wanted her out of there as soon as possible. It was a mistake to let her in at all. It wasn't easy to live each day with that doubt lying dormant in his mind, craving conditions that would set it loose, nurture it, and allow it to flourish. Every day, every second, he forced it to stay in its place, and he won because he could distance himself from the people who tried to tease it out. But she was here, and she was trying to get into his head. She was tempting him to set it free. He didn't need people feeding him, entertaining him, making sure his needs were met. He felt like hell, and that was alright. Carla was likely feeling like hell. God only knew what Christopher was feeling. Why shouldn't he?

Rachel rose slowly and deliberately. She opened the game board, gathered the scattered pieces, put them inside, and then snapped it shut again. When she was done, she tucked the box under her arm and hoisted her purse over her shoulder, shaking her hair, which fell neatly into place. But her eyes were moist when she looked at him, and her step was uncertain as she moved to the door on her spiked heels. He'd rattled her, and it felt good. She'd been too calm throughout this ordeal, too composed. She stopped in the foyer and turned to him.

"I didn't say I believed it, Nick. I never said that. I just think you should be prepared because we never really know anybody, do we? We'll get her back, but … I want you to be strong and, sometimes, being strong means being brave enough to face all the possibilities. If you want to find her, you need to open your mind. Keep the whiskey. You need it more than I do. I don't really like it anyway. I'm more of a wine girl myself."

Then she was gone. Nick stood in place for a moment, unsure what to do next. His eyes rested on the whiskey bottle. It had burned nicely going down, and he could feel it starting to numb his senses. It took the edge off, allowing his muscles and his brain to relax. He reached for it and ran his fingers along the glass, but before he could think it over, his fingers clenched its throat, and he marched across the room to the kitchen, where he poured the whiskey down the drain. He didn't need it, and he wouldn't need it. She was wrong. He knew Carla better than anyone, better than she knew herself, and he felt her. He felt her screaming out to him, willing him to find her. She was in danger. Maybe she had been in an accident. Maybe someone kidnapped her and Christopher. But she was not free. Christopher was not free. They needed him, and he would not drown their pleas with a bottle of whiskey.

Nick returned to the table to collect the glasses, but he was distracted by a black messenger bag that was draped over the back of her chair. In her rush, Rachel had left it behind. He found a file containing offer papers for a house inside, and the paperwork was incomplete. She would need these, but he didn't want her coming back here. He sighed, grabbed his cell phone, and sent her a text. He would drop them off at her office in the morning, he said. At least the errand would get him up and moving. He was on his laptop, searching through newspapers all over the country for any stories involving an unidentified woman or a baby, when his phone buzzed, indicating he had a text. It was Rachel.

I'm sorry to bother you, Nick, but I need those papers tonight, and I don't have time to come get them. I'm up to my ears in work with a closing on retail space tomorrow and the offer I left at your house. Could you bring them by? I'll be upstairs, but just open the door and holler when you get there. I'll come right down. I won't keep you. I promise. And I am sorry, really. I didn't mean to upset you.

He didn't want to go anywhere, but he couldn't be that cruel. Her intentions were good tonight. Who else would have thought to bring over a mancala board? Not only did she attempt to distract him, but she had also planned to spend the evening with him when she had work to finish, a transaction that would bring her more income. He responded that he was on his way, changed his clothes, grabbed his keys and the messenger bag, and left, leaving the door unlocked behind him. He knew he should lock the door, but he always changed his mind at the last minute. What if Carla came home? What if she didn't have her keys? He liked that idea, that it was possible he could come home to find her waiting for him, smiling with Christopher in her arms.

Chapter Nine

Carla was watching a small, brown ant crawl across the floor when Rachel's voice came over the speaker. She couldn't make out the words. She was too busy thinking about the ant and monitoring its progress. If the ant had broken into her room, there must be an opening somewhere, something tiny that could be made bigger. The ant was free. It could come and go through whatever entrance it had found simply because it was small. Why couldn't she make herself small? It wasn't fair. But her pondering was disrupted by a new sound that came over the speaker, the sound of a doorbell. Someone was here, right outside Rachel's door. Just one floor above her.

"Oh, I have a visitor," Rachel said with exaggerated sweetness. "I wonder who that could be."

Rachel left the microphone on while she ran down the stairs to answer the door. Carla could hear her footsteps fading away. The silence that followed was broken by a male voice, far away and muffled even more by a closed door. "Rachel," the voice hollered. "Rachel? Where are you?"

For a moment, Carla couldn't speak. Her throat closed and the room titled. That voice. Then a scream erupted on its own, and it wouldn't stop. She screamed and screamed and screamed without resting until her throat was raw and her lungs were on fire.

"Nick! I'm here, too! Nick! Help me! Help! Please, help!"

When nothing more came from her throat, she used her body. Carla jumped up and pounded on the door with her fists and her feet. She threw her entire body at it, but it wouldn't budge, and no more voices came over

59

the speaker. No one answered her calls. The room and the speaker were silent. Carla was spent. She felt bruised all over, and her voice was broken, but maybe he had heard. Maybe he was gone now, telling the police what he suspected and sending them to rescue her. Or maybe he had slugged Rachel and knocked her unconscious and was outside that door right now, digging his way to her.

She curled up on the mattress, exhausted. How long had she screamed and pounded? Five minutes? Twenty minutes? Nick had been here, right here. Maybe he was still here. Could he feel her? Did he hear her? Her heart quickened when the speaker finally crackled again. Would she hear a new voice, a friendly voice? Could this be the moment she was saved? But the familiar sound of Rachel's voice crushed her like an anvil thrown onto her chest. She couldn't breathe. Couldn't move.

"Wasn't that kind," Rachel said. "Nick came by to drop off some papers I left at his house this evening. We'd been drinking whiskey, and you know how that goes. Alcohol makes me a little forgetful. We had a good time playing mancala. Thank you for that. We're getting closer. I can feel how badly he wants me. The blinders are coming off, and he's starting to see that he loves me, but you are still a distraction. He's a good man, and he took vows that bind him to you. It will take a while to convince him that it's okay to break those vows. He needs your approval, or he needs you to disappear. When the time comes, you need to disappear."

She was going to kill her. No matter what, she was going to kill her. How much time did she have left? "I'll disappear." Carla forced the words from her throat despite the pain. She hoped Rachel could hear her. Her voice wasn't much more than a hoarse whisper.

"I'll leave the country. You'll never see me again. Neither will Nick. I promise. Just let me go. Please."

"Oh, we all make promises when we are desperate," Rachel said. "Relax. I didn't say I was going to kill you, but I don't think I can trust you to disappear on your own just yet. I don't think I can trust Nick to follow his heart, either. These emotions are so new to him. He needs to love me more before you disappear. He needs to love me so much it hurts, and I need you for that. You sound a little hoarse. I suppose I should have told you that I can't hear you when the microphone is on. I have to click it off after I finished speaking, so he didn't hear a word. I hope you didn't yell too much."

Carla took a deep breath. Her throat was raw. The air rushing down her esophagus hurt. She needed water, but she didn't want Rachel to see her drink. She didn't want to show her weakness. She sat up on the mattress and hugged her knees to her chest. She lifted her head to the camera and hoped that her eyes were looking right into Rachel's.

"Okay. What do you need from me then?"

"Don't you worry yourself just yet. I'll let you know. Get some rest for now, and I'll see you in the morning. Night-night, sweetie."

Carla dropped her gaze to the floor. She wanted to curl up in a corner, to make herself as small as possible, but she wasn't convinced Rachel was no longer watching, and the lights were still on. So, she pulled out her journal and started to write. She wrote about her first week on the job at the Artic Hut, an ice cream stand on the edge of town that also sold hamburgers, hot dogs, and fries. They were sixteen years old. Rachel had worked there the previous season, so she was assigned as Carla's trainer. The job seemed easy enough, Carla perfected the wrist twist that resulted in the perfect soft-serve ice cream cone on the first day, and she had memorized the hard ice cream flavors by the second day, but she was still struggling to remember all the ingredients for banana splits, ice-cream brownie mounds, shakes and each type of sundae when carloads of kids from three different baseball teams pulled into the parking lot.

Dozens of kids piled out, all between the ages of eight and eleven. They pushed and shoved for chances to order at the square, screened-in window. Parents stood in the background, laughing and talking, paying no attention to the chaos their kids were creating. Orders were coming at her from all directions for all sorts of things Carla had never made before. She heard one kid call out for a chocolate shake, which was simple enough, so she turned to grab the silver shake cup. But then another kid shouted that he'd gotten to the counter first and then another and another. The tears welled in Carla's eyes. She didn't dare turn back to face them. Rachel had been on the grill, tending to a new batch of burgers. She looked up at Carla and winked. Then she set down her spatula, marched to the window, and took control.

Within a minute, Rachel had the kids lined up, one behind the other. She made it clear that those who violated the line, complained, or cursed would not be served. Then she turned to Carla and motioned that she should take over the register. Carla took orders and cash while Rachel reached her arms deep into the ice cream bins and created works of art. The rush last only fifteen minutes, but it felt like hours. After the last vehicle pulled away, Carla grabbed Rachel and pulled her into a hug. She thanked her over and over again.

"I was useless. I should be fired."

"No biggie," Rachel said. "You'll get used to it. Just remember you hold the reins. Somebody has to put them in their place when their parents won't. The parents do that all the time. They give their kids money and then fade into the background, acting like they don't even know them. You can make it up to me, though."

"How?" Carla expected her to ask for a shift swap. Rachel was scheduled for Friday night, but Carla was off.

"You can learn how to clean a grill," she said, shoving a grill scraper in Carla's hand. She picked up a charred burger from a platter next to the grill and bit into it. Rachel winced, and they both laughed uncontrollably. Carla scrubbed that grill cleaner than it had been in years, and when their boss came at closing time, Rachel made no mention of the rush or the tears. Rachel was good once. It was still in her somewhere. It had to be.

Carla tucked the journal back under her pillow when the lights finally clicked off, indicating it was bedtime for most normal people in the rest of the world. It was still possible that Nick heard something, that he suspected something. She needed to remember that. Maybe these walls were not as soundproof as Racheal assumed.

When she finally fell asleep, she dreamed of the ant. She dreamed that his entrance was followed by another and another and another until the floor, the walls, even the camera were covered in a blanket of ants. The blanket swelled, thickening, displacing the air and making it difficult to breathe.

Then they marched forward and crawled onto her body, nibbling away at her flesh. She stomped, slapped, screamed, and brushed them away, but it was useless. There were too many of them. Exhausted, she stood in place, enduring the pain and scanning the room until she spotted the lead ant, the one who had come first and seemed to be in charge of the rest.

"Why are you doing this to me?" she asked. "Why won't you leave me alone? You're hurting me."

The ant looked up at her, puzzled.

"Why? You said it was unfair that we could come and go because we are so small, so we are making you small. I brought a whole army, as you can see, and more are on their way. We will carry you out of here bit by bit, and we won't stop until we are done."

Carla was overwhelmed with terror. The bites felt like millions of tiny pinpricks at once. Not one spot on her body was spared. She brushed a swath of ants off her forearm and caught a glimpse of the raw and bloodied flesh before they occupied the space again, shielding her view.

"But you'll kill me! I don't want to die."

"We are only doing what you wished," the ant said. "You should be more careful what you wish for. Now, this will be much easier and go much faster if you would stop killing off my crew. It is pointless. I'll just bring more."

Carla thought she had closed her eyes, but it was the ants. They were in her eyes, in her nose and mouth. She was theirs. When the lights came back on, the signal that morning had come, she was covered in a salty film of dry sweat. She looked for the ant. If she found him, she vowed, she would crush him.

Chapter Ten

It had been only a week since the Amber Alert was issued, nearly two weeks since Carla and Christopher disappeared, but already the press calls were winding down. This was not their usual coverage area. The newspapers had few readers in Maplewood Falls, and the television stations had no advertisers here. They would not be back unless something big happened. Nick had been a businessman long enough to understand that, but it was still discouraging.

He had spent the early morning hours at the store reviewing the inventory, working on the payroll, and paying his suppliers. It felt good to do something concrete for a change, something that forced him to focus. But he couldn't stay once employees filtered in and realized he was there, hiding in a corner of his office with his back to the door. The store opened at seven, and he'd made it until nine. But it got to be too much. It wasn't the words. No one said much of anything. They didn't seem to know what to say. It was the looks, a mix of pity and blame. In their minds, his employees and his customers were already taking sides, figuring Carla left him with the baby and that one of them was at fault. But they didn't know her like he did. No one did. The worst, though, were the people who believed she was dead. They didn't have to say it. It was in their eyes. It was their looks he dreaded the most.

It had seemed like a good idea to walk to the store at five in the morning when the streets were empty, and the sky was just beginning to lighten, but now, in the bright light of day, Nick wished he could hide behind his windshield. Cars idled in the bank's drive-through, leaving their drivers with nothing to do but scan the village streets while they waited for the next teller. People waved as they drove past him. The convenience store on the corner was abuzz with men and women in need of all kinds of fuel—gas, caffeine, cigarettes, and breakfast pizza. He felt exposed, so he was relieved when he turned onto the residential streets for the remaining three blocks. He wanted to be home, where he could close the doors and pretend none of this was real, that he was sleepwalking during a nightmare.

As he passed the familiar homes, he couldn't help thinking about the evening walks with Carla and Christopher, when neighbors would step off their porches or rise up from their gardening or leave their own kids playing in their yards to greet them and take a peek into the stroller. He complained about the disruptions sometimes but, in reality, he was proud. His baby, their creation, was beautiful and was worth abandoning everything else for. Carla would beam when people stopped them, remaining polite even when they inundated her with advice about everything from sleep to nursing to losing the baby weight. She seemed to know just how long to let people talk and how to end the conversations in ways that left them feeling like they'd been helpful. She knew how to discourage the most annoying oglers without insulting them, walking and waving at the same time as if to say, "I'd stop if I could, but the baby won't let me."

The argument with Rachel had gotten him thinking, reviewing his courtship with Carla, his proposal, all the decisions they had made along the way. Did she participate, or did she just comply? He couldn't remember ever arguing over any of it or mulling over it. She was in tears when he proposed, but they were happy tears. They didn't talk much about her move back home. It just seemed like the logical thing to do since they were getting married here, and he couldn't move the store to New York City. She worked out an agreement with her boss that would allow her to keep her job, and she seemed happy with that. Where was the sacrifice? If she was unhappy, she should have talked to him, not Rachel.

They argued over his decision to keep the store once, but that was a long time ago, before they got married. She was angry that he hadn't consulted her. She reminded him that he had planned on becoming an engineer, and then he got angry, asking her whether her feelings toward him had changed because he wasn't pursuing the career she approved of. That was bad. They both said things they regretted and later apologized for. He reminded her that he could always sell the store and go back to school. His job and the fact that he lived at home through college meant he had no student loans. He was free to do anything he wanted. It came up again a year or so later, but under calmer circumstances. She asked whether he would still consider selling. He explained that it wouldn't be financially smart to sell at that point. If he waited a few years until revenues were higher, the equity could provide them with a huge nest egg. Maybe they could even retire early. She agreed, and they never talked about it again. They were happy. They had a good marriage, and their finances were solid.

The red flag on his mailbox was down when he arrived, indicating the mail carrier had visited already and taken the bills he'd finally gotten around to paying. He grabbed the stack of catalogs, magazines, junk mail, and more bills and took them inside, tossing them on the kitchen counter along with his keys. The house was unbearably quiet except for the rhythmic beep of his answering machine, telling him he had a message. Probably his parents or Carla's, hoping for news he couldn't give them. Nick sighed. He didn't want to deal with them, but he couldn't stand the beeping anymore. He reached across the counter to hit "play," but stopped when a small manila envelope in the mail pile caught his eye. His name and address were hand-written, so it probably wasn't junk mail, but he didn't recognize the writing. He picked it up and turned it over—no return address anywhere—and his fingers rested on a small lump inside. His heart quickened as he ripped it open. He didn't know what he expected, but he'd take anything at this point.

Inside, he found a folded piece of white paper and something small and hard wrapped in tissue. He took a few deep breaths to calm down, and then opened the note. The handwriting was different from the envelope. His pulse quickened. It was Carla's. He'd know it anywhere. But any elation he'd felt upon seeing it was quickly replaced by nausea. His knees buckled, and he dropped onto a kitchen stool, trying to focus on the words, despite his shaking hands.

I am so sorry, Nick. I am safe, and so is Christopher. I just couldn't do it anymore. I couldn't pretend I loved you. Here are the rings with which we sealed our marriage. I know you paid a lot for them. I feel guilty keeping them, especially since they mean nothing to me. Take them and sell them. Get your money back. Forget about me. Forget about Christopher. Find someone who loves you in return.

He unfolded the tissue paper, and two rings fell onto the counter with a clang that seemed to echo throughout the house. There they were—the engagement ring with the tiny diamonds embedded among gold swirls and the matching wedding ring that set into the engagement ring, making it appear as if the larger diamond rose from the smaller ones. He reached toward them with trembling fingers, but stopped as the words from the note began to sink in. She said to sell them, to get his money back. She said she knew how much he'd paid for them. He'd paid nothing. They were her grandmother's, given to him by Carla's mother when he told her mother he planned to propose.

Slowly and carefully, Nick set the note he held in his other hand down on the counter and reached for the phone. He'd already contaminated the note with his own fingerprints, but he hadn't touched the rings. Carla had sent him a message, alright, but it wasn't that she didn't love him. He riffled through the business cards he kept in the phone stand until he found the card from Investigator Zittle, and then he dialed the cell phone number he'd scribbled along the bottom. It went right to voicemail.

"Investigator Zittle, this is Nick Murphy. My wife and baby are in trouble. I got a note in the mail. I don't want to touch it anymore in case it has prints. Please, please get over here right away. You have to believe me now. Someone took them. They have my wife and son, and I don't know why. We have to find them. I'm going to hang up and call Sawyer. We've got to find them, damn it, before it's too late."

He sat back on the stool and let his head drop into his hands. Finally, he had something, something to prove she was alive. Carla was alive when she wrote this note, and she probably was still alive today. It wouldn't make sense otherwise. Why would a killer keep her around long enough to write a note? Why take that chance? Wouldn't that be more dangerous than just ditching her body somewhere and getting rid of the evidence? Someone wanted to keep her alive, but wanted Nick to believe she had run away. This person wanted Nick to stop looking. Did that mean he was close? Did that mean Christopher was alive, too? What did they want with her? Who would take her? Maybe someone who was obsessed with her? A stalker? But who? Nick grabbed the notepad they kept near the phone and started writing, jotting down the names of anyone Carla had ever dated or who had ever asked her out. Then he added male editors she'd worked with, men she had interviewed, their male friends in town. The list was growing and was becoming impossibly long. It would be of no help to police if he couldn't narrow it down, but he could stop writing. He didn't want to leave anyone off the list who might be a suspect. He was still writing half an hour later when Zittle came to the door.

Chapter Eleven

"What did you do?" Rachel's voice was firm and level, terrifying. "That note was supposed to convince Nick you'd run away. Instead, he called the police, and they're all over it. They came by the house last night and questioned me for an hour, asking for names of anyone I thought might be obsessed with you. I was late getting to Nick, and he didn't answer the door when I knocked. This cannot happen."

Carla swallowed hard. Rachel had not fed her dinner or breakfast, and all the skipped meals were catching up with her. When she did feed her, it wasn't enough to make up for all the calories she'd denied her. She was getting thinner already and weaker. She'd taken a huge risk, writing that note. What had she been thinking? Of course, Rachel would find out. No one suspected Rachel was involved. They'd have no reason to withhold details of the investigation. She would have to find a way to turn this around.

"I don't know, Rachel." Carla curled up against the door, hugging her knees and holding vigil by the food slot. "I really don't. Maybe my handwriting was shaky. Maybe he just doesn't believe I'd do anything like that. Maybe they think I stole Christopher now, and they are after me. Did they tell you anything? Did Nick say anything about what he believes? Do they think I abducted my own son? Think about it. It's not just me who's missing. It's Christopher, too, and this is an open investigation. He would have to call the police if he got any word from me at all. It doesn't mean he doesn't believe the note."

"Move over where I can see you," Rachel said. "Nothing is coming through that slot anytime soon. Not until I know what's going on, whether you betrayed me. I trusted you, Carla. I have fed you and kept you safe and warm. If I find out you tricked me, you're dead. We're all dead, and I'll make sure Nick suffers. You will be responsible if he suffers."

Rachel couldn't see her? Carla barely dared to breathe. The room was small, a perfect rectangle. She had assumed the camera could see everything. Where else was the camera blind? Carla crawled to the right, staying along the wall until she'd reached the mattress, which was positioned, so the short end shared the wall with the door. She climbed onto the mattress and leaned against the wall, stretching her legs out in front of her. She'd been sleeping the opposite way each night so she could see the door and the food slot. It had never occurred to her that the camera might have blind spots or that Rachel couldn't move it remotely to adjust her field of vision.

"I don't want to see your feet. I want to see your face. I want to see whether you are telling the truth. Flip around. Now."

She couldn't see her. This was huge. Carla could scrape away the material surrounding the door and shove the debris under the mattress without being seen…if she could find something to dig with and a way to dig without making too much noise or attracting Rachel's attention. For the first time since she woke up surrounded by these walls, Carla felt hope. Real hope. It was slim, but it was there. She quickly flipped and scooted back so she faced the door and tried to stuff that hope deep down where it would be safely hidden. Rachel would be studying her face. She couldn't let on what she was thinking. She concentrated on Christopher, and the tears started to fall.

"This could be good. Did you think of that? Maybe the cops think I was having an affair, and he doesn't believe I'd take off with some other guy willingly. Maybe the cops are just humoring him by questioning you. You could make someone up. You could tell them you saw me with some guy, but that you didn't think anything of it until now. What can I do to make it better, Rachel? How can I help?"

"How can you help?" Rachel said. "Sex. I need to know what turns him on, and I mean what really turns him on. Just to break that barrier. Once we cross that line, I won't need your help anymore. All the guys I've been with? They were just practice for the big game. I'll blow his mind away and, unlike you, I'll do it whenever and wherever he wants. After that, he won't be able to resist anymore. He won't want to."

Carla dropped back into the mattress and covered her eyes, suddenly nauseous and light-headed. She did not want Rachel to see her face right now, to see how repulsed she was at the thought of Rachel naked with her husband or trying to be. Would he respond? She'd like to think he wouldn't. He loved her. Love was stronger than sex, wasn't it? Their sex life took a dive after she had Christopher, but only for a while, and Nick was supportive. He was as enamored by Christopher as she was and just as tired between home and the store. Things had picked up recently when Christopher started sleeping for longer stretches. They weren't as impulsive as they used to be. Sex took a little planning, but it was still good. But what if he thought she was gone? What if he missed the clue in the note, and he did believe she abducted Christopher? What if he felt betrayed?

"I need time to think," Carla said without moving. "I don't want to make a mistake. I do know this though. He doesn't like a lot of make-up. Cut back on the make-up and make yourself a little vulnerable. Don't always be so perfect. Let him think you need him sometimes. People like to be needed now and then."

She could do that much. She could give Rachel baby steps.

"I'm sending in paper and a pencil. I want you to write down everything you can think of—how he likes to be kissed, where he likes to be touched, what time of day he likes sex best. And I want to know everything that turns him off, too. I'm going to turn off the water until you're done. If I'm happy with what I see, there will be water and a turkey sandwich in it for you."

Carla lunged for the bathtub, sank to her knees, and flipped on the faucets. She closed the drain and cupped her hands, drinking in all that she could as it flowed, full force, from the tap. If she could just fill the tub even a little bit, she could make it last.

"For every minute you keep that water on, you will go an extra hour without water. And drain that tub, too, or I'll never turn it back on."

Carla forced back the tears. The memories of old stories came back again—campfire tales about unearthed coffins with scratch marks on the insides of the lids, indicating the extent of the desperation when the victims regained consciousness six feet underground; news stories about kidnapping victims sealed into rooms or in underground boxes with no food, water or air and found too late; the short story she once read about a kid who planned his own funeral and burial just for the thrill of it. His friend buried him with a pipe for ventilation, intending to dig him up the next day. But another friend, who was unaware and mourning, placed flowers in the pipe, cutting off his air supply and killing him.

Carla's heart raced so fast, it hurt. Sweat, water she couldn't afford to lose, threatened to drench her clothes as she imagined the walls closing in, the air thinning, and her mouth sucking on the pipes for one last drop of liquid, enough to keep her alive just a little longer. She had to stop thinking. She would do as she was told. She would give Rachel what she wanted. She had no choice. But it wouldn't be that easy with Nick. Rachel would have to seduce him, and to do that, she would have to catch him in a moment of weakness. That was the key, to figure out a way to weaken her husband so he would have sex with her best friend even though his wife and baby were gone.

Chapter Twelve

No more sitting around, waiting for something to happen. Nick grabbed his keys from the counter. His wife and baby were out there, and they needed him. The envelope containing the rings was postmarked from Rochester, more than an hour away, but that didn't mean anything. Whoever took Carla and Christopher would know better than to mail it from the place they were holding them. The sender wanted Nick to go to Rochester to distract him, but he wasn't about to fall for it. The police were probably working that angle already anyway. Instead, Nick decided to head for the junkyard. Maybe the police missed something, something he would recognize that they might have assumed was irrelevant.

It had been three weeks since Nick last saw his son, and he found himself staring into every car that passed him in the opposite direction as he drove, looking for that familiar, toothless smile. Sometimes he watched the national news, waiting for coverage of big, public events that attracted crowds. He paused the TV every few seconds, studying strollers and baby carriers in the stills. He couldn't bear to watch any coverage that involved missing or injured children, though. He wasn't ready for that. Nick wondered whether Christopher had changed. Had he sat up on his own yet? Was he eating more than baby cereal? Was he even still alive? No, he couldn't think that way. He tightened his grip on the steering wheel so much his hands hurt, and his shoulders ached. The pain felt good and brought him back to the moment. Christopher was alive. He had to be. Nick had to be positive for Christopher's sake. For Carla's.

As he headed out of town, a sheriff's patrol car came toward him with its lights spinning and flashing, and he was filled with hope for a moment, but then he remembered they were not involved in the case. The patrol car sped past, probably after a speeder Nick hadn't noticed. Sawyer and the state investigators weren't as available or attentive as they had been in the beginning, not with Leland Boise's skeleton in their hands. Nothing like this ever happened here. Why now? Why Leland and Carla and Christopher at once? Nick knew he should be disturbed by the discovery of Leland's remains, bothered in the same sense as the rest of the community. He could feel it all around him, a heavy discomfort, a sadness, and sudden unease with both the unsolved murder and their own moral negligence when it came to Leland and his situation. There were other Lelands in town, other kids who were lonely and poor and uncared for, but it was easy to turn a blind eye in a community like this, a village with wrought iron benches that allowed downtown visitors to enjoy coffee or ice cream under the shade of the trees that lined its streets. A place where a carload of kids could be paddle boarding on the Finger Lakes within half an hour while their parents toured the local wineries to kill an afternoon. A place where struggling farmers were viewed as quaint, part of the authentic landscape that drew day tourists to the shops and restaurants. The Lelands of the community bussed tables after school and bought their clothes from the thrift shop, in part, because they had no way of getting anywhere else to shop. They fell asleep in class and dropped out junior year to work full time so they could pay rent. They had no cell phones and no internet to help them escape. It was easiest on everyone to let kids like Leland blend into the background, but the knowledge of his murder forced people to see him clearly for the first time. Nick knew he should feel the same. Leland was just a few grades behind him, but he didn't have the time or energy for that kind of self-reflection now.

The junkyard was nine miles out of town on the road to Corning, home of the famous glass factory, where half of Maplewood Falls worked. Police had found the Subaru on the fringe of the junkyard, around a curve from the main office, which was the entryway for customers bearing screwdrivers and wrenches to aid them in their quests for cheap used parts for their aging vehicles. Over the years, neighbors had clamored for fencing around the junkyard, calling it an eyesore. Nick had once signed a petition expressing his agreement. Now he was glad they'd lost that battle. If the junkyard hadn't been so open and accessible, the kidnapper might have dumped the car somewhere less visible.

Nick pulled over at the spot where the car was found and stepped out into the tall grass. It wasn't hard to find the exact location. The grass and weeds had been crushed by the Subaru and by the flatbed tow truck that pulled it out. Really, it was a stupid place to ditch a stolen car. The rusted, dented, and crushed vehicles that belonged to the junkyard were a good fifty feet away. The Subaru stood out as something that didn't belong, making it easy to spot from the road. The junkyard owners knew their inventory well. They were quick to spot the abandoned vehicle, but they waited a few days to report it, figuring it had broken down and that someone would come by to retrieve it. Investigators had used dogs to search the area for bodies. Nick was grateful he didn't know that until after they were done. He wasn't sure he could have handled it.

He started his own investigation at the edge of the area police had already searched. Whoever left the car here would have had to walk to another vehicle, one that was either on the side of the road and driven by a second kidnapper, or to a car that was hidden elsewhere ahead of the kidnapping. The volunteer group that had adopted this stretch of road had cleaned its shoulder just over a month ago, so there wasn't much garbage to sort through. That would make it easier. Police interviewed the junkyard owner and his employees, and they'd put out a plea to anyone who might have seen a suspicious person in the area that afternoon. They'd gotten nothing from anyone. Whoever did this had slipped away unnoticed, leading investigators to believe that two people were involved. But what if it was only one person? Where could that person go?

The neighboring cornfield was the most obvious means of camouflage. Police went through that as best they could, but it was huge, a good twenty acres. There was no way they could have searched all of it. Nick tried to think like a criminal as he waded his way through thistles and hay and buttercups and approached the stalks. He would want to go deep just in case someone found the car right away and suspected foul play, deep and fast. Before immersing himself in the field, he took note of landmarks—the rolling, wooded hills to the west and the more open sky to the east, where the farm continued on the other side of the road. The junkyard was to the south, and he knew the cornfield met up with a creek to the north. The sun was high in the noon sky. It was easy to get lost among the stalks, which were well above his height at this time of year, almost ready for picking. Without a sense of direction, he could wander for hours.

Nick stopped for a moment, overwhelmed by the sight and the smell of the fields. Every summer, near the end of July and all through the month of August, he and Carla ate corn on the cob at least three times a week. They bought it fresh from stands, or he brought it home from the store, where he sold produce from local farmers whenever it was in season. They would boil it, grill it, soak it overnight and throw it on a campfire. Nothing was sweeter than fresh-picked corn, and nothing tasted better on a warm summer night. He missed her.

He decided to go row-by-row, up one and down the next, a process that would take him all day. It was overwhelming, methodically scanning the ground for something a kidnapper might have left behind, but at least he was doing something. He'd gone in to work again this morning, this time until ten. The employees were getting used to his presence, but word had spread that police were now investigating his family's disappearance as suspicious, though police were careful to tell no one why. Customers who previously expressed sympathy now gave him wary looks, like kidnapping was contagious and he was a carrier. If not for the fact that the next nearest grocery store was more than half an hour away, they probably would have stopped shopping in his store. Nick couldn't concentrate on work anyway. This was better. This, he could focus on.

More than three hours later, Nick had found nothing but a crushed water bottle with a "use-by" date that was three years old. It had clearly been run over by a tractor at some point, so that ruled it out as evidence. His legs ached, and his throat was dry. He had planned to give it half an hour more, working his way back toward his entry point along a diagonal path, when his eye caught a glimpse of something white high up in the next row over. He pushed through the corn and spotted a McDonald's bag. It was caught among the leaves of two stalks, like it wanted to be found. How would a McDonald's bag make its way into here? It was unlikely any farmer would drive thirty-five minutes to the nearest McDonald's to satisfy a Big Mac craving while checking on his corn, and it was too deep into the field to have come from the road. Then again, why would a kidnapper munch on fast food while fleeing?

Nick reached up and grabbed the small bag. It couldn't have held more than a burger and fries. He nearly missed the receipt inside the bag. It was face-down, and it blended in with the white of its bottom. Carefully, he drew it out and looked it over. His hand began to shake, and his knees gave way beneath him. Kneeling on the earthen floor, he forced his eyes to focus and read it again. He had to be sure. It was for a Coke and a large order of fries, and it was dated June twenty-fifth, the day Carla and Christopher disappeared. The time stamp read two thirty in the afternoon, three hours after Carla's lunch date with Rachel.

Chapter Thirteen

Nick had worn a light jacket despite the heat. He was always cold lately. Rachel said it was because he wasn't eating enough. He'd been trying, but he couldn't seem to lift a fork or a spoon to his mouth. Everything felt too heavy. But right now, he was grateful he had something he could leave behind so he could mark the spot where he'd found the receipt. The trooper who had accompanied him back through the cornstalks spotted the jacket easily and waved as the helicopter passed overhead. Despite the din from the helicopter, Nick could hear the voice of its passenger over the trooper's handheld radio. They were lucky to have the help of the police helicopter, especially since it was getting late. The chopper was on its way back from another assignment, and the crew offered to take a look from above.

"A few yards further east, and you'll be at the rail trail. If this person was fleeing, I'd guess the suspect knew where to go and followed the rail trail out of the area. It's a long way into town, but the suspect could have stashed a bike ahead of time or posed as a runner. She would have blended right in."

By now, they knew the suspect was a woman and that Christopher and Carla were not with her. The McDonald's video showed a white, middle-aged man of average height with a full head of graying hair making the food purchase and then sitting at a table near a window that looked out onto the parking lot. He wore a golf shirt and cargo shorts. The man pulled the fries out of the bag and subtly slid a thick envelope he'd taken from an inside jacket pocket into it. The man ate a few of the fries, but he stopped when something in the parking lot caught his attention. He left the fries on the table, grabbed the bag, and went outside.

The parking lot camera is not as clear, but it shows the man walking up to a Subaru that looked like Carla's. A woman wearing sunglasses and a sun hat got out and greeted him. Hair the length of Carla's cascaded from beneath the hat. The woman opened the passenger door and pulled out an infant carrier. The carrier was covered with a blanket, making it hard to tell whether a baby was inside. With only black and white footage, Nick could not positively identify the blanket. Christopher had lots of blankets that were appropriately sized for his car seat, and this one was a solid color, like many of his. The man acted casual, like they were a set of divorced parents exchanging baby duties. He even seemed to laugh once. But, after he took the carrier and peered under the blanket, he gave the woman the McDonald's bag, which anyone watching would have assumed held food. He waited while the woman looked into the bag. Then he took the carrier to a nearby sedan, opened the door, and set it inside.

The woman appeared to be about Carla's height, but, unlike Carla, her hair was perfectly straight. Carla sometimes flattened her curls, but she'd been air-drying her hair since Christopher's birth, letting her natural waves go wild. She was also wearing shorts in the video. Rachel said Carla wore jeans and a t-shirt the morning she disappeared, and the clothes Rachel described were missing from the house. And the woman was built more thickly than Carla, not overweight, but rounder in the hips and chest. Those were the differences Nick noted for the investigator, but he didn't need to look that closely to know the woman in the video wasn't her. He just knew.

Bile had burned in Nick's throat as he watched the video on the trooper's cell phone and spoke with the investigator on his own phone. He felt it again now as he stood in the cornfield where the suspect once walked or ran. This woman must have chosen Christopher long before this attack, kidnapping, assault, whatever it was. How long had she been watching them? This wasn't a random act. This woman had time to arrange the hand-off and to find a wig that matched Carla's hair color. She had time to ditch the car and make Carla disappear. She planned this and planned it well.

But it was the end of the video that rattled him most. The woman seemed nervous, glancing in all directions before getting back into the Subaru. The man, however, walked brazenly toward his car after their transaction, peeking into the infant seat again and smiling. Then he drove away. He drove away with Christopher. He didn't seem worried someone would follow him or take the baby from him, and Carla was nowhere in sight. The investigator said Christopher was likely safe, probably a victim of black-market adoption, but he wouldn't answer when Nick asked about Carla. If this woman stole Christopher for the money that she would make off the sale, then she wouldn't need Carla. Carla was disposable. And if she'd taken a baby, she would be nervous, very nervous that someone would find out. If she was that careful in her planning…he couldn't allow himself to think about it.

Nick learned all this as he and the trooper stood guard over the spot where he had found the bag and receipt. They had waited ninety minutes in the field for Investigator Zittle and two troopers to arrive with a camera and other equipment. Getting the McDonald's video had been the top priority. Nick stood where he was told, being careful not to ruin any evidence. It wasn't long before they found sneaker prints, likely too small for a man, in spots that were well-protected from the elements by the corn stalks. There were only a few, and they were scattered, but they seemed to be heading right where the helicopter pilot had suggested. It would be impossible to follow them beyond the edge of the rail trail. The trail was well-used. It had been more than three weeks since Carla and Christopher disappeared, and it had rained at least four times. The best prints they found were between the lushest stalks where the leaves had shielded them from rain.

Anger overwhelmed Nick until he could feel nothing at all. The person who took his wife and baby, the person who sold his baby for cash, had been here. In this spot. She had ditched the bag and run through this field with the money in her hand, her bra, a purse, whatever. She had no heart. She was not human. If he found her, Nick would kill her, and he would experience no remorse whatsoever.

Chapter Fourteen

Sawyer stood in the back of the conference room and watched Nick as the investigator leaned into him. Nick sat slumped in a chair, looking like hell. His hair was disheveled. His eyes were swollen and red. His skin looked almost opaque, like he was malnourished and hadn't slept for weeks. Investigator Zittle rested both hands on the arms of Nick's chair, trying to get him to focus. There was just nothing left in Nick. He was numb.

"No one, and I mean no one, can know about any of this, Nick. I need to see that you understand. Whoever did this knew the area. She knew Carla. It could be anyone. It could be her own family, for all we know. But if Carla is still out there and if whoever did this knows we're onto them, they might harm her. Right now, we still have a chance, but I need your word that you will tell no one what we found today. Not even those closest to you or closest to Carla. Do you understand?"

Nick managed a nod.

"I want to be nice about this. I want to be understanding, but if any of this gets leaked, I'm coming after you. There are plenty of charges I could come up with. You can't get all emotional on me, and you can't slip. I know this has hit you hard, but you have to pull it together if you want us to find them. You'll have to put on an act. I've talked to the McDonald's manager, and he has promised to keep his mouth shut, too. He's the only one outside police who knows about the video, the only one besides you."

Zittle pulled back and threw up his hands in frustration. Nick remained motionless, almost catatonic. Sawyer was about to intervene, to offer to take

Nick home with him, where his wife could keep an eye on him and make sure he was okay when Nick stirred. He sucked in a long breath and rubbed his face with his hands. Then he locked eyes with Zittle with an intensity that seemed to unnerve him. When Nick finally spoke, his voice was flat but firm.

"Tell me there is a chance. Tell me Carla might still be alive and that we might get Christopher back. I need to hear that from you."

Zittle looked at Sawyer with raised eyebrows. Then he turned back to Nick.

"I'm not going to lie to you, Nick. Chances are slim that we'll find Carla alive. But until or unless we find a body, we're operating under the assumption that she is alive. And we have a plate on the sedan that took off with the baby. After looking more closely at the video, we do know there was a baby in the carrier. A partial face is visible when he checks under the blanket. The sedan was rented under a false name, but it was rented and returned at the Rochester airport. We're looking through the videos, and we're checking all records for flights that took off that day for a man and baby traveling alone. We're also checking with cab drivers, other rental agencies, and bus lines. We'll find him. It's only a matter of time. Even if you can't save Carla, you can save Christopher, and you might be able to protect other babies from the same scam. We need your help, Nick. Christopher needs your help."

Sawyer held his own breath, waiting for Nick's reaction. No one had come out and said yet what they knew was likely true, that Carla was dead. She was a liability. She was a threat. She was evidence. Whoever did this killed her, no doubt. If Sawyer were in Nick's place, he'd be locked in a padded room by now. But Nick stood, straightened his hair with his fingers, and smoothed his shirt. He took a deep breath and looked at them both.

"I guess I'd better get some sleep and start eating again. It's show time, and I'm not very convincing, the way I look and feel right now. Sawyer, no way am I going to sleep without help. Can you call Dr. Wade for me and ask him to prescribe something, and would you mind bringing it by the house later? I'd do it myself, but I think I'd fall apart."

"No problem," Sawyer said. "Do you want a ride home?"

"No thanks. I think I'll walk. The fresh air will help. Thanks for everything, Sawyer. I don't know what I'd do without you."

Nick reached for the doorknob, but then he dropped his hand and turned to Sawyer with a suddenness that startled both the police chief and the investigator. His expression—the confusion, the bewilderment, the sadness—weighed on Sawyer. He wished he could do something to bring him relief.

"She was happy, right, Sawyer? I mean, I know now for sure she didn't run away, but there was this doubt that crept up in me sometimes. She had a good job in her field, and then we had Christopher. That was what she wanted, what she said she wanted. I think. Could you tell? Was she happy? Be honest with me."

Happy. Sawyer never did like that word. What did it mean anyway? Not sad? Content? Giddy all the time? It was too relative. Sawyer would describe himself as happy, but his wife might not. He complained sometimes about money, about stress, the usual things. He wished they could afford a bigger house where the boys could have their own rooms, like their sister. Someday, they would find that unfair, that she had her own room simply because of her gender. He wished he had time to coach baseball or take Heather on three-day weekends to some cabin in the mountains, just the two of them. He could see that Heather might think he was unhappy, especially after late-night conversations triggered by sleep deprivation brought on by sick kids or thwarted plans or raises that weren't approved. But was he unhappy? He didn't think so. They were just bumps on the road, obstacles to be navigated. So, who was he to judge? Who was he to say the longing he saw sometimes in Carla's eyes, the sadness, was anything but a bump? He sighed.

"No, Nick. I don't think she was unhappy."

Nick nodded slowly and stared at the distant wall for a moment, seeming to consider and digest Sawyer's words. Then he left, and the room was silent. Sawyer watched through the glass in the door as Nick made his way down the hall and out of the building. Zittle shrugged and collected his notebook.

"Keep an eye on him," he said. "He's going to lose it when it finally hits him.

And, hey. Now that he's gone, I've got a question about that dead kid. Can you confirm for me that the total missing from the grandmother's house was twenty-one thousand dollars? We've raked that site clean, and we only recovered twenty thousand, six hundred. Might just be she rounded up the total."

"I'll look into it," Sawyer said. "I was just a kid myself, but the former police chief is still around. I'll have a talk with him. He was the kind who knew everybody's business. Worked until he was seventy-one. Can you believe that? He's in his eighties now, and I still see him out hunting every fall."

"Get back to me as soon you know," Zittle said over his shoulder as he left the room. "I've got a strange feeling about this one."

It was getting late, almost dinner time, and Sawyer still had a few hours of work to do. Even though state police were in charge of the two big cases, he had been devoting a lot of time to them and neglecting the smaller stuff. There were reports to review and schedules to revise to allow one officer time to testify in a burglary case that was going to trial next week. Sawyer had promised to speak about safety and active shooter drills at the school board meeting next week. He also needed to take a closer look at the budget to squeeze more money out for car repairs. Sawyer called Heather and asked whether she would mind if he stopped home to see the kids and then took off again.

"They're not here," she said in a voice that seemed flat and dismissive. "I'm behind on my schoolwork, so I called the sitter. She's taking them to the beach for dinner at the concession stand and some play time."

"I'm sorry, Heather. I know I haven't been around much. I—"

"Look," she snapped. "I just fell behind because I wasn't feeling well. Let's not make a big deal out of this. I knew what I signed up for when you became a cop. I can't be chipper all the time, okay? Right now, I have a lot to do and not much time before the kids are back."

She sighed.

"I'm sorry. I'm just a little stressed."

"It's okay," Sawyer said. "You have a right to be. How about this? I'll work through dinner and be home in time to give the kids baths and put them to bed so you can keep working. It's almost six now. I can come home at eight."

Heather agreed, and he hung up, but he couldn't help feeling there was something more going on. All this talk about happy marriages and spouses and careers—it was getting to him and messing with his head. Their marriage was fine. She'd been sick for a few days and had fallen behind, just like she'd said. He needed to quash this paranoia now. Whatever happened to Carla, they knew now her disappearance was not voluntary. It had nothing to do with the state of her marriage to Nick. It was time to get past that.

Sawyer called the sub shop and ordered delivery. He opened the schedule on his computer and dove in. If he couldn't finish tonight, he could work from home after everyone was in bed. He knew he wouldn't sleep well anyway, not with the panic that kept rising up in him. It wasn't his case. He shouldn't feel responsible, but he couldn't help feeling that Carla might actually be alive, despite the odds, and that every second wasted brought them closer to a murder investigation instead of a kidnapping.

Chapter Fifteen

I t had taken Carla two days to find a tool she could use to dig at the door frame. She couldn't actually search the room because Rachel would see her. So, she had to sit in the chair and pretend to stare at nothing at all, keeping her face as blank as possible while her mind explored the possibilities and her heart raced. In the middle of the night, when the room was dark, and Rachel was, hopefully, asleep, Carla felt her way along the floor to the sink. She opened the cabinet door and reached behind the basin, feeling for the flat, vertical metal bar that was attached to the knob near the faucet that opened and closed the drain. She wasn't exactly sure how it was attached, and it seemed to take forever to loosen it, but when it came apart, it fell to the cabinet floor with a clatter. Carla left it there and scurried back to her mattress, fearing that at any moment, she would hear Rachel's voice over the speaker. She didn't dare retrieve it until the next night. But now she had it, and now she was digging. Bit by bit, the rubber-like seal was coming loose.

Carla had done what she was told. She had jotted down everything she could think of when it came to Nick and sex. As a writer, she had crafted countless articles about sex throughout her career—"How to Get Your Partner in the Mood," "How to Ensure an Orgasm," "Is Recreational Sex Making a Comeback?" For some of those articles, she'd drawn from her own experiences and, every time, she had managed a certain kind of professional detachment. But this was different. This manual for Rachel, it should have been disgusting, revolting. It should have made her ill. Instead, Carla found herself reliving moments with Nick, taking pride in her ability to turn him on even when he was in the foulest of moods. She found herself wanting him, wanting to run her fingers along his chest, feel the clenching of his muscles as he drove himself in her, feel the heat of his breath on her neck. When she had to give it up, turn the paper over to Rachel, it was like she was ripping a piece of her flesh away with her own hands. She hadn't meant to be so vivid, so precise, so helpful. It had just happened, and now that document was in Rachel's hands. She shuddered to think about her reading it, about her practicing or planning sex with images of Nick in her head. Carla wanted to trust him, to believe that it would take more than a certain touch or a particular way of posing to persuade Nick to give in. She wanted to believe that Nick would only ever want Carla because she was Carla. But she had to will him otherwise. Rachel had to succeed because Carla needed time. Rachel turned the water back on after Carla gave her the notes, but she still had not fed her. She would feed her, she said, after she tested Carla's advice and determined whether it would work.

So, Carla kept digging, pulling, and pushing away at the seal bit-by-bit and watching the video screen to determine the time of day. It wasn't too hard to figure out. Carla remembered that the neighbor across the street worked at the bank, which was open from eight-thirty to four-thirty. She always parked out front, so Carla could tell about what time it was each weekday by the neighbor's comings and goings. That helped her figure out when Rachel might leave and about when she would return. Of course, that schedule was likely a little off since Rachel was busy with Nick, but at least it gave Carla a framework. Every few minutes, she scooped up the scrapings and slid them under the mattress, resting the metal bar on the floor along the wall out of the camera's sight. She was tempted to move faster, but she held herself in check. The smallest screw-up—the slightest bit of debris left in view, the bar accidentally left in her hand, any excess of noise that might be heard by the microphone—and that could be the end. While she dug, she moaned and cried softly or sang to herself, trying to cover up the sound. And she was careful to dig only in short intervals with longer intervals spent on the chair or the mattress. She didn't want to arouse any suspicions.

Her hands, fingers, and wrists ached, but she found encouragement just as she was about to give up on that first day. A few hours into digging, the bar slipped, pushing farther beyond the seal until only about two inches of metal remained visible. Nothing further seemed to block it. Since then, Carla made sure to poke wherever she dug until the bar passed through with little resistance. It appeared that this was just a sealed door covered by some type of soft insulation, just as she had hoped. If she could remove all the caulking, she might have a chance, but it was slow-going. Rachel had applied the rubbery seal from the other side of the door in large, uneven amounts. In some spots, she had been less successful, making it easy for Carla to push through without digging, but in other areas, the material had oozed through to Carla's side, dripping down the door. She had to scrape through thick gobs of the stuff before she could push through. She prayed that those bits of seal did not fall anywhere where Rachel could see them.

Whenever Carla saw the neighbor's car pull up in the video, she stopped for the day. Part of her felt foolish, knowing the video was a year old, but she would rather play it safe. She had already accomplished more than she thought possible with about half the seal removed. Two days, maybe three, and she would be done. It was getting late, and she would have to stop soon, maybe in an hour. She rubbed her palms, which were purple and sore in the center where the end of the bar pushed against them and got back to work. But then her heart sank. The metal bar hit something solid about halfway down the door. Carla started poking on the other side in the same place. Another barrier. Of course, Rachel would have to hold the door in place somehow while she sealed it. The door had no hinges. She poked some more and determined it was rectangular, about four inches wide. It felt like wood when the metal bar made contact. A two-by-four, maybe? Rachel would probably have nailed it to the door and lifted the door into brackets on either side. This would be harder than Carla thought. She would need enough force to push the brackets out of the wall or break them. She prayed that in her rush, Rachel had done a lousy job securing them.

She still didn't know exactly what covered the door on the other side. From reaching into the food slot and feeling around, Carla figured it was fiberglass insulation about two feet thick. If that was the case and if there was nothing else after that, she could tear it when she pushed the door open. Regardless, she would need to do it when she knew she had time, a few hours at least. If there was something more blocking her way beyond the insulation, she would need time to put it all back together and come up with another plan.

The room was quiet until long after dark when the slot at the bottom of the door opened, and Rachel slid something in. Carla crawled off the mattress and over to the tray, feeling the contents with her fingers. It was a sandwich, a bag of chips and an apple and something else, a thin, flat, rectangle about four inches long and maybe an inch or two across, wrapped in paper. She held to her nose and took in its scent. It was chocolate. And that could mean only one thing. As hungry as she was, Carla pushed the tray aside, fell back onto the mattress, and let it all go. The tears came fast, and her sobs shook her body in waves. She didn't remember falling asleep, but when she awoke the next morning, she felt as though she'd swum across an ocean and back. Her muscles ached, and her eyes burned. She looked at the Hershey's bar on the tray and held her stomach as dry heaves overwhelmed her.

On the napkin was a note.

Hershey's chocolate is cheap, a quick and sweet energy boost, like last night. If tonight goes as planned, I'll bring you some Godiva. Wish me luck, bestie!

'If tonight goes as planned ...' So, she had not succeeded. Something had happened, but Rachel could easily have interpreted the slightest touch as intimacy in her state of mind. There was still time, but probably not a lot. Rachel would try to take it further and, if Nick resisted, she would lose it. They would all be dead. And what if he didn't resist? What then? Rachel wouldn't need her anymore. She would turn off the water and leave her there to die. She didn't want to die. Carla's right wrist was swollen, and her left wrist wasn't much better. But she ate the food Rachel had left her and pushed the tray back through when Rachel demanded it. She checked the video every few minutes to determine whether it was past the time Rachel would normally go to work. When she was sure it was late enough, she slipped the metal bar out from under the mattress and started to dig again.

Chapter Sixteen

I t was clear from the exterior of Rachel's house that it was just that, a house. A place to eat, sleep, and shower. The lawn was mown, but no flowers or shrubs lined its edges, and the wide front porch that wrapped partially around one side of the house offered no seating for visitors. A sign on the front door warned against solicitors. The interior had the same feel as what Sawyer remembered. He had helped state police question Rachel and search for clues after Carla was reported missing. Artwork hung in strategic places on the walls, but there were no photos of family or friends. The living room furniture was elegant and clean, but it lacked the kind of wear that would reveal the favored spots by the fireplace or in front of the TV. The kitchen was uncluttered, but it also looked barely used, with countertops free of appliances, containers, and holders for utensils. No dirty dishes from her lunch with Carla and no take-out containers smelling up the garbage. Everything was clean, practically sterile.

The house had no life.

Rachel was leaving for work when Sawyer knocked. She motioned for him to enter, but she was jittery, obviously bothered by the intrusion, and anxious to get to her real estate office. She was good at her job. Rachel was their agent when he and Heather moved back to Maplewood Falls. She was tough, threatening to push back the closing if the sellers failed to eliminate the smoke odor in the house and clean up the dog feces that littered the backyard. She negotiated a price that was fifteen thousand below list price and got the sellers to throw in a one-year home warranty. So, he wasn't surprised that she was annoyed by the possibility that he would make her late.

"I won't take much of your time, Rachel," Sawyer said. "I just wanted to pick your brain a little more, see if you remember anything else from the day Carla disappeared. She told you she had a dentist appointment. Did she say where, whether it was her regular dentist or a specialist? We assumed it was her regular dentist and turned up nothing, but maybe it was someone new. Did she say why? A sore tooth? An infection? Maybe she broke a tooth after she saw Nick last and before she came here? It's the little things that might help us find her, the things that might seem trivial to you."

"Not that I mind talking to you, Sawyer, but aren't state police handling this?" Rachel asked as she ducked into the half bathroom off the foyer with a tube of lipstick. "Why are you here asking questions and not that state investigator guy who came before?"

Rachel emerged from the bathroom with glossy, deep-red lips that made her dark hair seem even darker. Her eyes flicked toward him every now and then as she packed the make-up into her purse and flung the bag over her shoulder, like she was keeping him in check. She had managed, with her body language, to prevent him from going any further than just inside the front door. Sharp. That was the best way to describe Rachel. She was sharp—always focused, always thinking, and always aware of her surroundings. Probably intimidating to people who didn't know her well.

"His name is Zittle, and he is spread thin between Carla's disappearance and the discovery of Leland's remains. I'm helping him out, is all. We can talk at your office if you'd rather. I'm guessing you're in a hurry."

Rachel slipped into a pair of high heels and took her keys off a hook near the door to the attached garage. Sawyer was only supposed to explore the kitchen, bathroom, and living room of Rachel's house when he was here last, rooms where Carla had been. They had no reason to look elsewhere. But he had given himself a quick tour of the rest out of curiosity. It was an old house with a choppy layout. To the left, the foyer opened to the living room and to the stairs leading to the bedrooms. The garage and the basement stairs were to the right of the foyer, with the garage slightly forward of the house, where her keys had hung. The eat-in kitchen was straight ahead. Her foyer felt like the entrance to a labyrinth.

"I don't want to talk at my office. I don't have anything to say. I'll call you if I think of anything. I promise, but now I really have to go. I'm meeting clients at eight-thirty." Rachel smiled and swung her keys on her finger playfully. "Lock that front door, would you? You can leave through the garage with me."

As Sawyer locked the door, he heard a crash. He turned to find Rachel standing near the garage door, red-faced, with water stains on her pants and shoes. An empty Doritos bag, a paper plate, an oddly squat cup, and a chocolate bar wrapper were scattered on the floor, and a brown plastic tray had landed near her feet.

"Damn it! Now I have to change."

Rachel's face was flushed, and her fists were clenched at her sides. Even her purse was a victim. Water clung to the leather and dripped from it onto the floor. It wasn't much. The water stain on her clothes was small and would dry. She could wipe her purse off and be on her way, but she seemed excessively irritated by the whole thing. He reached around her to pick up the tray and the cup, but she slapped his hand away.

"Hey, no need for that," Sawyer said. "I was just helping clean up. What happened?"

"What happened?" Rachel glared at him. "I am a busy person. I am working. I am doing what I can to help Nick. I'm so worried about Carla that I'm not sleeping and I'm eating junk instead of real food. That's what. I ate dinner at my desk last night, so I could get some work done, and I brought the tray downstairs when I was done. But I set it on this table for some stupid reason and forgot, and then you came along, and I forgot again. And now I am a mess, and I am going to be late for my meeting. So, no, I don't want your help. Please leave. Now."

Her voice was controlled, but barely, and her eyes were on fire as she stared at him. He'd never seen Rachel angry, and it was a side of her he hoped never to see again. He understood she was stressed between her meeting and Carla's disappearance. Everyone involved was stressed, but that was a quick one-eighty from the woman he'd been talking with moments ago. It was unsettling.

"Fine," he said. "I'll let myself out. I hope your day gets better, but I need to talk to you as soon as possible. Come by my office sometime today if that's better for you."

"I will if I am able," Rachel said in a level but firm voice, "but I have lost a lot of time because of Carla and that baby, and that means I have lost showings and listings. So, forgive me if I am not extremely eager to sit down with you and review everything that I have already told you and the state police."

"Christopher," Sawyer said.

"What?" Rachel wiped some of the water off her purse with a napkin she'd picked up from the floor.

"That baby's name is Christopher."

For a moment, Rachel looked like she might explode, but then her face softened, and she tossed the crumpled napkin onto the accent table. She reached out and touched Sawyer's arm, raising her eyes until they met with his.

"Of course," she said. "Christopher. I guess commissions don't mean much in comparison to everything else that is going on. I didn't mean to be so rude. I'm just frustrated. Like I said, I haven't slept much since Carla and Christopher disappeared. I can't help thinking maybe I could have done something, been a better friend. Maybe if I had been listening more, this wouldn't have happened."

She reached past him, unlocked the front door, and opened it for him

"I will stop by. I promise. But I really do have to get going. Please keep me posted if there are any updates."

Sawyer remained parked out front for a few moments while he answered a text from Investigator Zittle and checked his email. The garage door opened, and Rachel's car pulled out. She reversed a little faster than she should have, producing a squeal with her tires as she turned onto the street.

When Sawyer finally returned to his office that afternoon, he asked his secretary to request a copy of Rachel's interview from state police. He had read it before, but maybe he missed a clue or a hint. Carla must have said or done something more that was out of the ordinary. The fact that she mentioned a nonexistent dentist appointment indicated that whatever triggered the events did not begin after she left Rachel's house. It was already in motion.

"Get the neighbor's statement, too, would you?" he asked.

Maybe the neighbor who saw Carla leave noticed something odd—a change in turn signal when she pulled out of the driveway, a pause to reflect as she clicked Christopher's car seat into place, a quick glance in an unusual direction, anything at all. He sighed. It was funny. Sawyer had always thought of Rachel as a successful person, a person other people might envy. She made good money and had always seemed so put together. But that tray, the fact of it and the contents of it, seemed sad. Pathetic even. It tainted his image of her somehow. Nobody was what they seemed anymore. No one at all.

Chapter Seventeen

Nick was numb, physically and mentally. His baby was gone, in the arms of another set of parents who might or might not know he was kidnapped. And he knew what Sawyer and the investigator were not telling him, that they were sure Carla was dead. Dead. The word sounded so strange in his head. He could not speak it. He would not. He would not give in to that kind of power. He could feel nothing one way or another. Not hope. Not devastation. Nothing. He was done. The sun brightened the living room, despite the drawn drapes. It would be a gorgeous day, a perfect day for drifting on the lake in a pontoon boat, nursing an ice-cold beer. Carla would like that, though she wouldn't touch the beer for fear of tainting Christopher's milk. They hadn't been on the lake since the baby was born. The summer had just begun when they disappeared. They'd had all kinds of plans, so many firsts to experience with Christopher. But the lake-perfect days were passing by without them. They'd never get them back.

He'd woken up in the recliner again, but he knew he didn't sleep much. Sleep was elusive these days. He should go to the store and check on things, but that all seemed unimportant. The store would survive another day without him. He took a shower, brushed his teeth, and shaved, but he had no clue what to do next. He sank back into the chair's soft leather and closed his eyes. He had no idea what time it was when Rachel came through the door, uninvited once again and unwelcome after what she'd done the previous night, the way she had behaved. The way he had behaved. He needed her out, out of his house, and out of his life, but he was too drained to do anything at all.

"Nick?"

She set something down on the kitchen counter, her purse maybe, and came into his view. She was dressed for work. Good. She wouldn't stay long. He did not want her here. His lips still burned from last night, from the shame of it. He never should have let her in then, and he should have locked the door this morning. Why was she here? The scene had been running through his head all night, tormenting him.

"About last night, Nick," she said, keeping her distance. "I'm sorry. I don't know what else to say."

Sorry. That was how the conversation started last night. She burst into the house, much like this morning, and apologized for ever suggesting Carla had run away. She said she never once believed Carla would intentionally leave him, but that sometimes she preferred to believe Carla left on her own rather than facing the alternative, the possibility that she and Christopher were taken, victims of something too horrible to comprehend. She stood in almost that same spot, her shape silhouetted by the kitchen lights. He came close to telling her about McDonald's, about the exchange. He wanted to throw it in her face, but he had promised he wouldn't tell a soul. She kept talking last night, and she got to him.

"I need this routine, Nick," she said. "I need to take care of you, so I can take care of myself. This is selfish on my part, I know. But please, Nick. Try to understand where I am coming from. Give me another chance. Just let me be around you, around everything that is Carla. Everything that is Christopher. I need this."

He could understand that, that need to be surrounded by everything that was Carla and Christopher, to feel them in the air. So even though he'd never liked her, even though her presence so often irritated him, even though he wanted to be alone, he let Rachel stay last night. She had brought subs from Subway—Italian for him, chicken with cheese for her—and two cokes. No whiskey. No mancala. No conversation, at least not for a while. She checked messages on her cell phone while they ate. He stared at nothing at all. He softened. He let down his guard. He even swallowed a few bites.

He didn't know what made him do it, why he let her kiss him after they ate or why he kissed her back. There was something about her that attracted him that night, something in her voice, the smell of her skin, her touch. They had both risen from the table at the same time, and she moved toward him, intending to clear his place just as he moved to clear hers. They nearly collided, and she was so close, he could breathe in her breath. It smelled of cherry bubble gum, like Carla's. She put a hand on his arm to steady herself and laughed, tilting her head back, exposing her throat. And then she brought her face down, her lips brushing his. She pressed harder and pulled him toward her.

He forgot himself for a moment and forgot it was Rachel who had kissed him. He kissed her back, hard, desperately. He kissed her and reached his hands under her blouse, cupping them over her breasts, wanting to believe she was back, that the nightmare was over. But then she whispered in his ear, and he remembered. The voice was not Carla's. This was Rachel, the same Rachel who had just apologized for being insensitive. He pulled away, but he didn't have to order her out. She left on her own. He thought she understood he didn't want her back, that he wanted nothing to do with her. But here she was again.

"You need to leave, Rachel."

He was wide awake and alert now, and he was angry. He stood and walked toward her, blocking her from stepping into the living room from the kitchen. This was his home, Carla's home. Christopher's home. Rachel had no rights here.

"Why are you here? Why are you always here?"

It was the way she kissed him last night that threw him, the way she touched him when she caught her balance. The way she teased him first with her lips and then took what she wanted. It was something Carla would do before Christopher was born, before they settled into married life when they were still dating and still daring enough to make love in his office in the middle of the afternoon with customers wandering the aisles and employees at the cash registers just twenty feet away, maybe needing more one-dollar bills for their drawers or a rain check issued or a break to use the bathroom.

He was always reluctant at first, afraid they'd get caught and his uncle would fire him. But she would tease him like that. She was irresistible, and he always gave in. He thought that was unique to Carla, that trick of hers. But maybe it wasn't. Maybe it was a trick all women used on men, a tip they shared. Tease them first, and then pour it on. Had Rachel planned it? Did she know how he would react?

Nick's anger with Rachel grew quickly into something else. Anger with everyone—Sawyer, Investigator Zittle, Carla, Christopher, his employees, his customers, everyone. It was as if he'd been pulling his emotions back in a rubber band, like a slingshot, and Rachel's appearance had startled him into letting go. He was free. His anger was free, and he felt more alive than he had in weeks. It felt good. He grabbed Rachel's purse and threw it at her, but she flinched, and its contents scattered about the tile floor. Then he tipped over the garbage can and threw his coffee mug against the wall, shattering it. He wanted to break something else. His eyes searched the room, but then they settled on Rachel. She was cowered in the corner of the kitchen near the stove, protecting her face with her hands. A shard from the mug had nicked her arm, and blood trickled to the floor. She looked terrified. He had done that. He made her feel that way. He cut her. The energy drained from him as quickly as it had surfaced. What had he done? He grabbed a towel from the dish drainer and sank to his knees beside her, pressing the towel against the wound.

"I am so sorry," he said in a voice that shook. "I'm so very sorry. I don't know what came over me."

Rachel took the towel and pushed his hand away. She stood slowly and shook a few more shards from her clothing. Then she rinsed the cut in the sink and patted it dry with the towel, all in silence and without looking at him. He moved behind the breakfast bar into the living room, trying to create enough physical distance to ensure her that she was safe from him. Would she call the police? She had every right to. She'd done nothing wrong, nothing but kiss him the night before. And he had kissed her back. He was just as guilty. Maybe he'd been too hard on her. The kiss wasn't intentional. They were both upset and confused. They were aware it could happen now.

It wouldn't happen again. He wouldn't let it.

"Rachel, please. That wasn't me. I promise—"

"Hydrogen peroxide." She turned and gave him a weak smile. "And a Band-Aid. If you want to be helpful, quit talking and get me something to fix this thing up. But put some shoes on first. I don't have time to take you to the ER to get shards of cheap ceramic removed from your foot. I'm already going to be late for work."

Nick did as he was told, returning with a container full of bandages of varying shapes and sizes along with Neosporin. He carried a spray bottle of hydrogen peroxide in his other hand. He offered to help, but she declined, motioning for him to put it all on the counter.

"Look, let's forget it," Rachel said as she sanitized the cut and stretched a bandage across it. The injury wasn't as bad as he'd feared. Once the bleeding stopped, it was hardly even noticeable. He righted the garbage can and picked up Rachel's purse, gathering the items that had fallen out and placing them back inside. Then he swept up the remaining bits of ceramic and threw them away. The mug was one of his favorites, a souvenir from their trip to the Grand Canyon four years ago.

"The kiss, that whole thing, was an accident. We're both upset. I'm sure you are sleeping even less than I am. That does things to people, makes them a little crazy. Maybe even drives them to do things like this." She raised her injured arm. "I'm not going to stop being your friend simply because you lost your temper. You're going through a rough time, and I get it, probably more than anyone. I hope you'll still be my friend, too."

What could he say? She was right.

"I don't know what came over me. I just exploded with no warning, like an overstressed pressure value. You didn't deserve that. You just happened to be here when it happened. I can't apologize enough."

"You don't have to," she said. "Let's just get back to normal. The new normal. Hopefully, the temporary normal. I'll come by tonight with some pizza because I honestly don't trust you to eat on your own, but I won't stay. You need some space. Eat the pizza, take a sleeping pill and get some rest. You'll feel better in the morning, at least physically, and that will help. You need to stay strong for Carla and Christopher, and you're not doing that now. You're falling apart. You can't afford to fall apart."

He nodded in compliance as she gathered her things and left. She was right again. Nick fixed himself a bagel with cream cheese and took it into the study, setting the plate on the desk while he pulled open the blinds. Then he fired up his laptop and typed the words "black market babies" in the Google search bar. It was time to face the possibilities, to prepare himself mentally and physically for whatever might come.

Chapter Eighteen

Sawyer scanned the statements again. Nothing. Rachel had to have noticed something more, something that would lead them to this female impersonator and the man who took the baby. She said Carla was acting strangely. How, exactly? Did Carla know someone was after her? Was someone threatening her, trying to force her to give up the baby? And Nick. To Nick, the morning Carla and Christopher disappeared was like any other. His description of Carla was the opposite of Rachel's. She was happy, bubbly even, excited to meet with her friend. But, sometimes, when we are that close to somebody, we don't notice the signs. Maybe Carla was too happy. Maybe she was faking it.

Sawyer had tried to run it by Heather. Heather and Carla were not especially close, but they were friends. Heather was a year younger than Carla, Sawyer, and Nick, but she and Carla played soccer and basketball together for years. Toward the end of his senior year, when she and Sawyer had been dating for several months, they sometimes all went for pizza together or hung out at parties. They attended each other's weddings and, when Sawyer and Heather returned to Maplewood Falls three years ago, just before their youngest was born, Carla reached out to her, bringing cookies for the kids on move-in day.

But something had shifted in Heather since Carla and the baby disappeared. Not right away, but a few days later, about when the car was discovered, and it was more than some physical illness. Heather had always listened eagerly to Sawyer's cases. She seemed to find the holes where he didn't see them. At first, she offered her own perspective on Carla, insisting on foul play. Heather had seen Carla several times since the baby was born, and they had talked about the aftermath—the hormones, the lack of sleep, the pounds that wouldn't melt away. She showed none of the typical signs of postpartum depression and readily admitted to the negative stuff, Heather said. She didn't pretend to be constantly happy, nor did she seem depressed.

"She was grounded, Sawyer," Heather said. "I know grounded when I see it."

But lately, Heather seemed withdrawn, distracted. She didn't ask for updates, and she didn't seem to listen when he tried to give them to her. She had no interest in Leland Boise's case and seemed to get annoyed when he talked about work at all. She had gone nowhere with the kids for the past week—not to the park nor to the beach—and that was unlike her. She was a social person, and she liked to keep the kids active. When he stopped off at home for dinner last night, she was still in the sweats she'd worn to bed the night before. She had ordered pizza for dinner, something she usually did only when Sawyer pleaded. He tried to talk to her about it, but she insisted nothing was wrong. She was just tired and worried about the kids, she said. This whole thing was too close to home, for both of them. What if the same thing happened to her? What if someone took their kids?

"I couldn't handle it, Sawyer. What if someone took me away from the kids? What then?" Her voice trembled with a fear that was real. He needed to find Carla and Christopher, to set the balance right again.

Sawyer surveyed his desk and sighed. Two different cases. Two notes and one envelope. He stared at the photos of the handwriting on his desk. Somehow, he'd had the crazy notion that two of them would match—either the strange handwriting on the envelope and the note in Leland's pocket, or the note from Carla and the note in Leland's pocket. If the two cases were connected, it might have given him more clues. Whoever killed Leland might have guessed his body would be unearthed by construction. Maybe he should pursue the potential connection to Carla. Maybe Carla killed Leland. Maybe that connection was the reason Carla disappeared and, maybe, the whole missing mother-and-baby scenario, right down to the man's involvement and the McDonald's video, was all a ruse. She could have paid the man to enact the scene. It was far-fetched but possible that Carla set up her entire disappearance.

But the writing in the two cases was nothing alike, and preliminary analysis results confirmed it. They were two separate cases. He was letting his imagination get the best of him, letting it distract him. Sawyer had three stacks of yearbooks on his desk from the year Leland disappeared and had started going through them. No matches so far, at least not as far as his untrained eye could see. Still, something about the note from Leland's pocket bothered him. It was familiar—either the handwriting or the message. He wasn't sure.

He'd found the former police chief building a deck on his house with the help of his grandson. He looked healthier than ever, and his mind was still sharp. He knew of no documentation that proved Leland's grandmother had twenty-one thousand dollars in her house, but he said he was confident the number was correct. She counted her money once a month, he said, and she had added an extra fifty-two dollars that week to bring it to the even amount. She told the chief Leland was a selfish boy and always had been. Leland had asked for cash a few days earlier, saying he needed a real haircut, but she told him she would cut it for him. She guessed that was why Leland stole the money, because he was angry that she didn't pay for his haircut. It really didn't matter, Sawyer thought. Maybe there was twenty-one thousand. Maybe there was less. Or maybe he spent some of the money before he ended up at the warehouse. It would be impossible to track that spending now.

The more Sawyer learned about Leland—the more people he interviewed—the more he understood how wrong he had been about him. He'd thought Leland was lonely, that he had no friends, but that wasn't the case. Leland did not have a traditional group of friends, peers who were all friends with each other and hung out together. His friends were different. They were scattered throughout the area and among age groups, and they were not necessarily known to each other. Mrs. Beecher, the high school art teacher, was among them. She had only been in the district a few years when Leland came into her class. She said he was incredibly talented and that she had looked forward to seeing how his art would evolve through high school. "He spent his study halls and his lunch period in my room. He was a good kid and a good conversationalist. He liked to talk to adults," she said.

Leland had won an award or two in middle school for his art, and he could have won some in high school if he had let her enter more of his work into contests, she said. But he was shy about it. He seemed to be afraid of attention, unable to handle too much at a time. He had an analytical nature, which probably contributed to his artistic success, she said.

"He saw things other people didn't," she said. "At such a young age, he could sketch complicated emotions into faces. That's not the kind of thing you can teach. We had talked about art school, and he was thinking about it, but then he disappeared. I googled him now and then, thinking his name might turn up online, but I got nothing. I guess now I know why."

Mrs. Beecher still had a few of his pieces in her classroom. Sawyer had hoped they might contain clues, but he found nothing. One was of a horse that almost looked like it was in motion. The muscles were perfectly sculpted with acrylic paints. He could almost feel the heat coming off them. The other was a portrait of a child, a toddler with chubby cheeks and eyes that seemed alive. The eyes left Sawyer feeling unsettled, which was probably Leland's intent. An odd choice for a teenager, he thought. Mrs. Beecher said it was unfinished. He had started it the day before he disappeared.

"I'm guessing he had a young cousin or niece he fell in love with," Mrs. Beecher said. "Or, knowing him, the portrait could be a stranger's kid he saw on the street who captivated him. He did this all in one day. He even stayed after school to work on it. I would have loved to see the finished piece."

Leland liked animals, too. He often dog-sat for the neighbors two houses down from his grandmother's, a young couple that liked to travel a lot. The wife said they intentionally stocked the refrigerator with freshly cooked food and told him they were leftovers that needed to be eaten or they would go bad. They liked him, and he always wanted to hear about their travels when they returned. He sometimes stopped by just to check in, they said.

"He was so skinny, and his grandmother was so odd. I felt like I had to feed him. Honestly, when he disappeared, I suspected her, " the wife said. "But I can't imagine she would have been with it enough to bury him and keep it a secret for so long."

Sawyer had thought that angle through, but the former police chief said the grandmother was so angry when she realized her money was gone that he couldn't imagine she knew anything about it. It's possible she wanted him out of her life, but even if she did, why would she bury him with the money? She could have hidden the money elsewhere and kept it, or claimed he stole a couple hundred dollars, not the whole thing. It didn't make sense. The note didn't fit into that scenario either.

There were other people Leland spent time with—younger kids at the skateboard park, a man who drove the Amish around and sometimes offered Leland a lift when the weather was bad, the pastor of the Methodist church, who talked for hours with Leland about theology and spirituality. The summer before he died, Leland worked on a farm, making a little regular money of his own. He had probably spent every dime on the basics as quickly as he earned it.

Leland had weaved himself subtly and artfully into the fabric of the community in ways that were far more mature than his years. Sawyer was getting to know a different Maplewood Falls through Leland, one he had been blind to all through his youth and even after moving back. But no one seemed to hate Leland. There was nothing shady about him, certainly nothing worth killing him over. It was getting late, close to dinner time. Sawyer needed to get home, but he pulled one more yearbook off the stack and flipped it open, revealing dozens of signatures and notes on the inside of the cover and the facing page.

"Party down, man. Life's too short!"

"I'll always remember science class. Good luck!"

"Another year down the drain. Let's make next year rock!"

He'd been through three so far and had found a few that were close. He'd set those books aside with Post-It notes marking the pages. But he knew they wouldn't be matches. Something told him that when he found the right handwriting, he'd know it. He started flipping through the fourth book, past photo after photo of girls baring their shoulders and glancing sideways into the camera, and boys with excessively short hair, the only acceptable style in their school that year. He passed by his own photo without stopping. Sawyer had paused and lingered on that page too many times in the previous yearbooks, stunned at how young he looked and how mature he'd thought he was at the time. Just four years later, he was a cop in Syracuse, and he was engaged to Heather. Then along came their daughter and their first son, and then, finally, their second son. It just didn't seem that long ago.

Heather was firmly against living anywhere near Maplewood Falls after the first two kids were born, even though his hours were long and, in the beginning, he worked the night patrol. She said she was tired of their hometown and of the people in it. She had made lots of friends in the Syracuse area, and she enjoyed exploring the local trails and parks with the babies in tow. She loved the coffee shops and the huge mall, Destiny USA, was like an indoor city. She and the kids could spend hours in there without getting bored when it was too wet or cold to play outside. Why would she give that up? But when she got pregnant for the third time, and the police chief position came open, she said she was ready. She was even excited. It was good to be home, where they had help with the kids, and the kids had cousins to grow up with. But these cases…he'd had others that had depressed him—fatal car wrecks involving people he knew, suicides, domestic violence. It wasn't always fun becoming acquainted with the darker sides of people he grew up with. But this was worse. Carla was gone. Her baby was gone. There was no closure in sight, no explanation he could give her husband. And Leland was dead, not living free in some big city. Someone had killed him.

Sawyer picked up the statement from Rachel's neighbor and read through it again, pushing the yearbook to the side. Her name was Anne, and she was a retiree in her late sixties. She said she was returning from errands when she saw a blonde woman with a baby carrier rushing from the house and getting into a car that matched the description of Carla's. The driver pulled out of the driveway quickly, barely pausing to look for traffic. That was it. That was the extent of the woman's statement. But wait. When she described the woman, the neighbor said she was wearing shorts. Carla was still in pajamas when Nick last saw her, but Rachel said she wore jeans to lunch. Anyone involved in her disappearance would have to be careful to describe the clothes she actually wore that day, wouldn't they? They wouldn't know who else might have seen her. A wrong description could draw unwanted attention. But the woman who left Rachel's house wore shorts, just like the woman at McDonald's, the woman who gave away the baby. Rachel was thin, but she was bigger than Carla in the hips and waist and couldn't have fit in Carla's clothes. She could not have taken Carla's clothes off her body and worn them herself. Carla was petite in that way.

Sawyer's stomach turned. This couldn't be. He stood and was about to close the yearbook when something caught his eye. It was a cartoonish drawing in Phillip Yager's yearbook on the back page, a lush set of lips with the words "You wish!" written underneath. No name. He stared at the writing and then at the photographs on his desk. There it was. A match. The loops, the flourish… the letters matched the envelope with Carla's note inside. He didn't need an expert to confirm it. He didn't need a name. He knew it in his gut. Sawyer grabbed his phone and dialed Investigator Zittle's number.

Chapter Nineteen

Nick spent the entire morning and afternoon online, researching the illegal adoption market, the way they get the babies, and who buys them. Most cases involved unwed women who lacked the resources to mother their children and were lured in by promises of food, housing, and medical care until their babies were born. They received a small amount of cash to help them get on their feet afterward. The "agencies" or lawyers promised a selective process that would place the babies with loving, well-adjusted families. In reality, they turned around and sold them to the highest bidders. The methods were illegal and unethical, but the babies would have been placed with agencies regardless and adopted by someone. The lack of vetting sometimes led to abuse, but no more often than in legal adoptions, from what he could find. Older children were a different story. They were more likely to be bought for domestic labor or forced into the sex trade. Nick avoided those articles. He couldn't stomach them.

There were a few stories about babies who were randomly snatched and then possibly sold. Enough to make Nick believe it was more common than the authorities might think. In Arizona, a baby was stolen while a mom was in a port-a-potty with her toddler. The port-a-potty was too small for both children and too dirty for the baby. So, she placed the infant seat just outside the door at the crowded swap meet, an exchange similar to a flea market. She was distracted for just a minute. When she emerged, her daughter and the infant seat were gone. That was in 2001. The baby was never found. A few other infants were taken from their own beds while their parents slept or from playgrounds while moms were busy with older kids. It made Nick wonder how many babies were plucked from homeless women or others who might be afraid to report the child missing or incapable due to addiction or mental illness. There could be a lucrative market in that. No medical bills to cover for the mom. Only pure profit.

Drug-addicted parents were a common source of cheap or free babies. Addicts will often do anything for their next high. A West Virginia woman tried to sell her three-month-old for five hundred dollars. A Tennessee couple tried to sell their baby for three thousand dollars on Craigslist. A Pennsylvania woman wanted seventeen hundred dollars for her baby girl. These were just the people who got caught. Nick was sure plenty more people got away with it. It made him sick just thinking about it.

The buyers were usually couples who wanted children fast, especially white infants. The waiting list for white infants in most legal agencies is huge and long. Prospective parents might have to wait years and, if too much time passes, they might grow too old and get bumped off the lists entirely. This was actually a comfort to Nick. People who bought black market babies were desperate for children. Sometimes, they knew they were buying babies illegally. Sometimes, they were duped into believing the adoptions were legal. But the babies were wanted and were loved. That was something Nick could cling to.

His eyes burned, and his neck ached when he finally pried himself away from the laptop and rose from his desk. It was getting late, almost quitting time for Rachel. She would be here soon with the pizza. He found himself salivating a bit at the thought of cheese, pepperoni, and spicy Italian sauce. He was embarrassed by this morning's temper tantrum, but it turned out to be a good thing. It woke him up, gave him energy again. Maybe he would ask her to join him for dinner. He couldn't eat a whole pizza himself anyway, and it would be rude not to after all she'd done for him. He needed to remember to pay her back, too. She had spent a lot of money feeding him lately.

Nick spent the next two hours doing laundry, cleaning bathrooms, vacuuming, and wiping down counters. He didn't want Carla returning to a filthy house. He couldn't bring himself to change the sheets on their queen-sized bed, though. Her pillows still smelled like her. So did her side of the bed. He needed that. He left the nursery untouched, too. Nick was putting the vacuum cleaner away when he heard a knock on the door. Rachel's car was parked in the driveway. She knocked again. He appreciated that she didn't just walk in again like she belonged there and that she stayed on the other side of the threshold when he opened the door. She tried to hand him the pizza and walk away, but he insisted she come in.

"Only for a slice, though, and then I'm out of here." She must have stopped at home before picking up the food. She had traded her work clothes for a pair of jeans and a loose t-shirt, an unusual outfit for her, and her hair was pulled back into a ponytail. Nick found himself staring. She looked less intimidating this way, less superficial.

Nick decided it was his turn to be nice. He'd grown so used to brushing Rachel off and ignoring her that he realized today he knew nothing about her. She was his wife's best friend, a huge part of her life. He should have welcomed her into their lives, not simply tolerated her all these years. So he asked Rachel questions about her job, her family, her interests. He found himself laughing at her stories and enjoying the conversation. They moved to the sofa, and he offered her a glass of wine. He could understand a little better now why she and Carla were friends. But then she reached out, walked her fingers playfully up his leg, and reached for his crotch.

"What are you doing?"

He jumped back to the end of sofa, the heat rising in his cheeks. She was on top of him before he knew what was happening, massaging him, making him hard with one hand while she slipped her other hand behind his head, pushing his mouth into hers. He resisted, but she forced her tongue inside, and he found his mouth opening wider, taking her in. Her fingers undid the snap on his jeans and worked the zipper down, releasing him, while she thrust her tongue harder and harder down his throat. The memory of last night, of Rachel's breasts in his hands, of his body pressed against hers, the scent of her hair and her skin, stirred something within him despite his shame and anger. He tried to force it down, the feeling rising inside him, the craving, but it was almost impossible. He tried to push her off, but he didn't push hard enough. He didn't want to push any harder. He wanted her.

Slowly, she raised her head, pulled off her ponytail holder, and let her hair cascade over her face. She pulled off her shirt and unfastened her bra, revealing hard, dark nipples that begged to be touched. Nick closed his eyes and let her unbutton his shirt, brushing against him, licking his chest, stirring the greed in him. He wanted to feel good, even just for a minute. He wanted to escape. Her tongue was moving further down his body. He was losing control. She was reaching for the waistband on his jeans, ready to pull them down when she said it.

"You're the only one, Nick, the only one I would ever do this for."

He opened his eyes and pushed her away.

"Why did you say that?"

Those were Carla's words, her exact words. She wasn't a fan of oral sex, so the few times they did it, she made it clear she did it for love, and she said it in those precise words in the same way Rachel said them. It all came to him in a blur of sensations—the perfume, the scent of her lotion, the ponytail, the jeans, her makeup, the mancala board, the whiskey. Rachel was becoming Carla, and it wasn't his imagination. She was doing it intentionally. She wanted to tempt him, to lure him in. How did she know these things? Had she been waiting all these years, watching Carla, listening, prying things out of her, things only best friends might share? This was sick, and he was a fool. She was ninth-grade Rachel all over again, showing up in strange places, stealing scraps of paper from his locker, watching his every move. She hadn't changed. She'd just been waiting for an opportunity.

Rachel sat on the floor with her legs tucked under her and her breasts bare, thrusting her chest toward him. She smiled and pursed her lips. Then she stood and sauntered toward him, reaching for him, like nothing had changed. "Oh, poor Nicky. I thought you liked it that way. I wanted to do it the way you like it. But I can be different. You have no idea how different I can be, and I think you'll like it a lot better."

She tried to climb on him again, and he pushed her to the floor. Nick was horrified. Who was this woman? He'd let her inside his house. He had done this. He quickly stood, zipped his jeans, and started buttoning his shirt. He stepped away from her as he spoke and moved out of the living room, closer

111

to the phone. She lifted herself up and followed him, still half naked, still acting like this was all a game between lovers.

"Put your shirt on and get out now, or I'll call the police."

She was almost on him again. He didn't want to shove her again and risk hurting her, but she wasn't giving him any choice. She was insane, but he would be the one in trouble if she got injured. She would pin this whole thing on him, and there were no witnesses. He had let her into his house, not just now, but several times a week since Carla and Christopher disappeared. She was here at all hours, morning and night. She could say they'd had an affair all along, but that he got tired of her. She could say anything she wanted. She could put the investigation at risk, make him a suspect again, throw investigators off the path of the true suspects. She was only a few feet away when the phone rang. Nick grabbed it, and Rachel pouted.

"Hello," he said.

"Nick, this is Sawyer."

"Good," Nick said, turning away from her, but speaking loudly so she could hear. "I need you here right away, Sawyer. Rachel is here, and she's acting crazy. She's half naked, and she won't leave. I need the police. I need someone to get her out."

"Be careful, Nick," Sawyer said. "She's the reason I'm calling. We identified the writing on the envelope. It's Rachel's. I'm on my way. Don't do anything stupid. We don't know what she is capable of or how she is involved in all this."

Nick turned when he heard the front door shut. Then he heard her car engine start and the squealing of tires as she peeled out of the driveway. Rachel and her shirt were gone. What had he done? What had she done with his wife and baby? Who was Rachel, really? Nick stumbled to the sink and vomited.

Chapter Twenty

Carla had just put the metal bar back in its place when Rachel's voice came over the speakers. Had she seen her? Could she see the sweat on Carla's face, the fear? She was so close. A few more inches to remove, and she'd be done. It would take her only another hour or so at her current pace, but she decided not to risk it, and she was glad. Rachel had been gone until after dark most nights, but here she was, and, in the video, it was only dusk. Maybe eight thirty or eight forty-five. A few more minutes and she would have been caught.

"Hi Carla," Rachel said. "No Godiva for you, I'm afraid. Nicky was a bad boy, and you were not a good friend. I was so close. He's got smooth hands, you know. They felt good on my breasts and in my hair, and those lips... He was hard, so hard, and so ready. But I used the words you gave me, and he didn't like it. He shoved me away, and he told the police. It was because of those words, Carla. 'Only for you, Nick.' Remember that? That was supposed to turn him on, make him feel like I was a good girl who was about to do something nasty just for him. But they didn't. They reminded him of you, and he felt guilty. He shouldn't have felt guilty. He wanted me bad. He's always wanted me. We were supposed to be together. It was the right thing. But you interfered again. You got in his head."

Carla fell back on the mattress, overwhelmed by a sudden and unexpected rage. She wanted to cry, scream and destroy something, all at the same time. How could Nick do this? How dare he? She wasn't angry he pushed Rachel away, putting them all in danger. It was that Rachel's plan had worked, at least somewhat. Nick had seen her naked. He'd touched her. He'd let her touch him, all while she was trapped in this prison, and their baby was god knows where. How long had she been in here? Maybe a couple of weeks? Was their marriage that weak? She knew she was partly responsible. She told Rachel how to seduce him, but she never really thought it would work. Carla should have been the missing ingredient. He should never have been tempted without her in the mix. He betrayed her. She raised up and pounded the wall with her fist, and kicked the mattress. To hell with what Rachel saw. She was tired of being Rachel's puppet. Another day and she'd be out of here. Then she'd find her baby and leave the town, leave it forever. Without Nick.

"Temper, temper," Rachel said. "I know. I'm mad at Nick, too. I'm sure you realize it's his fault you have to die, but if it will make you feel better, I'll let you in on a secret. I'm going to kill him, too, but I'm not going to kill myself. I just said that to motivate you. Neither of you deserves to live, not after what you've done to me. You were supposed to be my friend. When we were in junior high, I had visions of us as old ladies, never really growing old. We'd be the cool ones, the ones who jetted all over the world, new men in every country, disposable men. We would be free, but we would always be there for each other, Companions for life. But you ruined it. You messed up my life, my future. I dumped Nick when you told me, too, and then you scooped him up. What a fool I was. I loved him, but my allegiance was with you, with my vision. I should have kept Nick and dumped you. I really thought he would come around, though. Look at all the years I've wasted, believing it would happen. But now I have to make up for them. It's not really fair. I have to leave the country because it will be obvious that I killed you. I would have let you dehydrate like I planned, but I noticed when I came home, you were digging at the door with some rod or something I must have stupidly left behind. So there goes that plan. You might get out before you die if I do it that way, though I doubt you'd get far digging with that flimsy scrap of metal."

Carla stopped, covered her mouth with her hands, and collapsed onto the floor. She'd been caught. There was no hope. She was dead. Nick was dead. Christopher would never know either of them. She didn't mean what she'd said about Nick. It was her fault Nick was tempted by Rachel. She'd wanted it to happen for selfish reasons, to save her own life. She made it happen. And he stopped, didn't he? He stopped as soon as he came to his senses. Did he suspect Rachel? Did he know she kidnapped her? Carla's mind was reeling, and her body was trembling. What was Rachel going to do? She didn't want to die this way. She didn't want to die now. She couldn't.

"Please, Rachel." She stared up at the camera, wishing she could see Rachel's face, wishing she could grab her by the shoulders and talk sense into her. "There has to be a better way. I didn't know. I really didn't. Let me talk to Nick. He was just confused by the way I disappeared. Maybe if I tell him myself that it's okay with me—"

"Don't you get it?" Rachel hissed. "It shouldn't have to be okay with you. I don't want your sloppy seconds. He was supposed to understand that it was me he wanted in the first place. He was supposed to help me get rid of you, to prove his love to me. That was the plan. He would come over here and turn off the water himself. We would make love for three days straight in my bedroom, right above you, watching you die on my monitor. You were never going to live. Why would I have let you live?"

"No, Rachel." Carla could barely get the words out. It was unthinkable, all of it. Rachel was her best friend. They stayed at each other's houses, talked each other through their first periods, shared a bottle of vodka before the homecoming parade when they were fifteen. Rachel was the first person she told when she lost her virginity to Scott at sixteen, and the first person she told when she made love to Nick a year later and discovered what sex should be like. She was in her wedding. She had held her baby. The journal, tucked under her pillow, was alive with memories of the good times, of another Rachel. This couldn't be happening. She pulled the journal out and flipped through the pages.

"You don't mean it. Please. Let me read some of this to you. I 've been writing about us, about the good times. We had so many good times, Rachel. You are not well right now, but you can get better again. I'm your friend. Please."

Rachel laughed—a light, carefree laugh.

"I'll be bringing you a present in a few minutes, a little trick I thought up to kill you quickly without burning my house down. I need some time to get out of here just in case Nick knows I'm up to something, so I can't attract too much attention. I turned off the water already, so you can't ruin my gift. Love you, bestie! That's what people call best friends, right? It was good while it lasted. Maybe I'll stop in Arizona on my way to Mexico, if that's where I decide to go, and see that little boy of yours. Don't worry so much. He'll have a good life. His new parents are rich, and they're raising him in Scottsdale.

Did I tell you he has new parents? An older couple that got tired of waiting for traditional agencies to give them a blue-eyed, blonde-haired, little boy. Adoption agencies discriminate against older couples, you know. It's hard enough for younger couples. Sometimes, they have to wait years for a white baby, but once you hit forty, forget it. White infants are worth a fortune on the black market. Nobody cares where they come from. Nobody asks questions. Christopher deserves a good home. None of this was his fault, really. He was just the product of your mistakes. I would never punish someone who didn't deserve it."

Then the speaker went silent.

Chapter Twenty-One

Nick didn't know what to do with himself. Every second felt critical, like this could be the second that made it too late, that cost him Carla. Sawyer was taking too long. He couldn't wait any longer. He grabbed his keys and ran for the garage, dropping the keys twice on his way out the door. He would track Rachel down and find out for himself what was going on. What had she done with Carla? This was his fault, all of it. He should have noticed. He should have picked up on the signs. Rachel was becoming Carla. She was trying to insert herself into Carla's life, dressing like her, talking like her, even smelling like her. She'd been trying to seduce him from the beginning, damn it. But he couldn't believe Rachel was capable of killing anyone. Maybe she sent Carla on a trip, told her Nick had arranged for a month-long spa vacation or lied to her about an emergency in some foreign country. Maybe Rachel gave her a drug that wiped out her memory, or maybe Carla hit her head while she was at Rachel's house and suffered amnesia. Maybe Carla wanted a break, and Rachel convinced her to take it, offering to bring Christopher back to Nick so she could be free of responsibility for a while. Whatever Rachel did, she didn't kill her. She couldn't have. Rachel was her friend, her childhood friend, and she couldn't have turned on her completely.

Rachel's house was the obvious place to look. She knew Nick was angry, but she thought it was because he didn't want to have sex with her. She had no reason to hide from him. He could pretend he'd changed his mind. He could turn the tables and seduce her and get to the truth. Nick opened the garage door, threw the car in reverse, and drove away, not bothering to shut the door behind him. There was nothing valuable in that house or garage anyway, not without Carla and Christopher.

Chapter Twenty-Two

Nick flung open the front door without knocking or ringing the bell. That was a mistake. He was supposed to pretend he was here to make up with Rachel. He needed to slow down and catch his breath. He needed to get his head into the role he was supposed to be playing. He took a deep breath and called out her name.

"Rachel? Rachel, it's me, Nick."

No one answered. He stood in the entryway and looked around for a sign that she was home, and there it was. Rachel's car keys were on the accent table next to the staircase that led to the next level. Along with the keys was a pile of unopened mail, her purse, and what looked like a passport. Was she planning to leave the country, or did she use the passport to get rid of Carla? He reached for it as he called out again.

"Rachel, I'm sorry. I was unfair to you. I want to talk, maybe go out to dinner, like other people do. I've had enough of this self-pity. You're right. It's time I moved on. I just need a slower pace. That's all."

Before he could grab the passport, the door to the basement opened, and out stepped Rachel, who offered him a smile. He pulled his hand back and tried to act like he had been stepping further into the house to look for her. His hands were shaking, so he shoved them in his pockets.

"Rachel, what were you doing? Are you okay?"

Rachel's eyes darted about before they settled on him again. She shut the basement door, smoothed her hair, and moved toward him as if she might hug him or kiss him. He stepped back and then silently cursed himself for it. He was supposed to be into her, to want to pick up where they had left off.

Nick reached for her, but she stopped, blocking his access to the rest of the house.

"I'm sorry, Rachel. I'm sorry for everything. You just caught me off guard. It's hard, you know? Carla is missing, but I have these incredibly strong feelings for you. I feel guilty, like I'm betraying her and taking advantage of you. If she were here, if I could just talk to her and explain how I feel about you, I wouldn't feel guilty anymore. Do you understand? I just—"

"Shh." Rachel moved closer to Nick and placed a finger on his lips. She took his hand in hers and led him toward the stairs leading up to the bedrooms. Nick hesitated. He was hoping they would talk it out, not hop right into bed. He knew he wouldn't be able to take the charade that far. He couldn't. She was supposed to believe that he would be all hers if he could just get rid of his guilt, if he could talk to Carla first. She knew where Carla was. She sent those rings in the mail. Where was she?

"Come on," Rachel said with a slow smile. "I want to show you something. Don't worry. I'll keep my clothes on."

Nick hadn't thought this through. How would he handle it if she made another advance? He needed to get her talking about Carla. Sawyer would come here after he saw that Nick and Rachel were no longer at Nick's house, wouldn't he? He said they suspected Rachel. It would make sense. He just needed a few minutes alone with her before the police arrived. He could get her to talk. He knew he could. She might clam up if they asked her questions, and then they'd never know where Carla and Christopher were.

"It all happened so fast, Carla leaving and all," Nick said, following her. "I didn't want to believe that she would leave me like that. But I guess you never really do know anybody. I didn't want to believe she was unhappy, but when I think about it, I can see that she loved her job. She loved New York. Marrying me, having a baby, that wasn't what she wanted, and maybe it wasn't what I wanted either. We didn't belong together."

"Oh, Nicky," Rachel stopped on the stairs, turned, and caressed his cheek. "It will all make sense to you. I promise. I just want to show you this one thing, and then we can talk, go out to dinner, whatever you want."

They continued up the stairs, rounded a corner, and went into a bedroom, where she ushered him to a desk and told him to sit before a computer screen. She leaned over him after he sat, reaching around his shoulders for the mouse with one arm and for the keyboard with the other. The scent of Carla's perfume still lingered on her skin and clothes, making him uneasy. This was a mistake, coming over here, following her upstairs. But he couldn't turn back now. Rachel clicked an icon that was an image of an eye, and a video appeared. Nick couldn't quite understand what he was looking at.

"Just watch for a minute while I freshen up. It'll all make sense to you if you keep watching."

It was a room with a mattress, a chair, a bathtub, and a toilet, and he was looking into it from above, but the black-and-white picture was unclear. He could make out movement, a figure close to the wall, but partially out of sight, with arms moving frantically. The figure—it looked like a woman—was whacking the wall with a rod or a stick over and over again. And then it hit him, so hard he could hardly breathe. It was Carla. That was Carla on the monitor, and she was trapped in a room, trying to get out. Before he could think or turn around, an intense heat sliced into his body between his shoulder blades and radiated throughout his shoulders and back. He turned to see Rachel standing behind him, holding a bloody knife, a pool of blood already forming on the floor. Dizziness and nausea overwhelmed him, and he slipped from the chair, crashing onto the hardwood. Nick started to rise up as Rachel dashed through the bedroom door, slamming it shut behind her. He stood unsteady on his feet and tried the knob, but it was locked. A deadbolt snapped into place. He was too weak or too much in shock to break the door down. His body slid to the floor, and he stared at the blood he'd left behind. How bad was it? He couldn't see the wound, couldn't see how deep or long it was or how much it was bleeding, but there was a lot of blood on the floor already. Would he die before he got help? Would she come back with another weapon? A gun? He'd left his cell phone at home in his hurry to get here, but he could use her computer. If he could stay alert long enough, he could get help and get them both to safety.

"Now it's her turn," Rachel yelled through the door. "This isn't the way I wanted it, Nick. I wanted to watch her die together. It was supposed to bond us, watching her die in the basement while we made love. But I know you, and I know when you are lying. You don't love me. You were trying to trick me to see if I knew where she was. Now I have to kill you both. It'll take you a while to bleed out, but you'll be too weak within a few minutes to break a window or holler for help. You would only bleed faster with the effort. You'll have some entertainment, though. Keep your eyes on the monitor, and we'll see who goes first—you or her."

"Rachel, no. You don't have to do this. We can be together. She doesn't have to die. No one has to die."

But it was too late. He could hear her feet on the stairs. Nick stood and stumbled back to the desk, falling into the chair. He looked around the room, he but didn't see a telephone anywhere. Rachel had no need for a landline. It was only her living in the house. He could shout out the windows for help, but they seemed so far away. Even if he made it to the windows and managed to open or break one, how long would it take for someone to hear him, and then to figure out what was going on? The bedroom was at the back of the house, and her property abutted a thick patch of woods. Her lot was large, affording her plenty of space between her house and the neighbors on either side. He clicked on the Chrome icon, and a blank page came up, covering Carla's image. What should he do? He could sign into Skype and make an internet call. Nick typed the letters into the address bar. *Page not found. No internet connection.* Nick looked for an internet icon and found none. The computer was an older model. There was no WiFi, and no ethernet cable plugged into the computer. This computer was probably dedicated to the cameras in the basement with no internet access. He had no way of communicating with anyone. Nick knew he should try for that window and start shouting, but he was so tired. He tried to get up, but he was too dizzy to stand for long. He made his way to the bed and fell into it. If he could just rest for a few minutes, maybe then, he could break the door down.

Chapter Twenty-Three

As soon as Rachel stopped talking, Carla began digging furiously into the crevices of the doorway with the metal rod, using all the energy she could find. What did it matter if Rachel saw her now? She'd already watched her dig. She knew what Carla was doing, and she wasn't worried. Either Rachel knew Carla wasn't going to get free no matter how much she tore away at the seal, or Rachel had other plans. Carla didn't want to sit around feeling sorry for herself, waiting to find out. She was so close, but her hands were cramped and sore, and her fingers were bleeding. What if it didn't matter? What if, after all this digging, the door still wouldn't budge? Carla stopped digging a moment and looked around. She would need something heavier than her own body, something she could ram it with, especially since there seemed to be a wooden brace across it on the other side. The chair. She set down the metal bar and tried lifting it. It was small for an armchair and cheap, probably framed with pine. It was heavy, but she could do it. Once, maybe twice. That was it. Carla's energy was nearly depleted, but she could do it—if she thought of Christopher, thought about how much she needed him.

Carla had returned to digging for only a moment when she heard the food slot open near her feet. She moved back just as three red sticks came flying through, spitting red sparks and plumes of smoke from one end and illuminating the room in a hot, red glow. Within seconds, they were emitting so much smoke and heat that she couldn't get close to them to toss them back out the opening. The smoke rose quickly, irritating her lungs and eyes and filling the room. Road flares. Rachel had thrown in road flares. Carla

123

threw herself in the direction of the bathtub and, with her eyes closed, felt for the faucets. She turned them quickly to full force, but all she got was a trickle. Rachel had shut off the water. The flares were too hot to stomp, and she had nothing to throw over them. She couldn't see them anyway. The room was already filling with smoke that reflected the red flames and completely disoriented her. Carla grabbed the towel from the edge of the tub and tied it around her face. Then she curled up in a ball in a corner of the room, getting as low to the floor as she could. It wouldn't be long before there was no clean air left, and she died either of smoke inhalation or from a lack of oxygen in the room. Road flares could burn for hours with enough oxygen, and the smoke had nowhere else to go except for the tiny vent in the ceiling. The vent. Rachel had probably blocked that off, too. It was getting hot in the room, and Carla was feeling dizzy. She had to do something. She looked up from her fetal position just as a plume of yellow and orange burst toward the ceiling in the area of the mattress. Her mattress had caught fire. What if it spread to the chair? She needed that chair. Without thinking, Carla stood, grabbed the chair and, with energy she didn't know she had, flung it at the door.

Chapter Twenty-Four

Investigator Zittle used Sawyer's radio to call for state police backup when they saw Nick's car in Rachel's driveway. Sawyer had already called for his own force. One officer was on her way, and the other was dealing with a potentially violent domestic situation. He would be here as soon as things calmed down.

"You never know what we're going to find in there," Zittle said. "Might as well play it safe. I'll go to the front door. You secure the back. Holler if anybody tries to leave. When your guys get here, I'll send two around the sides and take one in with me. Our nearest state unit is ten minutes away, so we're on our own for a while."

Sawyer moved cautiously to the back of the house and opened the gate, letting himself into the backyard. The fencing was at least six feet high. Rachel valued her privacy. That was clear. The fencing would make it hard for anyone to escape. The only way out of this yard was the gate he'd just come through. A lack of landscaping gave the yard a stark, sterile feel. The grass was mown and trimmed along the fence line, but there were no flowers or bushes or gardens. Nothing but grass and a small, concrete patio with a glass table and two chairs.

Sawyer moved along the fence until he reached the back of the house. He pressed his body against the vinyl siding and ducked beneath the first window, which looked into the kitchen. Then he rose up beside it and looked in, pulling back from the glass. He saw a few dishes in the sink, but nothing else. No movement. Nothing suspicious. He continued until he got to the patio with its sliding glass doors that offered a view of the dining area. Still nothing. Sawyer took a chance and tried the door. It wouldn't budge. He'd have to wait for the backup and let Zittle go in through the front.

Sawyer was about to move to the next window when he noticed a wisp of smoke pushing into the space between the dining area and the foyer from underneath a door, the door that led to the basement, from what he could remember. Then he saw her. Rachel came rushing from around a corner near the front of the house with something in her hand. She flung the basement door open, releasing low-lying billows of smoke that curled around her ankles, and she disappeared down the staircase. Sawyer grabbed his radio and put a call in to Zittle.

"We've got a fire in the basement or at least smoke. Call for help. Rachel went down there. I'm going to try to get in. She had something in her hand. It looked like a gun."

He didn't wait for a response. Sawyer pulled harder on the sliding door, but it still wouldn't move. The glass was too thick to break easily. He took his gun out of its holster and, without thinking, used the gun's butt to smash the window he'd looked into. Then he slipped on gloves and opened the window, knowing there was no way to get in fast without getting cut. He grabbed a chair from the deck, cleared as much debris from the windowsill as he could, and stepped through, slicing the skin on his forearm. Blood gushed from what appeared to be about a two-inch gash, but it didn't cut an artery, and there was no time to worry about it. Once inside, Sawyer heard Zittle crashing something against the front door. The smoke was thickening near the basement door. He ran through the house to the front and let Zittle in just as a shot rang out in the basement. One at a time, with guns drawn, they started down the stairs, careful not to make a sound.

Chapter Twenty-Five

The chair was heavier than Carla had imagined, but somehow, she found the strength to pick it up a second time and heave it against the door, which gave way under its weight. Fresh air rushed in as it collapsed, fueling the flames that were eating up the mattress and licking at the ceiling. The walls of the room were made mostly of concrete, so there should have been little left to burn, but the heat from the sudden burst of flame scorched her throat and skin. She'd had to drop the towel from her face to lift the chair. Smoke and heat seared her lungs, choking her. Carla stepped over the chair and fell into the remaining part of the basement, struggling on her hands and knees to see through the smoke. The flares were still burning, and the smoke reflected the redness of their sparks, making visibility worse. She needed to get her bearings. Then she heard a voice.

"No, no, no, Carla. This isn't how it ends."

Rachel was somewhere in the room, but Carla couldn't see her. She closed her eyes for a moment and tried to remember the layout. The video screen was on the opposite end of the basement from the door leading to the stairs. Rachel would not likely have moved toward Carla's prison with all the smoke, flames, and sparks. She was probably near the stairs and would expect Carla to crawl in that direction. Instead, Carla felt her way along the floor toward a side wall and stretched out on her belly on the concrete, turning her head to face the door. The smoke was still a few inches above the floor in places. From her position, Carla could see Rachel's shoes, black pumps with narrow, five-inch heels. Stupid choice for a smoke-filled room, Carla thought. If she could grab Rachel's ankles, she could easily trip her and escape up the stairs.

"Come out, come out, Carla. You can't survive down here much longer."

Rachel's feet were pointed away from Carla. So, her plan had worked. She was looking for Carla closer to the chair and the secret room. Carla had started crawling toward her, quickly and quietly, when she was overcome by the urge to cough. She put her hand over her mouth and tried to force the cough down, but it was useless. She couldn't hold back, and she saw Rachel's feet pivot as soon as her lungs let loose. The first shot nicked the concrete floor by Carla's head.

"I didn't want to destroy the house, Carla, but you've given me no choice," she said. "You are always ruining my plans. You and Nick both, and it's going to hurt like it should. I've got two cans of gasoline down here, and I have Nick locked in my room upstairs, bleeding to death. That pretty hair of yours, that pale skin, your blue eyes—all of it is going to burn to a crisp, and I'm getting out of here. I'd rather you baked slowly in that room where Nick could watch. I worked hard on that, you know. He was supposed to watch you die. But have it your way. You always did."

Carla rolled her body toward Rachel as another shot rang out. She lunged forward and grabbed Rachel's ankle as a third shot hit her in the left leg. Carla screamed in pain, and Rachel crashed to the floor. With Rachel out of the way, Carla could see the gasoline cans just a few feet from where the chair had caught fire. Rachel looked across the floor at Carla and smiled, aiming her gun at the cans. Then she fired, and as she did, Carla saw Rachel's head smack the concrete and bloodstream from the base of her neck, pooling beside her. Carla couldn't move, even as she saw the gasoline streaming toward the chair. Her legs, her arms, her head—she couldn't make them move. Something had happened to Rachel, and she didn't know what. Then two sets of strong hands encircled each of her arms on either side and pulled her to her feet. She couldn't see through the smoke, and she couldn't put much weight on her left leg, but she let them lead her quickly up the stairs and outside, throwing her onto the grass seconds before the basement, filled with gasoline vapors, exploded into flames.

"Nick." She tried to scream, but the words barely made a sound as they came out of her smoke-injured throat. She pulled on the shirt of the man lying on the grass beside her, catching his breath. It was Sawyer, the village police chief, and a friend. She tried to speak again and pointed to an upstairs window, yanking harder on his shirt.

"Nick," she mouthed again.

Sawyer sat up. He seemed puzzled, but then his face changed, and she could see the shock in his eyes. She pointed again to the upstairs window and then clasped her hands together in the prayer position and rested them against her cheek, as if sleeping, hoping he would understand her charade. He leaped to his feet and started toward the house, yelling over his shoulder. "Zittle, stay with her. Nick's upstairs."

Carla fell back onto the grass and focused on the stars above her as fresh air worked its way into her lungs. He had to get Nick. He had to reach him. In the distance, she heard the sirens of fire trucks and an ambulance. But with gasoline in the basement and a furnace nearby, the firefighters would be too late. The house would be engulfed in a matter of minutes. Her only hope was Sawyer.

Chapter Twenty-Six

Sawyer heard someone behind him as he stepped through the doorway and into the smoke, lifting his shirt up to cover his mouth and nose. It was Zittle. The knowledge that he wasn't alone settled his nerves a bit. Flames were shooting out of the basement stairwell. It wouldn't be long before the floor caught fire or the whole place exploded. This was a huge risk.

"I left your people in charge of her," Zittle said. "The fire department is right behind us. Where is he?"

Sawyer pointed toward the staircase and started up, turning down the hall toward the room with the window Carla had indicated. He threw the door open, but it was a guestroom, and it was empty. The smoke was thickening as he tried the knob on the door across the hall, and he heard the fire crackling below. The door wouldn't budge, and the deadbolt was in place. Who puts a deadbolt on the outside of a bedroom door? His hands shook as he turned the lock and pushed the door in. There was Nick, splayed out on the bed with a mess of blood on the floor and the comforter. He raised his head slightly when they entered. He looked weak and defeated. Sawyer bent down and looked for the source of the bleeding. He rolled him over slightly. A wound to his back, high up between the shoulder blades. Probably a stab wound. He'd lost a lot of blood, but he would probably make it if they could get him out of there.

"Carla," Nick whispered. "She's dead. Rachel killed her."

"No, Nick," Sawyer said, "She's outside on the lawn, and she's alive. Let's get you out of here."

Together, Zittle and Sawyer helped Nick into a sitting position. Then they sat down beside him on either side, threw his arms over their shoulders, and stood, lifting him up. The news about Carla seemed to give Nick a little energy. He stepped with them and took on some of his own weight. They had to move fast. Another minute or two, and they'd be trapped. They were working their way back down the hall when flames rolled through the smoke and up the stairs. It was too late. They couldn't go down. A window would be their only way out. They'd have to jump. Sawyer was about to turn back when water shot up the stairs piercing the smoke and the flames. A firefighter wearing an oxygen mask came up the stairs while water from a hose continued to flood the front door area and the walls nearest the stairs. The firefighter took Nick from them and indicated that they should go ahead. Sawyer and Zittle emerged from the house with the two firefighters coming out behind them, towing Nick and the hose. They stopped several yards back and watched, coughing the smoke out of their lungs as other firefighters doused nearby houses to prevent the fire from spreading, and Rachel and her house were devoured by flames.

Chapter Twenty-Seven

Carla shed the blanket and the oxygen mask the medic had given her when she saw Nick emerge from the house. She was weak and could barely stand, but she managed to stumble across the lawn and over to an ambulance, where a firefighter had taken her husband. A medic, with the help of the firefighter, hoisted Nick onto a gurney and rolled him onto his side. Then he started cutting through his shirt to reach a wound on Nick's back. Carla tried to speak, but her throat was irritated from the heat and the smoke, and her words became lost in fits of coughing. The tears came fast and hard as he grabbed her hand and released tears of his own. Someone slapped a blood pressure cuff on his upper arm and asked Carla to let go for a moment, assuring her his wound was not life-threatening. Nick winced as the medic applied antiseptic to his back. His clothes were covered in blood.

"You heard him," Nick said. "I'm going to be okay. You're going to be okay. I can't believe it, Carla. You were right here all along. She'd better be dead, or I will kill her myself. I missed you so much."

He reached for her again when the cuff came off. She'd had no human contact in weeks. Her voice and his touch made it all real. She was free. Rachel was dead. She couldn't hurt her anymore. But Rachel was the only one who knew how to find their baby. How would they find him now?

"Christopher," Carla said in a hoarse whisper. "Rachel sold him, to another family. I don't know where, Nick. I don't know where. Rachel's dead. How will we find Christopher?"

Nick tried to reach for her face, but he pulled his arm back in pain. Rachel had stabbed him, the medic said. The cut was deep and might require surgery to repair the damaged muscles and tissues.

"I don't know, Carla, but we will. The police have video of the man she sold him to. If we can get through this, we can find Christopher. Oh, God, Carla. You're alive. You don't know—I'm just—You're alive."

His body started shaking, which only worsened his pain. Another medic rested her hands on Carla's shoulders and gently urged her away from her husband. "You need oxygen," the medic said, slipping the mask over Carla's face once again, "and a hospital. We need to have a look at your lungs and that gunshot wound, okay? Your husband needs some attention, too. You'll be right behind him."

A firefighter came across the lawn with a second gurney and, together, they helped her onto it. A medic asked her about allergies and started an IV. The cool fabric of the sheets felt good, and so did the blankets they piled on top of her, but an intense fear set in as they rolled her toward the ambulance. It was all too confusing, and her head ached so much, especially with all the commotion around her, the lights, the shouting, the neighbors who had spilled out of their houses to watch. She couldn't think of anything but Christopher. It had seemed so unreal when she was trapped in that room, but now, out here, in the fresh air...it hit her hard. So hard, she wanted to scream, to fly off the gurney and run. Do something. Anything. Christopher really was missing. He wouldn't be in his crib when she got home. Her heart raced, and she tried to rise up, but the medic gently forced her down. The faster her heart beat, the harder it was to breathe. It hurt. It hurt so much. What was happening? Carla struggled to sit up, her chest heaving and throat tightening. She needed air. Someone grabbed her arm and held it in place. Out of the corner of her eye, she could see an injection going into the IV. Then something flowed through her veins, something cool and warm at the same time. No, she thought. Don't sedate me. He needs me. But it was no use. The sedative invaded her thoughts, and she couldn't break through.

She awoke in a small room with dim lights. The emergency room or maybe a regular room. She wasn't sure. She couldn't seem to sit up to look around. Nurses and doctors floated past her open door, talking to each other or staring ahead. No one seemed to notice her. She tried to call out, but she couldn't speak. Something was in the way, in her throat. Her arms wouldn't move either. They were strapped down. Before she could give in to panic, a nurse stepped into sight from her periphery, pushed a few loose hairs from her face, and caressed her cheek.

"Calm down," she said. "We put a tube in your throat to help you breathe in case your throat swelled because of the smoke inhalation, but you seem to be doing fine, so I'm going to remove it. We've had to keep you sedated and strap your arms down because you really don't like this thing. But you have to relax if you want it out. Can you do that?"

Carla grunted what she hoped sounded like a "yes."

"Okay then. It's going to feel kind of funny coming out, but keep in mind that it will be over within a matter of seconds. I'm going to count down from five and then gently glide it out." She leaned over Carla slightly and gripped the tube. "Five, four, three, two, one."

And it was done. Carla was free just like that. She coughed a few times, but then moved her neck freely from side to side. The nurse freed her arms, and Carla sat up. It was a private room, much like the room she was in after she gave birth to Christopher. She didn't remember coming into the hospital or being examined or being brought here. The sun was shining brightly through the open blinds. Morning sun. An IV remained attached to her arm along with a clip on her finger that led to a monitor. A blood pressure cuff was wrapped around her other arm. Her leg ached a little, but only slightly. She pulled back the covers to find the bullet wound covered with gauze and hospital tape. Carla looked at the nurse, not sure where to begin with her questions.

"You're lucky," she said. "The bullet just grazed you. Your leg will be fine, and so will the rest of you. You've been here at the hospital for about thirty-six hours and, with the doctor's permission, you'll be leaving soon. Your husband didn't need surgery. Just an awful lot of stitches, internal and external. The doctor kept him overnight and pumped him full of antibiotics, but he will be released this afternoon with strict orders concerning his movements and the treatment of the wound. He'll need to let that wound heal. Now try to relax, and if all is well, I'll take that IV out in an hour or so."

The nurse covered Carla back up and pressed a button on the bed to raise her head, but Carla swung her legs over the edge, nearly yanking the IV out of her arm.

"I can't do this," she said. "I can't just lie in this bed and wait while my baby is out there. I am going to go see my husband, and then I am leaving. I know I have a right to do that. You can't make me stay."

It hurt to talk.

"Hold on." The nurse reached across the bed and pulled the IV stand closer to Carla. "I'm a mother, too. I'd be freaking out if my child was missing, and I wouldn't want to stay either. But I'll make you a deal. You give me one hour to check your oxygen levels and make sure you're okay without the tube, and I will expedite the process of discharging you against the doctor's advice. One hour. That's all I'm asking. You won't do your baby any good if you collapse on the way out of here, and you need to wait for your ride anyway. Your mother is in the cafeteria. I made her go get a bite to eat."

Carla sighed and drew her legs back onto the bed.

"You're right. One hour. But no more."

One more hour would give Carla some time to think. She couldn't just go running around looking for her baby. She needed a plan, a strategy. It could be years before the police found him, if they ever found him at all, and every day she waited would make it that much harder to trace him. Rachel had mentioned Phoenix, maybe stopping by there to get a peek at Christopher before she fled the country. That was something. Rachel had no reason to lie about Christopher's whereabouts. At that point, she assumed she'd be leaving Carla to die. She would tell the police, but she couldn't just sit back and let strangers take complete control. She had to do something. She needed to get to her laptop as soon as possible. Carla had promised the nurse she wouldn't leave, but she didn't say she'd stay in bed. She yanked the IV out of her arm, removed the finger clip and the blood pressure cuff, and headed for the shower, grabbing a bag with clothes her mother must have brought for her on the way. She wanted to be ready to go the second her hour was up.

Chapter Twenty-Eight

The doctor was waiting in Carla's room when she got out of the shower. He seemed to expect that she would be in a hurry to leave. He tried to convince her to stay for at least a few hours, but when she refused, he pulled out a clipboard with all the discharge papers and instructions attached, handed it all to the nurse to go over with her, and let her go. Nick was released soon after, so they left the hospital together with Carla's mother, Loretta, driving. Carla's mother had had some time to process all that had happened while Carla was sedated, but she was still a mess. She was struggling with the fact that Rachel had spent so many nights at their house and eaten so many meals at their table over the years. As teenagers, she had often left the two of them alone together while she met friends for dinner or went on the occasional date. She had believed they were safe together. She had trusted Rachel, she said.

"I should have known, Carla," Loretta said as they buckled into the car, with Carla in the front seat and Nick trying to get comfortable in the back. "I am so sorry. I should have picked up on the fact that something was wrong with her. That's what mothers are supposed to do. They are supposed to protect their children."

Loretta clamped her hands over her mouth as soon as the words escaped, immediately realizing her mistake. Then she burst into tears and turned to Carla. "I am so sorry, honey. It's not the same. You couldn't have done anything differently. Rachel was your friend. She's been your friend since childhood. How could you know she would take your son? I didn't mean it to sound that way. It's not your fault he's gone."

"It's okay, Mom," Carla said, her voice still raspy. "I just want to go home."

They rode the rest of the way in silence. The streets, their neighborhood, the house—it all looked so familiar, but so different at the same time. The air was hot, not just warm. Summer was in full swing. Kids played under sprinklers, rode bikes, and walked down the street in groups. Life had gone on without her, without Christopher. The thought was comforting and unnerving at the same time. The first thing she did after they walked in the door was head for the nursery, but she found she couldn't go inside. Not yet. Her mother's words echoed in her mind: Mothers are supposed to protect their children.

It was strange to be home, and it was so lonely without Christopher. The house felt empty, though it was full of people at first. Her mother stayed the first night to make sure they were able to take care of themselves, especially since Nick was still in so much pain, but she left after Nick's mother arrived from Florida. She continued to stop frequently at first, but she was starting to come less often, realizing there wasn't much she could do. The police were in and out with question after question. Neighbors and acquaintances came by with food and flowers, bringing their curiosity with them. Where were all these people when she was missing? Nick said Rachel was the only one who visited regularly, and the mention of her usually stopped any further conversation, but Carla understood people. She knew that people are selfish by nature, protective of their time and emotions. There is no commitment involved in stopping by with a pan of lasagna for two people who have each other to pull through tragedy. But becoming involved when it was just Nick, when there were no answers in sight, was a risk. Who knew what they might get pulled into?

Carla slept on the sofa for now, in part because she didn't want to hurt Nick by disturbing the bed with her nightmares and with the tossing and turning that came with them, and in part, because she preferred the openness of the living room. It was comforting to see the light from the kitchen in the middle of the night and to hear the usual house noises—the hum of the refrigerator, the sound of the occasional car passing by. She often woke up in a panic, forgetting she was home, but those sounds and the feel of sofa cushions under her body helped bring her back to reality. The relief that washed over her was short-lived, though quickly displaced by helplessness, sadness, and depression. Those were feelings she could not and would not shake until she held Christopher in her arms again.

Carla was sitting on the sofa with a blanket wrapped around her shoulders, unable to sleep any longer, when Sawyer called out a soft "hello" and came through the front door. They had told him not to bother knocking or ringing the bell anymore. It was too much trouble to answer it, and he had been around enough to be treated like family at this point. It was just after seven, and he was in uniform, probably on his way to work. He apologized for coming so early and then sat beside Carla on the sofa and toyed with his hat in his hands.

"I wanted to check in and see how you guys are doing," Sawyer said. His skin was pale, and his eyes were webbed with red, like he'd gotten no sleep for days. With three kids, an unearthed skeleton, and a missing mother and child, he must have been going out of his mind, Carla thought. When she felt better, she would have to make it up to him. Maybe watch the kids a couple of times so he and Heather could have a date night or have the whole family here for dinner so they could enjoy a meal cooked by someone else. His kids loved Christopher. They doted on him constantly. The thought of Christopher pulled her back into her emotional slump. She could feel the tears rising and welling in her eyes. Of course, she couldn't watch Sawyer's kids. Who would want her to watch their kids after what happened to Christopher?

"I'm sorry I haven't been by more often," he said, "but I've still got this Leland case to take care of. I'm getting nowhere. It just doesn't seem right that a kid so harmless gets murdered so brutally, and no one knows or cares."

Carla knew Leland by face in high school, but she couldn't have told anyone anything about him, not even his last name. She knew she was no different than the rest of the people who frustrated Sawyer. Leland's disappearance was a day's gossip at most. After that, he was gone from her mind. Nick told her there were rumors that her disappearance and the discovery of Leland's bones were related, that maybe she killed him and ran away, knowing her secret would be revealed as construction continued at the site. She wanted to be angry with those people, but she found she didn't have the energy. It would be better not to know who spread those rumors. She wished she'd never heard them.

"Are you getting anywhere? Whoever did it must have left some evidence, right?" Carla asked, happy to have something other than her own issues to talk about. "Any chance Rachel was connected with him somehow? I wouldn't have thought her capable before, but now, I think she'd be the first person I'd look at."

"We're not closing any doors right now, but we have nothing that points us in her direction. Honestly, we don't have much of anything at all. State police are leading the investigation, but I think they are getting ready to wrap it up unless new evidence surfaces. I'm doing what I can on my own, but I'm really at a loss. It's a shame. I wish I'd known him better or known him at all."

Carla heard the shower turn on in the second-floor bathroom. Nick's mother was up. Moments later, Nick came down the stairs, wincing when he tried to go too fast. Stairs were hard for him because they used so many muscles, including the back and shoulders. He was doing better, though. The wound was starting to heal.

"Hey, Sawyer," he said when he reached the bottom. "Know anyone who can take my mother to the airport tonight? She's ready to leave, and I'm ready for her to go. She means well, but she treats me like I'm ten, and I don't think I can handle her crying episodes anymore. If she sees anything that reminds her of Christopher, she loses it. It's hard enough for us, you know? Her flight leaves at eight."

"I'll get somebody," Sawyer said. "Don't worry about it."

Nick edged his way onto a kitchen stool where he could still talk with Sawyer but would be able to easily get up and down. Carla couldn't even imagine what he'd been through, but she was finding it hard to reach out. Whenever he touched her, she thought of Rachel and how Rachel touched him, how he touched Rachel. She knew she had played a role in that. It was what she had wished for, a ploy to buy more time. Still, she couldn't shake that feeling of betrayal and the anger that it stirred within her. His injury was her excuse for not holding him tighter, not kissing him the way she used to, but she wasn't sure he bought it.

"You look like hell, man," Nick said. "You need to get some sleep. I've been meaning to ask how Heather is doing. She came by the store last week before all this happened, and she looked almost as bad as you do now. Has she been sick? I tried to get her attention, but she was spaced out, lost in thought or something. And she was in and out of there in minutes flat."

Sawyer drew in a deep breath.

"I don't know what's going on. She's been like this since Carla and Christopher disappeared. If you feel up to it, Carla, maybe I could bring her by so she can see you for herself. This whole thing really shook her up. I think it hit too close to home. She's always felt secure and confident, in control of everything. This sort of shattered that illusion, and she's having trouble bouncing back."

"Of course, Sawyer. Anytime. I'd probably feel the same way if the tables were turned," she said. Carla pulled the blanket tighter around herself. She would have to lie to Heather because she knew the truth, that no one is really ever safe. How do we really know people? How can we trust anyone? She trusted Rachel. She had always trusted Rachel. She would have trusted her with her life. And then there was Nick. He loved her. She loved him. She thought that was all that mattered, that nothing could come between them. But there it was. Rachel died, but she would always be there, haunting them.

She knew there were things Nick wasn't saying, too. He was trying so hard, but whenever she talked about Christopher, his face hardened a bit, and he looked away. He blamed her. He would never say it, but he did. Wouldn't she feel the same way if he had been the last one with Christopher? She knew she could not have prevented his disappearance, but she blamed herself, too. She couldn't expect anything different from Nick. So, there it was. Nick was the only person she wanted to be with, and she knew he felt the same. She loved him, but what could they do? Where did they go from here?

"Any more news about the search for Christopher?" Nick asked, though they both knew Sawyer would have told them immediately if there were any new developments at all.

"Nothing yet, but don't be fooled into thinking nothing is happening. We can be fairly certain he is safe, and no one wants to jeopardize that. State police have pulled in the FBI, so they have all their resources as well. They want to take this slowly, so they don't tip off the people who sold him or the adoptive parents. Nobody else knows what you told us about Arizona, Carla, and you have to keep it that way. The fewer people who know right now, the better. Just keep acting like you have no idea where he is. Keep up the social media pleas. Keep distributing flyers. Make it look like you don't know anything."

"We know," Carla said. "But just sitting here, doing nothing, it feels wrong."

"I understand, but you have to trust us."

That word again. How could he ever understand? How could anyone else understand unless someone stole their baby, too. Not just someone, but a confidant, a lifelong friend. How could anyone understand what it is like to have someone you trust and love drug you, and then seal you behind walls, threatening to kill you, torturing you? She was tired of people telling her to be patient, to let the police do their jobs, to focus on getting better. She would not get better, she could not get better, until Christopher was found.

"I'd better get going," Sawyer said. "I've got a couple meetings this morning. You two take it easy, okay? I'll try to come by again tomorrow, and I promise I'll let you know as soon as I hear anything at all."

Carla and Nick sat in silence for a moment when Sawyer left. Then Nick got up and slipped onto the sofa beside her. She knew that was a sacrifice. The sofa was old, and the cushions sank with his weight. It would hurt for him to get up again. He rested his head on her shoulder, and she found she appreciated his closeness.

"You know I love you," he said.

Carla looked at the rings that had been returned to her fingers. They shined with the same brilliance as before, but now she couldn't look at them without wondering whether they'd been blinding her all along. She reached for Nick's hand, his skin and his warmth so familiar. The smell of him was inviting.

    "I know," she said. "I know."

Chapter Twenty-Nine

Sawyer had left work early and brought home take-out. Even Bryce liked Chinese. He left Heather to herself, trying to take all the pressure off of her that he could. After he tucked the kids in for the night, he came downstairs to find her already in bed. He stayed up for a while, catching up on bills and watching a little TV. Then he carefully climbed in beside her, knowing, even with her back to him, that she wasn't asleep. He could tell by her breathing and the stiffness of her curled-up figure.

"I know you don't want to talk, Heather, but we have to," he said.

She didn't respond.

"What happened to Carla, it was a one-in-a-million thing. I asked her if we can come by, so you can see her for yourself and see that she is okay. She was excited. I think she'd really like to see you. She could use a friend right now."

Heather surprised him by flipping over to face him.

"Couldn't happen to me?" she said. "It's a one-in-a-million chance, but it happened, didn't it? To someone we know. What if that was me? What if someone suddenly took me away, and I was gone? What would you do then? Who would take care of the kids? They would grow up without their mother or with someone else filling in. I can't stand the thought of that, Sawyer. It could happen to anyone. Besides, she's not okay. Her son is gone. What if I were separated from our kids? What then? Would I be okay? Would you be okay?"

The strength of her reaction surprised him. It was not normal to be this

143

affected. He gently pushed her hair away from her eyes and caressed her cheek. Even now, with no make-up and her eyes swollen from a day's worth of tears, there was a beauty about her, a strength underneath it all. It was still there somewhere deep inside her. He needed to help her bring it back to the surface, but he had no idea how. She sighed.

"You don't know what it's like for me, knowing what's going on all the time, but not being able to do anything about it. You investigate these things. You can take action, but all I can do is sit here and worry—worry about Carla and Christopher, worry about you, worry about the kids. I can't keep doing this. A teenager is dead, and the killer is still out there. You don't even talk about that case. What if you get too close and that person comes after you?"

The relief at hearing Heather's voice was almost enough. She hadn't said that many words to him at once in weeks. Of course, she was upset. Talking about his cases made him feel better, but he never thought about the fact that he was shifting that burden to her. And she had no one to give it to. She was stuck with it, unable to change or fix anything. His previous cases were minor in comparison—a domestic dispute here, a burglary there—but two major crimes back-to-back? That was a lot to put on her.

"Oh, babe, I am so sorry. I wasn't thinking. That wasn't fair of me," Sawyer said. "The FBI has some leads on the baby and, with state police involved, I doubt they'll need me at all, And the Leland case—that's not going anywhere. We have nothing. No real leads. No real evidence. Whoever killed him is probably long gone. State police will probably file it with the cold cases soon. I have to wrap up things on my end, but then I'll be home more. I can help, and we can figure this out."

Heather took his hand in hers.

"I'm sorry. I don't mean to be this way, but I'm glad we talked. I'm starting to feel better already. I don't want you to stop sharing things with me. That wouldn't be much of a marriage. I just need time. I don't know why it's all bothering me so much. Can you give me a little more time? I love you so much, Sawyer, and I love our kids. Maybe we could take a vacation. I think it might help if I could get away from here for a while. "

They hadn't been on vacation since before Bryce was born. That might be exactly what they needed. He had time coming and, with things settling down, he could probably take his vacation before school started back up again. Maybe they could go to the ocean. Sophie and Andy had never been to the ocean, and they were at good ages. Bryce would be happy just to play in the sand and touch his toes to the waves. They could drive to Virginia Beach in a day if they started off when it was still dark and the kids were sleepy.

"That sounds like a great idea," he said. "I'll look at my schedule tomorrow and text you with some dates."

She leaned over and kissed him on his forehead.

"Thank you for being so patient with me. I don't know why I let this get me so down. But it's all going to be okay. I know it. I'm glad we talked."

Heather rolled back over again, within a few minutes, he could see her back rise and fall with the steady rhythm of deep sleep. Sawyer wasn't tired yet. He was still thinking about Leland. He was being truthful when he said state police would likely shelve the case for now. He couldn't blame them. It was fifteen years ago, and they had learned nothing new since the day his bones were discovered. There was no other DNA, and there were no suspects. None at all. If it weren't so personal, he would shelve it too. But he felt an obligation. He and the rest of the community had let Leland down, first, by doing nothing to help him when he lived with his grandmother, and second, by doing nothing when he disappeared. He couldn't abandon him again.

He climbed out of bed and settled in an armchair in the living room. A survival show was on TV. He watched without listening, deep in thought and heavy with sleep. At two in the morning, he woke up and made his way back into the bedroom. Heather was still fast asleep, but there would be no more for him. He lay there, trying to clear his mind and trying to decide whether their conversation was too easy, whether there was something else Heather was hiding from him, something more than a vacation could cure.

When the first hint of sun appeared, Sawyer climbed out of bed and started a fresh pot of coffee. He would probably have another hour to himself before the kids woke up. The fight he'd witnessed in the parking lot involving

Leland was bothering him. No one else seemed to remember it. He pulled his yearbook from the shelf and began flipping through it again. He didn't know the names of the guys who had surrounded Leland, but maybe he would recognize a face. Sawyer started with the senior class and worked his way backward. It amazed him that there were certain people he attended school with for twelve years—thirteen if he counted kindergarten—yet he never knew them. How was that even possible in a school so small? He paused as he passed Rachel's photo. She was odd in high school, but she had always seemed confident, put together. As they grew into adulthood, her oddities seemed a side effect of her ambition or maybe they were what made her successful. She was confident, bold, smart, and good-looking, but she never seemed to stay in a relationship for more than a few months. While others in the class married and had kids, divorced, and had more kids, she remained happily single. Now he understood why.

He sighed as he flipped the pages, running his finger over the photos of each member of the junior class as though touching them might spark a memory. But when he came to the end of the sophomore class, his finger stopped abruptly. That was him, the kid who made the first move, the one who pushed Leland the first time. It was the grin that gave him away. It was more like a smirk, the same kind of smirk he wore that day. It came back to him more vividly now—the bulky, sandy hair that was always slightly overgrown with bangs that swooped over his eyes. The sharp chin and angular body. The turtlenecks and patch-covered jean jackets that were fashion remnants of the previous decade, but somehow still looked right on him. His name was Daniel Walsh.

Chapter Thirty

Nick did it again. He walked into the kitchen to find Carla there and instinctively looked around for Christopher. His heart sank when he realized he wasn't there. Each time that happened, it was like losing him all over again. This was not what he had imagined, having one home and not the other. They had been a unit in his mind ever since they had gone missing. They were supposed to return as a unit. Nausea threatened to overtake him, bringing silent accusations into his throat. He knew the moment would pass, but for now, he couldn't talk for fear those accusations would escape, the allegations that she planned this, that she hated being a mother and wanted Christopher gone. It was irrational. He knew she loved Christopher and wanted him back as much as he did. He knew that Rachel was to blame for it all. But the emotions crashed into him like ocean waves, and he was helpless to stop them.

Carla sat hunched over her laptop at the kitchen counter, too focused to notice he'd entered the room, so he backed up quietly into the hallway to allow himself time to recover. He needed a moment to come to his senses, to remind himself what she'd been through, to remember how happy he was to get her back. They would get Christopher back. They would be a family again. She turned in his direction just as the doorbell rang.

"I'll get it," Nick said.

It was the state police again. How many more times could they do this?

"I'm sorry, but I need to talk to Carla again," Zittle said. "She might have remembered more since we last talked, and every bit of information is crucial. We never know what might lead us to Christopher."

Carla slammed her laptop shut and stood to greet him.

"It's okay," she said. Her voice was still a bit raw from the smoke when she hadn't spoken in a while.

"We can talk in the den."

Nick watched her go. She was so thin. She was drowning in her clothes, which hung on protruding shoulder bones and hips. Her cheeks were drawn, and her lips were chapped from dehydration. She needed to eat, and she needed to rest, but he knew that was impossible. Not with Christopher still out there. She was depressed and distraught, and she needed him, but he had no energy to give her. No physical energy and no emotional energy. He was saving that all for Christopher.

He wanted to take another pain pill, to fall back asleep again and wake up when this was all over, but he knew he had to control the urge. The pain in his shoulder was duller now, though it was still difficult to raise his right arm. His mother was gone, and Carla's mother only stopped by occasionally. The parade of visitors had ended as well. The house was theirs again. That should have made Nick happy, but it didn't. The visitors had distracted both Nick and Carla, making it possible to pretend the tension didn't exist, that he never touched Rachel and that Carla was as happy to see him as he was to see her. But Carla's initial happiness had faded as the reality of his actions with Rachel sunk in. His own irrational anger toward Carla never lasted more than a few minutes and was always followed by a rush of gratitude for her return, but it seemed like her eyes were empty sometimes when she looked at him.

The doorbell rang again. This time, it was Scott Duval, a reporter from the Rochester newspaper and an old friend of Sawyer's. Carla didn't want to talk to the press, but Nick knew it was important. They needed to keep her story alive for Christopher's sake, even if they couldn't tell the press everything. If the reporters stopped caring, so would everyone else. Besides, Scott had been around from the beginning, somehow convincing his editors that the story was relevant to their readers despite the distance. He deserved some respect in return. It was his fourth time making the trip from Rochester, so they could talk face-to-face.

Nick offered him coffee, but Scott told him to sit at the table and got them each a cup.

"You look better than you did in the hospital, but not much," Scott said. "How's that knife wound healing?"

"It's deep, but I got lucky. No major tissue damage." Nick shook his head. "I almost wish it was worse. Then I'd have an excuse for not reacting. It's just a big cut. I should have turned around and grabbed the knife and held it to her throat. She was five-foot-four and couldn't have been more than a hundred and twenty pounds. If I had done something, maybe then we'd know where Christopher is now."

"You were in shock, and you lost a lot of blood. From what I heard, you sucked down a few pints in the ER. You didn't even know for sure what had happened to you. You can't do this to yourself. You can't rewind and do that twenty-twenty hindsight thing. It won't get you anywhere."

Nick could hear Zittle's voice from the other room. He was asking Carla to describe again the moments before she passed out, to try to recall everything she saw in Rachel's house, any papers or photos or phone numbers. Nick wished he'd stop. Just stop. He started to raise his hands to his face, but he couldn't even do that. The pain was unbearable. He stared into his coffee as he spoke.

"She hates me," he said. "She tries to hide it, but I see it in the way she looks at me."

Nick couldn't believe he was saying this to a reporter, but who else could he tell? His parents? Sawyer? There was no one else. Somehow it seemed easier to tell someone he wasn't so close to. He sank back in the chair and dropped his hands in his lap.

"And sometimes, I think I hate her."

Scott said nothing for a moment, but he took his notepad off the table and flipped it closed.

"Look," he said, finally. "I can get what I need today from Investigator Zittle when he is done talking to Carla, but I have to tell you, I've done a lot of these stories, stories about bad things that happen to kids. Parents blame each other. They can't help it. When you've lost control of everything else,

149

it feels good to get angry. It feels even better to blame someone else. The anger keeps the sadness at bay. Most times, it ends in divorce. Don't let that happen to you and Carla."

"But how? I don't even know where to start."

"I don't know. Talk about it, maybe. Be honest. Most of the stories I wrote—the parents didn't get their kids back. Christopher isn't dead, as far as anyone knows. You have a good shot at getting him back. Remember that. Maybe it will help."

They sat in silence for the next five minutes until Zittle emerged from the den. He didn't seem surprised to see Scott there, but he didn't seem happy either. Scott stood and greeted him.

"I was told you were here. Got time for a few questions?"

"I'll talk to you outside," the investigator said. He waited until Scott left, and then he turned to Nick.

"I'm done with Carla for now, but I need to talk to you again, and an FBI agent will be here later. She's probably going to have more questions. So, don't go anywhere. And don't talk to the press again without talking to me first. The wrong kind of publicity could do more harm than good right now."

Then he was gone, and so was Scott, and he and Carla were alone again.

Nick took both coffee mugs to the sink and turned to see Carla's laptop still on the counter, where she'd left it. Why had she slammed it shut? What was she afraid of? He was about to reach for it when she came into the kitchen and slipped back onto the stool.

"How are you feeling today?" she asked, resting one hand on the lid.

"It hurts, but it's better. My range of motion is improving. Did you find anything interesting?" He motioned to the laptop.

"No. I was just reading through some of the Facebook posts. It's amazing. These people I haven't heard from in years, people I forgot I was even connected with online, suddenly proclaim to be my best friends. They share the posts and the news stories and write something like, 'praying for my dear friend, Carla, and her baby boy,' and then they get all sorts of attention. Condolences, prayers, all that stuff. It's sick, really. It's all about them. They want attention, and they are using us to get it."

As she talked, her hand remained there, firm and heavy. She wasn't reviewing Facebook posts. "Carla, we have to trust the cops. You know that, right? This is their job. They are good at it. They have access to information we don't have."

And there was that look again, that empty stare. Was it specifically for him, or was she just drained of everything, for everyone? He reached out with his good arm and touched her hair, but she gently pushed his hand away.

"Please don't. I don't want to be touched, not now," she said. "I'm sorry."

He felt the redness rush into his face and the words swelling in his throat, threatening to explode with full force. Then he remembered what Scott had said. He was right. He was angry with himself. He was ashamed and embarrassed, and it would feel a whole lot better to take it out on Carla. He needed to take control. He swallowed his anger, but there was no way he could take a whole day of this behavior, and he couldn't talk to her right now. The timing wasn't right. He left her behind in the kitchen and climbed the stairs to the bathroom. He popped the lid on his pain pills and took one, knowing that in another hour, he would be asleep.

Chapter Thirty-One

It wasn't easy to find Daniel Walsh. Sawyer was able to get his personal information from the school and find his driver's license information without a problem. But Daniel had a habit of moving without legally changing his address. Turned out, he was well known to Social Services. Every time they came knocking on his door with allegations that he'd beaten his kids, he picked up and moved his family to the next county over. He hopped back and forth on a regular basis, successfully alluding to the overworked and overloaded social workers in both counties. He had trouble holding down jobs, too. He was known to a couple of employers in the area, but he never lasted more than a year or so at any of them. Sawyer finally caught him leaving a lumberyard forty minutes out of town, where he filled in hauling supplies when the demand was high. He threw his hands up in defeat when Sawyer approached him.

"Look, man," he said. "I got nothing. I told the judge I'll pay the fine when I get a job. This doesn't count. This guy hardly pays me, and I only work when he needs me, and that's like a few days a month. My kids got to eat."

Daniel, or "Danny" as he was known about the area, hadn't changed much over the years. He had the same build and the same face except for his skin, which was leathery, probably from years of sun and smoking. Sawyer didn't have to ask Liam Walsh whether this was the grandson who knew Leland Boise. He could see Liam in Daniel's thick hair, his eyes, and his mannerisms. Was this why Dean Mills had suggested Sawyer leave the case alone that day he saw him with Liam and the other men at the diner? Did Liam's grandson kill Leland? Sawyer felt no need to keep a hand on his gun. If Danny Walsh was dangerous then, he was not now. He was so thin and lacking in muscle, Sawyer could probably carry him to the patrol car if he had to. If he was guilty of beating his kids, he'd better watch it because they would soon be big enough to fight back.

"This is another matter," Sawyer said. "I'll leave that to the sheriff's deputies."

Sawyer handed him a photo of Leland Boise.

"Remember this kid?"

Danny shifted on his feet and stared at the photo, his eyebrows furrowed.

"Isn't this the dead kid? The skeleton they found? Why are you asking me? I didn't know him." He shoved the photo back at Sawyer. Sawyer studied Danny's face. He looked irritated, but not scared and not panicked. He spat on the ground and started to walk away, but Sawyer shifted, blocking his way.

"I don't got time for this shit," Danny said, shoving his hands in his pockets. "You got no jurisdiction here anyway."

"But you did know him." Sawyer took his time speaking, watching for any change in Danny's demeanor. "I had the pleasure of watching you make his acquaintance in the high school parking lot way, way back. You reached your hand out, both hands actually, and shoved him a couple times while your friends cheered you on. Is it coming back to you now? It wasn't too long after that somebody killed him."

"I told you I didn't know him," Danny said, the irritation growing more obvious in his voice. "I knew who he was, the freak. We were just messing with him, and he broke my nose. Threw a punch out of nowhere, and who got suspended? I did. But I didn't kill him. Why would I kill a guy just because he broke my nose? I'd break his nose, that's what I'd do, but that was my last chance. One more incident, and I was going to be expelled. My dad would have beat the living crap out of me."

He cast his eyes down with his last words and spat again. Was he thinking of his own kids? Danny looked up abruptly, almost as if he'd heard Sawyer's thoughts. He stared hard at Sawyer and spoke through a clenched jaw.

"Shit. You're just like everybody else, aren't you? I see it in your face. You think because my dad beat me, I beat my kids. Are you gonna come arrest me every time you see one of my kids crying? You gonna call Social Services if they come to school with bruises on their arms or legs, figuring I did that? You gonna take them away from me? Nobody is taking my kids away from me. Not you and not nobody else. I didn't kill that kid, and I don't beat my kids. Arrest me if you're going to, but I don't have to take this."

He moved around Sawyer and, this time, Sawyer didn't stop him.

A few weeks ago, he would have cuffed Danny and brought him in—handed him over to the sheriff's department and to Social Services. But the whole thing with Rachel was impacting his judgment. Maybe Danny didn't beat his kids. Maybe he was telling the truth. When you grow up in a small town, you tend to let the community define you and, unless you get out, you become trapped by that definition. Danny had a reputation for making trouble even as a kid. He was rough, and his family was rough, so that's how Maplewood Falls defined him. He was beaten, so he must be a beater. But maybe he wasn't. Maybe that was why he hopped from county to county. Maybe he was trying to escape the definition, but he didn't know how or have anywhere else to go.

Sawyer would keep Danny on his list, and he would tell the other agencies where he found him, but he needed to start thinking differently, unlike the rest of the community and unlike a cop. He knew that Leland had a job on a farm that summer, haying or something like that. It was a long shot, but maybe his employer knew something. There was no mention of an employer in his file, though, and nobody was bragging about the connection now that his remains had been found. Most likely, the investigation never went that far. His former employers might have lost or sold their farm over the years or retired down south or even passed away at this point. No internet search was going to help. He'd have to go farm-to-farm within walking or biking distance of town and ask around, but not today. Today, he had a sudden urge to go home and hug his kids.

Chapter Thirty-Two

The police and FBI had come and gone twice more last night, and Carla was exhausted. She'd gone over and over the whole ordeal—the drugging, her captivity, her escape, every verbal exchange she'd had with Rachel—so many times, it was becoming unreal. The victim advocate had suggested therapy, but the constant grilling was probably just as effective. Her brain didn't have room to deal with all that anyway. Right now, Christopher was all she could think about. It was so lonely here in the house without him. Everything she touched and smelled reminded her of him. Every room felt empty, hollow. And the nursery...the nursery was unbearable. Nick had left it just as it was that morning. She couldn't eat. She couldn't sleep. And she couldn't talk to Nick about it.

A wall had come up between them in the past week, a wall fortified by his retellings to the police about all the time he'd spent with Rachel, about the kissing, about what he almost let her do. Carla had wanted that. She had begged for that, knowing their lives depended on it, but she couldn't help feeling betrayed. She had been missing less than a month. Nick didn't know where she was or where his son was, or whether they were even alive. How does sex come into play during that kind of stress? How could he be seduced while his wife and child were missing? How much did he really love her? She'd given up so much to be with him, and it had taken so little time for him to start forgetting. She knew she'd played a role in it. The advocate had talked to her about that, about the little things Rachel did at Carla's instruction that reminded Nick of Carla and had probably messed with his mind. He was vulnerable, she said, and Carla had given Rachel the

155

weapons she needed to attack, intimate and personal things that made him feel close to her even when she wasn't there. He was desperate for Carla and, in his weakened psychological and physical state, he had let himself believe that Rachel was Carla. Carla knew some part of this was her own doing, but, as much as she loved him, she still couldn't forgive him. Not now. Forgiving required too much attention and energy. She needed all her energy for Christopher right now.

Nick's condition was improving, and he begged her to try sleeping in their room. They could keep the door open and the hall light on, he said. She tried, but when she went to bed, he was always already asleep, knocked out hard by painkillers. She got up each morning before the sun, never really sleeping at all. It wasn't just the trauma. It was a new fear, a fear of being intimate with Nick again. Could she handle it? She didn't want to know. She was afraid that if they tried to become physical again, that would be the end of it, and she didn't want it to end. She loved Nick, or at least she thought she did. And then there was Nick. She knew what he wasn't saying, what he didn't dare to say. It hung thick in the air between them. It was Nick who finally took the lead.

"Let's do this," he said. "We're both overwhelmed and exhausted and dealing with a lot of confusing emotions. It won't do us any good to hash things out now. It will only distract us from the search for Christopher. Let's call a truce. Let's take care of each other and work together to find him. Once we have him back, we can try to sort things out. If you want to. I know I love you. I know I love you more than I have ever loved anyone except maybe Christopher. Can you accept that for now? Can you decide later whether you still love me?"

Carla felt no attraction when she looked at him, nothing like she used to feel. She had no physical desire for anything with Christopher missing—not for food and certainly not for sex—but she didn't even want Nick's arm around her or his hand on hers or the warmth of his body near her. Maybe she felt she didn't deserve it. Christopher was in her care that day. She was his mother. She didn't protect him. She failed him. Or maybe it was this room, this house. This was where he had kissed Rachel just days before, where he lifted her blouse and fondled her breasts, where Rachel unzipped his pants and whispered those words in his ear. Here, in the house that Carla and Nick had bought together, the house where they had conceived their child. Nick wouldn't talk to the investigator while she was in the room, but she read the statement later, and she sometimes overheard the conversations. She made herself digest every word even though it made her stomach turn. Rachel was a good trainee. She did everything Carla had suggested, even whispering that phrase to him. Carla had wished for that moment. She gave Rachel those words in hopes that they would awaken Nick, that he would remember they were her words and understand what was happening. Those words, that encounter, had saved Carla's life. She should be grateful. They should be celebrating her cleverness and his sharpness. It was a clue, and he had picked up on it. Still, she couldn't get back to where they used to be. She didn't know how. But she could pretend. She had honed that skill when she was sealed in the basement.

"I'll try," she said.

That night, Carla made dinner, and they sat together at the table, picking at their food and talking about the efforts to find Christopher. State police had brought in the FBI since Christopher had been trafficked over state lines, and that gave them some level of comfort. Agents had come and gone several times already. What was missing, though, was a sense of urgency. Everyone seemed to agree that Christopher was likely safe with his adoptive parents. At this point, they didn't want to put out any flyers in Arizona or contact Phoenix police just yet for fear that someone involved in the illegal adoption would catch wind of it and destroy evidence. The FBI agent assigned to the case told Carla and Nick it was best to work slowly and discretely. She told them exactly what Sawyer had said a few days before.

"If we do things right, no one will know we have any idea what happened to Christopher until we have him in our custody," she said. "If we act rashly, the adoptive parents might flee with him, or the people who sold him might take him back. I don't even want to talk about what might happen then. I know it's hard, but patience is vital here. We are doing more than you realize. We just can't tell you everything."

But Carla didn't believe her. She was still finding it hard to trust anyone.

"We can't wait, Nick," Carla said. "Look at all the kids who are still missing years later, kids who were stolen by their own parents. If they can't catch those people, what makes you think they will find Christopher? I find it hard to believe that we're top on their list. Too many kids are missing, and too few people are looking for them. They have said it themselves over and over. They don't believe Christopher is in danger. Why would they devote all their resources to finding him?"

"Carla, they have said that this is likely something bigger than Christopher. Other kids are probably being bought and sold. The FBI needs time to go through Rachel's emails, social media, hard drive, all that stuff and figure out how she managed to connect with that guy in the first place. They will find him. They want to find him. You need to believe that. There is nothing we can do anyway. If we go looking for him, even if we just hint at the Phoenix connection, we might blow their investigation. We can't take that chance."

So, Carla did more pretending. She promised she wouldn't do anything without permission from the FBI. She did the dishes, and they each spent a little time on their own, still not knowing how to function alone again under one roof, but being respectful of each other's needs. But that night, Carla slipped out of bed as soon as Nick fell asleep and went to the den. She had been doing research for a while now, planning this all carefully. While Nick was asleep, she created a new profile on Facebook and searched until she found what she was looking for. Then she sneaked into their room and pulled some clothes from her dresser and their closet. She packed a bag and hid it.

Once again, Carla barely slept. It took everything out of her to stay in the bedroom away from her laptop. It wouldn't help to keep checking, and Nick might wake up and discover what she was doing. At six-thirty in the morning, Carla got out of bed, got dressed, and pulled out her laptop again. Nick had awoken in pain at about five a.m., and the drugs the doctor had given him were strong. He would probably sleep soundly until late morning. She needed to concentrate, and she didn't want him popping into the room when she wasn't prepared. He would try to stop her. It was better if he didn't know.

Her hand shook as she clicked again on the link for a Facebook group for couples in the Phoenix area who had adopted children in the months of April, May, June, and July. She had requested to join the night before, answering all the questions required of newcomers. She was certain her request would be rejected. Her newly created account had no history and no virtual friends associated with it, but she had explained in a message to the administrator that she had created a new account specifically for this group because she was concerned the birth mother would find her. She apologized for being so paranoid, saying she was sure she'd relax as their little girl grew up. It was a lame excuse, so she was shocked when she saw that her request was approved. The group had more than three hundred members and probably wasn't particular.

Carla had been careful to add things like hometown, type of employment, and schooling in her profile as well to differentiate her account from spammers. She had also fully described her supposed efforts to have children through in-vitro fertilization and their decision to give up. Now that she was in, she doubted it would matter. First, she posted a "thank you" to the administrators of the group for letting her in. Then she revealed her "true" reason for joining and prayed they wouldn't delete her post and remove her.

I apologize. I am not an adoptive parent. I joined this group, hoping to find the couple who adopted my nephew. My sister did not want her son, but she did want money from the adoption, so she went with an agency that was a little shady and that she had no way of reaching after she gave up her son. But she intentionally withheld critical medical information for fear that they would refuse to take him. That was wrong. I am sorry about that. The thing is that my nephew could potentially have an inherited heart problem that causes the heart to misfire and can lead to instant death. Our family just learned of it when our otherwise healthy fourteen-year-old brother, the youngest in our family, died six months ago. Most of our family members—aunts, uncles, cousins, nieces, and nephews—were tested after he died, and two of them have it. One of those people is my daughter. She is only three, and I thank God every day that we had her tested and were able to have a pacemaker implanted. A pediatrician would have no reason to test for this without a family history. I need to pass on this information along with the report on my brother. I can even just fax or email it to a pediatrician's office if the adoptive parents prefer to remain anonymous. I fully supported this adoption. My sister is not fit to be a parent, and I have three children of my own. I have no desire to invade the privacy of this new family, but I could never forgive myself if this baby died because I failed to intervene. Here is a photo of my nephew. All I know is that he was adopted by loving parents who desperately wanted a child and who live in the Phoenix area. Please. I beg you, private message me or have a friend do it, or create a new account and do it. I don't care. I don't need any information about you. Just a fax number or email address for a clinic or some other place where I can send this information, so my former nephew, your son, can live.

She added a photo of Christopher, his date of birth, and the approximate date he was given up along with a silent prayer that the news of a kidnapped child in New York would not make headlines in Phoenix. In this moment, she was grateful the FBI had decided not to go all-out in seeking the public's help. With the Facebook page still up, she pulled out her credit card and made a plane reservation. A one-way flight to Phoenix, departing in two hours. Nick was still in pain, but he could get around fairly easily now. He'd even been talking about going in to the store tomorrow for an hour or two. He would be fine without her. Then she grabbed the bag she had hidden in the closet and took one last look at the Facebook page before she shut down her laptop. No replies, but the administrators had not yet deleted it. That was good. Of course, it was even earlier in Arizona. Most likely, no one was awake to read it yet. She slipped her laptop into the bag, left a note on the dining room table, telling Nick she had gone for a walk to clear her head, and then waited ten minutes for an Uber she had requested. It would be several hours before Nick saw the note and another hour or so before he began to suspect that she was gone. He would have no way of knowing when she'd written it.

It was a long drive to the airport. She would just barely make it through security on time, but she was doing something, and that was what she needed.

She promised the driver a good tip if he hurried and settled into the back seat of the car. Then she pulled out the onesie she had tucked into her purse. It was a simple white onesie made of soft cotton. She put it up to her face and pulled Christopher's scent deep into her lungs. The onesie had been in the hamper next to the changing table. It was what Christopher had worn that night, before she changed him, fed him and took him to Rachel's house. She had taken her son to Rachel, handed him over to his kidnapper, never suspecting any danger despite the signs. Rachel was not simply sad or disappointed when Carla told her she was pregnant. She was angry. What kind of friend gets angry about a pregnancy? She had not come to her baby shower and had never given her a gift. She feigned interest in Christopher whenever she saw him, but the act lasted only a few minutes. Carla thought Rachel just wasn't the motherly type, but now she understood. Christopher was a permanent link between Carla and Nick. He destroyed Rachel's illusion that she and Nick would divorce and Rachel and Nick would become a couple. How could Carla not see Rachel for what she was? How had she remained friends with her all those years? What kind of a mother was she, putting her son in such danger? Once she had Christopher back, she would never leave him again. She would give him the love and protection he deserved. She would never let go.

Chapter Thirty-Three

Nick slept later than he intended. It was almost noon by the time he woke up, but he knew immediately Carla was gone. The house had that same kind of emptiness, a sadness of sorts. At first, he thought she had left him, but then he saw the note and knew she'd gone after Christopher. She would leave him, though. He was sure of that. How could she ever forgive him for what he'd done? Yes, Rachel pulled him in with the perfume, the mannerisms, the familiar teasing, the soft looks that had belonged to Carla, but he knew it was Rachel. He couldn't deny that. He didn't understand why he kissed her or why he let her come on to him. It was all so confusing in that moment. It felt good to let go, to allow himself to pretend Rachel was Carla, and to give in. It felt good to pretend for even just a second that everything was fine and that Christopher was upstairs asleep in his crib. Rachel had created that allusion for him, and she had aroused him to a point where the promise of physical release, the ability to escape in sex and forget about everything else, overwhelmed him and took priority over reality. He was living that allusion, but then she broke it with Carla's own words.

He could not explain his actions to his wife, and he couldn't justify them. There was no justification. Carla would not understand. He wouldn't understand either if the tables were turned. But he loved Carla. He loved her so much it hurt. He wanted their son back. He wanted their lives back. He wanted to undo this whole mess, but he didn't know how. After the fire, after she escaped and he was rescued, she held him so tightly that he almost believed they could be a family again. But then she let go, and she hadn't held him since. Their talk had helped. It provided some relief from the tension, getting things out in the open like that. He didn't try to touch her anymore, and he knew he wouldn't until after Christopher was found. She didn't want to be consoled. She wanted her son, and he understood that. But what would happen after he was found? Would she ever really desire him again?

She still refused to discuss her own feelings about his interaction with Rachel or to talk over ways they might help the police. So, he wasn't surprised when he woke up and found she was gone. He wasn't surprised when he saw her laptop was missing. He wasn't surprised when he pulled up their checking account on his own computer and saw that she'd bought a plane ticket. But he was worried. The man who bought Christopher from Rachel must know by now that Christopher was a kidnapping victim, if he hadn't known already. He would be nervous, and he would be trying to cover his tracks. He might be part of a larger and more powerful organization. Carla had no idea what she might be getting herself into. Nick pulled himself together and picked up the phone.

"Sawyer," he said. "I need your help."

Then he sank into the recliner and waited. How many times had he sat in this same spot already this summer, waiting, wishing she would come through that door? When Carla first disappeared, he was lost. He was frightened for her and for Christopher, constantly fighting his imagination, trying to suppress the scenes that played in his head over and over, the horrifying possibilities. But this time, she left by choice. She decided to put herself in danger with no thought for him and what he had been through. His fear and anxiety turned to anger, and it felt good to be angry. So, he fueled it while he waited for Sawyer with memories of every time she had ever wronged him, enjoying the warmth of its flames. He let himself hate her until he couldn't anymore. No matter what she'd done, he wanted her back safe and healthy. That was his reality. So, by the time Sawyer came through the door half an hour later, Nick had already checked the airline schedule and found that a one-stop flight for Phoenix had departed around nine that morning. The layover was thirty-three minutes. She would have caught her connecting flight and landed by now, which would make it harder to find her. What made her go there? Did she think she could just wander around Phoenix and its suburbs, hoping for a chance encounter with Christopher and the people who had him? Even in her current state, she wouldn't do that. Carla was a planner. She always had been. Something had changed. She had information of some sort, and that worried him more.

"Don't be stupid, Carla," he said aloud to their empty house. "I can't lose you again."

Chapter Thirty-Four

Carla had not done a good job of covering her tracks. It wouldn't be hard to figure out that she had flown to Phoenix, but so what? She was an adult, and she was no criminal. She had a right to fly wherever she wanted. She wasn't stupid, though. Nick would worry and call the police, but Phoenix was a big city. As long as she paid for everything with cash, she should be able to wander around undiscovered for a while. She had emptied Nick's wallet before she left, and she had taken the cash she had tucked away for Christmas with her. Then she made withdraws from different bank machines at each airport, taking out the maximum each time. She just hoped that her plan worked, that someone would respond to that Facebook post. She had no backup plan except maybe wandering the malls and hanging out in front of pediatricians' offices, hoping to catch a glimpse of her son. That didn't seem very practical or productive.

The airport was huge, much bigger than she realized. She'd wasted too much time getting from the gate to the exit. She wanted to get out there as quickly as she could. If the FBI got involved, they could find her at the airport with a phone call. She had assumed Nick would sleep in, but what if he didn't? What if he called the police right away, and they decided her actions were interfering with their investigation? What if they were looking for her already, concerned that she'd gone off the deep end and was a danger to herself? She'd been through a lot. That would be a reasonable assumption. Her plan would be ruined. She didn't want anyone else involved. It would be too easy for something to go wrong.

Rather than take a cab or an Uber from the airport, Carla hopped on a hotel shuttle. She knew she was being paranoid, but cab drivers might talk to the police, and a cell phone request for Uber would leave a record on the app. Hotel shuttle drivers have so many passengers at once and transport so many people in one day that the driver might not remember her. Plus, the shuttle was free. She chose the Sheraton as her destination because it was a large, downtown conference hotel. Most likely, no one would notice that she didn't check in or if they did see her come and go, they would assume she was there for a conference, but was staying elsewhere. She sat in the lobby for fifteen minutes, pretending to look for someone each time the doors opened. When she was sure the shuttle had left, she started walking.

The downtown neighborhoods changed quickly from upscale to somewhat downtrodden. The sun was brutal, and it was midafternoon, the hottest time of day. The pilot said it was ninety-eight degrees when they landed, but the dry heat thing was true. Ninety-eight degrees in Phoenix was far more bearable than ninety degrees and humid back home. This sun burned, and it sucked up all the moisture in her, but it didn't encase her in a layer of sweat. Her skin could breathe. She stopped at a food truck near the edge of the business district and bought a cold bottle of water. As long as she stayed hydrated, she knew she would be okay. It was an odd city. In the more upscale downtown area, everything was green. The grounds of each business were either lush and thick with grass or filled with carefully selected gravel and a variety of manicured desert plants. But the more she walked, the more barren the landscaping became. Cracked asphalt and hard dirt surrounded stucco-plastered buildings with cracked and peeling paint. Bars covered some of the store windows. Most people were in passing cars, not on the sidewalks. There were more trees than she expected, though. Even the most run-down home seemed to have a paloverde, an ironwood or a mesquite.

The site of the gunshot wound throbbed from all the day's stress, so she was relieved when she found a squat, privately owned motel with a vacancy sign out front after walking only half an hour. The man behind the desk was about her age and spoke in a thick Hispanic accent. He didn't demand an ID once she offered a week's payment in advance, but the way he stared at her...it was unnerving, like he was leery of her. She supposed she deserved that, given her behavior. The office was separate from the motel itself, which was a long strip of eight or nine rooms. Only one car was parked out front, and each room had a white, plastic table with two matching chairs outside its entrance, where guests could get some fresh air. She checked the bathtub for roaches and the sheets for bed bugs. No scorpions on the walls or underfoot. All was clear. The room even came with a coffee maker and a microwave, which was good because she was suddenly distrustful of any food or drink made for her by others. She knew she shouldn't be. She'd told herself a million times that only Rachel would do that and that Rachel was dead, but there could be other Rachels in the world, couldn't there? She had never suspected Rachel would hurt her. Rachel was her friend. It could happen again.

Carla took in the room with its dark green curtains and shiny bedspread that was covered in a paisley of dark greens, dark reds, and black. The room was depressing, but much better than being sealed in a basement. She tried the doorknob for the seventh time in ten minutes just to make sure it wasn't locked, another new habit she had formed. She worried more about being stuck inside than she did about people breaking in. Where to sit? Both the bed and the chair gave her the creeps. Who knew who had done what on them? But she would have to get over it if she wanted to find Christopher. She finally took a deep breath, plopped down on the bed, and opened her laptop, figuring that as gross as the bed was, the motel's dryer would probably have killed any germs or bacteria previous tenants had left behind. Mind over matter.

Still no response on the Facebook post, but at least the moderator didn't take it down. No word from Nick either. He would be awake by now, and he had probably found the note. She felt bad about leaving him in the dark, but if she had told Nick, he would have tried to stop her, worrying it would jeopardize the investigation or that it was dangerous. He had already warned her several times to let the police handle it, almost like he knew she was up to something. But how dangerous could the adoptive parents be? Carla still wasn't sure what she would do if she found them. Grab Christopher and run? That wouldn't work. She might be perceived as some crazy kidnapper and get herself locked up until she could explain. By then, they would be long gone with Christopher. She could try to reason with them, explain who she was, but what if they were aware it was an illegal adoption? She didn't know these people or what they were capable of. She would probably have to call the local police and stay close to the adoptive parents until they arrived. She didn't dare text Nick, though. She wasn't an expert in technology, but she was afraid someone would be able to trace her location. That is, assuming anyone cared where she was. The police might tell Nick they can't help, that she left of her own free will and that there is nothing they can do. The FBI became involved in the case because there was enough evidence that Christopher was taken out of state, but she doubted they would waste resources on finding her. She was alone in this. That was the only way it could work.

The rumble in Carla's stomach reminded her that she hadn't eaten in at least twenty-four hours. She remembered passing a convenience store just before she reached the motel, so she locked up the room and walked two blocks until she reached a Circle K. She grabbed another bottle of water, a bottle of diet Coke, a bag of pretzels, and some trail mix, which she was tempted to eat on the way back. A slight breeze cooled her on the walk. It was almost pleasant outside, and it occurred to her just how much safer the city neighborhoods seemed here than they did in the east. There were no alleyways for people to hide in. Most of the buildings were no more than a few stories high, and the few houses she'd passed were ranch-style. No one hung out on the street corners, leering at her as she walked by. A few kids with skateboards traveled up and down a side street with their backpacks still on, showing off their skills, probably on their way home from school. The driver of a pumped-up car beeped at her and whistled, but he never slowed down. What would her son be like if he grew up here? Where was he being raised? In an upscale subdivision with gardeners maintaining a lush green lawn despite the desert heat and a pool with a shaded hot tub attached? Or in a simple home in a neighborhood like this? Did his parents adopt through the black market because they had fistfuls of money to spare and they wanted a child quickly, or did they scrimp and save because the world is still an unfair place and they were rejected by other agencies because they were gay or lesbian or too old or the wrong color? Why adoption? Were they both infertile? Could they not get a sperm donor or an egg donor and have children on their own? Did they believe they were saving Christopher from foster care or from cruel and unloving parents? Did they even know their adoption was illegal? What was their story?

Carla sat on the motel bed and drank down the water within seconds. She hadn't realized how dehydrated she was. She ripped open the bag of pretzels and had eaten only a few when she saw that she had a message request from someone who was not her friend on this new Facebook account. Slowly, she rested the bag on the bed. She dropped down on her knees, not caring about the stains on the thin carpeting, and leaned over the bed so she could see her computer screen better. Her hands and fingers trembled as she clicked on the message from someone who called herself simply Belinda Ann. No last name. It looked like a newly created profile.

I saw your post, and I can't thank you enough. I can't give you my contact information because my husband and I agree that it's unhealthy for the baby to have an open adoption. I would greatly appreciate it if you would fax or email the information to Sand Hill Pediatrics in Scottsdale at the number or email address below. We already have an appointment, so the sooner you can send it, the better. We appreciate that you reached out like this. Your nephew is a beautiful boy and healthy in every way, as far as we know. Hopefully, he has been spared this genetic problem, but we will do everything possible to keep him healthy if he is affected. We can't thank your sister enough for bringing him into this world and giving him to us. Our life is complete with him in it. We hope your daughter is well.

The words and the screen blurred as tears filled Carla's eyes. Christopher was alive. He was safe, he was healthy, and he was right here in the Phoenix area. She rested her head on the bed and tried to absorb the words she'd just read. Her body ached for him. Her heart ached for him. Would he still know her? How long did it take for an infant to forget his mother, the mother whose body provided his only nourishment from conception until just before he was taken? Would he know her smell, her touch, her voice, or would he recoil and scream and cry and plead without words for his new parents? Would he still love her? Would he still want her? She needed to do something. Now. But what could she do? She was tempted to write back and tell them who she was, but she knew she couldn't do that. She would lose him. This was torture, knowing he was here, but not knowing where, not knowing how to reach him. She needed to distance herself, just like she would for a story. She needed to pull away from the emotion and gain some perspective.

Carla stood and drew in a long, deep breath. No more tears. She needed to think and act. She typed "Sand Hill Pediatrics" and "Scottsdale" into the Google search bar on her phone. There it was—the address and the phone number. Now she just needed to pull herself together enough to make the call and sound convincing. She would have only one chance. She couldn't afford to blow it, but she needed a burner phone. She grabbed her purse and her room keys, slipped on her shoes, and started walking. She would have to move fast. It was getting late, and the doctor's office might close soon. She had passed a shop on her way to the Circle K that sold electronics. It was only two blocks away.

Chapter Thirty-Five

Sawyer couldn't do anything more about Carla's flight and the baby. The FBI office in Phoenix had been notified. It was their case now. He could go home. He'd finished all his paperwork for the day. It was early, but he had started at seven in the morning. He had put in a full day today and plenty of overtime the week before. But home wasn't the haven it used to be. Heather was getting more and more depressed, despite their talk. She never wanted to leave the house anymore. He had to hire a friend's daughter to drive the kids back and forth to the YMCA program, and Heather was ordering take-out more than she was cooking, which meant they were burning through the household budget faster than they should. He tried to talk to her about it again two days ago, but she insisted it had nothing to do with him or their marriage, that she was simply feeling down and needed time. He suggested that she try counseling or therapy or even just see her regular doctor, but she flew off the handle.

"Lay off me." She'd been folding laundry on the dining room table, but she turned to face him, her eyes boring into him. "I'm not crazy. You smother me. You don't let me breathe. I said I needed time. Give me time."

Heather turned back to the white basket and pulled out a pair of soft pink pants that were a favorite of Sophie's. She snapped them in the air to get the wrinkles out with much more vigor than necessary. Sawyer came up behind her as she folded them and slipped a hand around her waist, burying his face in her long waves of hair. Immediately, she shrugged him off and turned to face him again, gently pushing him back a few steps.

"Look. I'm sorry I snapped. This whole thing with Carla and Rachel, it

171

really shook me up. You were right about that. I can't even imagine how I'd feel if someone took one of our kids. I can't imagine how Carla feels. I don't want to." She drew in a long breath. "I am doing better. I really am. Talking helped, but I still need to process some stuff, and that takes time. I'll be fine. We'll be fine. It was never about you. But I don't want to talk about it anymore at this moment, and I can't be your sounding board right now. Give me a few more days. Then we'll talk again. Okay?"

But it seemed to only get worse. She had been taking baths frequently for the past few weeks, but now it seemed she was always in the tub. She'd lock the bathroom door as soon as he walked into the house and stay in there for an hour or more while he picked up after the kids and gave them the attention they'd been craving all day. When Heather finally emerged from the bathroom, she was always cocooned in her robe, with water dripping from her long hair and her pale skin free of makeup. She would have looked beautiful except for the shadows under her eyes and the hollows in her cheeks. She would answer his questions, but she asked him nothing, and she showed no interest in anything at all. There were no more conversations in their household.

She wasn't acting like a mother anymore. It could be some sort of delayed post-partum depression triggered by the kidnappings. It could be the stress that came with being a sounding board, like she'd said. Then again, he might be looking in the wrong direction. He hadn't been home much to help out these past few weeks, and she was already overwhelmed with work, school, and the kids. Maybe she had taken on too much. She loved the kids. He knew that, but she seemed incapable of functioning anymore. There was one other thing he hadn't considered seriously enough: Maybe she was cheating on him. He didn't want to think that way, but it would explain a lot. He'd give her a few more days, but he was going to have to do something soon. They couldn't go on like this. It wasn't good for their marriage or the kids. It wasn't safe. It was all taking a toll on her, on the whole family.

But what Sawyer needed now was something else to focus on, and Leland's file was right there in front of him. State police still had no leads whatsoever. He was a good kid. It was that simple. Never got in any trouble. No complaints about him from teachers or neighbors. He'd finally tracked down Leland's employer from that summer, the Ellises, who had a farm a few miles outside town where he fed cows, cleaned the barn, and did other odd jobs. The Ellises had nothing but praise for him. Leland was always on time, and he worked hard. He bought a used bike to get back and forth to work, and he brought a sandwich each day for lunch, never taking more than twenty minutes for his break even, when Cindy Ellis urged him to rest longer. The one thing that didn't fit was the necklace, she said. The package fell out of his back pocket while he was working, and Cindy picked it up. It was a heart pendant—amber, framed with silver. Cindy said he blushed and grabbed it from her, insisting it was a gift for his grandmother. But it didn't look like the kind of gift you'd give a relative, she said. It looked like something for a girlfriend. But there was no other evidence that Leland ever had a girlfriend, not even a crush. Leland was full of secrets, but he had hidden them well.

Leland had probably bought the necklace locally. It was unlikely that he had a computer or a credit card that would allow him to order anything online, especially back then when personal computers and laptops were even more expensive. He was too young to drive, and it was an awfully long bike ride to the next community with a jewelry store or even a Walmart. So, he could start with the Karvets, who sold guns and jewelry from the main floor of their house on the edge of downtown and then try Zane Williams, who sold and repaired jewelry from a small shop in the Tops grocery store plaza. It was unlikely either owner would remember any sale from that long ago, but it beat sitting around and doing nothing. He grabbed his keys and left, feeling energized for the first time in days.

Chapter Thirty-Six

Carla wished she'd bought something to steady her nerves—some wine or beer or a shot of something. Maybe one of Nick's pain pills. Her hands were trembling, and she was afraid her voice would shake, too, giving her away. It was four fifteen. According to Google, the pediatrician's office was open until five. She tucked her own cell phone in her purse and used the burner phone instead so they wouldn't know who was calling. Nick knew she was gone now. He had called her cell phone at least four times, and he had sent her two texts, asking where she was and begging her to contact him. Sawyer had called twice. Carla closed her eyes as the burner phone rang through to the pediatrician's office and focused on Christopher. He needed her. She had to remain calm for his sake. If this didn't work, she would have to stake out the doctor's office for god-knows how long and hope they didn't have him covered up with a blanket in an infant carrier when he arrived. Who knew how long she might have to watch the office doors, how many days? Someone might see her loitering and have her arrested. It wouldn't work. She needed the appointment time. It seemed like an eternity before she heard a voice on the other end.

"Sand Hill Pediatrics. How may I help you?"

"Hi. I have some critical medical information to fax to your office for a couple who recently adopted a baby. I'm afraid I don't know their names and I can't give you mine because we are all trying to remain anonymous to each other here, but I can't get to a fax machine until tomorrow afternoon or Friday morning, and I don't have access to a scanner. I want to make sure I'm not too late for their appointment. They said they already made one."

The line was silent for a moment, and Carla was worried the woman had hung up. She was relieved to hear the voice again, but the woman's tone was cynical. "So, you can't give me any names, but you want me to find out when they have an appointment? How am I supposed to help you?"

"Please, this is important. A potentially life-threatening heart condition runs in the family that the mother did not reveal to the adoption agency. The agency refused to pass on the information, claiming the chances he inherited it are slim. My guess is they don't want to be sued. My baby brother died of this before we found out, and my daughter has it, too. My daughter will be fine because we knew about it, and she got a pacemaker. This boy would be my nephew. I don't want his parents to suffer the same heartache as we did when we lost my brother. The couple wants a closed adoption, and so do we. I got a message to them through a mutual connection, and they said to fax the documents to your office. I'm not positive, but I believe the mother's first name is Belinda. The baby is about six months old. It's a boy."

Another pause. Carla's hands were sweating so badly she feared the phone might slip from her grasp. She prayed she'd used the same details as she'd given Belinda. The appointment might be days away. If the doctor's office and the adoptive parents shared notes in the meantime and caught discrepancies, they might contact the adoption agency and double-check. That would be the end of it. She would never see Christopher again. Then she heard a sigh.

"Hold on. Let me see if anybody knows anything."

Carla forced herself to relax, practicing the breathing she learned to help her meditate during her labor with Christopher: Four-second breath in, eight seconds out; four in, eight out; four in, eight out. If you breathe correctly, the physical symptoms of panic cannot set in, she reminded herself. Four in, eight out. Panic is physical. Control the physical reactions, and you control the panic. The voice returned.

"Can you get it to us by Friday morning at ten?"

"Absolutely," Carla said, resisting a sudden temptation to laugh. "I can't thank you enough. You might have saved his life."

"Do you have our fax number?" she asked.

Carla repeated the number from the Facebook message, and the woman confirmed it. "Thank you so much," she said. "I might be cutting it close, but the documents will be there."

The second she clicked "end," Carla let the laugh loose. She rolled on the bed and giggled and laughed until her sides hurt, punching the air with her fists. She'd found Christopher. She knew where he would be at ten o'clock Friday morning. Today was Wednesday and it was evening. The appointment was less than two days away, less than forty-two hours away. Already, she could feel his warmth in her arms. Her laughter triggered tears and the tears were relentless. Soon she was on her knees, with her hands folded on the bed, gasping for breath and thanking a god she'd rarely prayed to. He was alive, he was well, and soon, he would be home again.

She had planned to call Sawyer when she found him, but she wasn't so sure that was a good idea anymore. What if the police screwed up? What if the FBI screwed up? This was a black-market adoption. The adoptive parents might have known that. If they suspect anything at all, they might back out and skip the appointment or even skip town. But what would she do when she found him? She couldn't just grab him and steal him back. She might get arrested, and by the time the cops figured it all out, Christopher and his adoptive parents could be long gone. Or worse, Christopher might get hurt. Maybe she could call the police just before the appointment, giving them time to get there, but no time to investigate further and risk screwing it up. At the very least, she needed to let Nick know she had found him and that he was okay. She could text him from the burner phone. That would work. He wouldn't be able to trace it.

Nick, you won't believe it. I used a fake profile to track down Christopher's adoptive parents on Facebook through an adoption board, and I found out about a doctor's appointment Friday morning. I know where our baby will be! He is healthy, and he is fine! I'm still trying to figure out how to handle this. I am worried about bringing the police into it because I don't want to blow it. By now, you know I flew to Phoenix. I can't tell you anything else because I know you love me and that you love Christopher and that you will tell Sawyer, believing that you are helping. I have to figure this out before I get anyone else involved. Please trust me. I love you! Our baby is coming home!

As Carla hit send, she heard a tap on the motel room door. No one knew she was here, and she had only checked in today. It couldn't be the cleaning person. Another tap and then a knock. She dropped the burner phone on the bed, not daring to even breathe.

"Hello?" It was a man's voice. A soft voice. "This Phoenix police officer Bill Schmidt. I'm looking for Carla Murphy. I know you checked in, so if you don't open the door, the manager will. We got a call for concern about your safety."

Carla's heart sank. How could they have found her? She did everything she could to cover her tracks. What had she overlooked? Her legs felt heavy, and the energy that had fueled her when she found Christopher was gone. Now she had no choice. She would have to put her trust in the police and the FBI and hope and pray all went well. Maybe this was a sign. Maybe this was the right thing to do. She stood, smoothed her shirt, ran her fingers through her hair, and opened the door. Before she could say a word, a strong hand grabbed her shirt and shoved her back inside, pushing her against the motel room wall, and then another hand clamped over her mouth. A tall man with a broad barrel of a chest stood before her. She could barely see past him to a second man who pointed a gun at her head and shut the door.

She tried to scream, but the first man pressed harder on her mouth and pushed his whole body into her. He let go of her shirt and pulled out a roll of duct tape with his free hand, ripping a piece off with his teeth. He had it over her mouth before she could release a sound. Then he flipped her around, pulled her arms behind her back, and tied a rope around her hands. When he was done, he threw her on the bed. This was it. This was how she would die. Her chest felt like it might shatter, but her mind was surprisingly calm. She closed her eyes and waited for them to rape her, shoot her, whatever they were going to do. She just wanted them to get it over with. Again and again, she told herself Christopher is safe. He is healthy. Even if Nick never gets him back, he will be fine. The adoptive parents love him, and he will be surrounded by that love. That's all that matters. But instead of shooting her or raping her, the first man reached for the burner phone.

"Look at this. A burner," he said, slipping the phone into his pocket. "She made sure no one could find her. Good of her to help us out like that."

He walked around her, took her laptop from the bed, and sat down with it at the desk while the other man—shorter, but just as muscular—kept the gun trained on her. She watched him, quietly cursing herself for leaving Facebook open and for sending the text to Nick. The message from Belinda Ann was right there for him to see. He studied it for a minute, wrote something, clicked a few times, and then came around the bed to face her.

"Thank you. You've made this so much easier. We thought we'd have to kill you and the couple who adopted your kid, and that would have been a huge mess. But if nobody else knows who the parents are and the parents don't know they bought the baby illegally, then we're good. We just need to get rid of you."

Carla stared up at him, too scared to move. They hadn't checked the burner phone for messages. She prayed Nick wouldn't text back. At least not now. What would happen to Christopher if they killed the adoptive parents? How would they kill her? When would they kill her? Would anyone even know she was dead? Phoenix is a big city. Bodies must surface all the time. Would she be two paragraphs in an online newspaper, years from now, with a small headline that read *Unidentified Body Found in Desert*, or would they make it look like suicide and leave her body to be found right away? Would she die a crazy woman who had been traumatized by kidnapping and couldn't live without her missing son? No, she had to stop thinking that way. Maybe they would take her somewhere else. Maybe she could escape or get someone's attention along the way. She could breathe through her nose, but it wasn't enough. She needed more air. She had slathered Chapstick on her lips when she returned from the store to protect herself from the hot sun and dehydration. She was glad of that now. She could feel gaps at the top and bottom of the tape with her tongue. She needed to gain control. She needed to calm down just like she did when she called the doctor's office. Panic would do no good.

But the first man wasn't done talking.

"When you are trying to sneak away unnoticed, you need to remember

178

that someone might have been following you from the beginning. That was your mistake. A lot of people would lose some serious income if you had screwed this up for us. Our regional representative made a poor decision buying a baby from a kidnapped mom. That's not the way we do business. We steal or buy them from unfit mothers—drug addicts, homeless women, that sort of thing. But too many people care about babies like this. Our man won't be a problem anymore, though. He can't talk to the police if he's dead, can he?"

He stopped and stared at her a moment, like he was letting it sink in, the fact that he had killed before.

"I sent your son's new parents a message, too," he said. "I apologized and let them know that you made a mistake. Their son was tested at birth, which is why he was not available for adoption as an infant. The agency kept him in its care until the results came in, and then ordered follow-up tests to be sure. So, they won't be looking for any paperwork either."

The man with the gun seemed to be trained to do nothing but guard her. He was silent. He just stood there with no expression, keeping the gun pointed at her while his partner talked. It would be hard to escape him.

"On a positive note, your boy brought in a lot more money than most. Blue eyes, blond hair, chubby little legs, and belly. A lot of the babies we get are thinner than they should be. Some of them are addicted. They need to be weaned and nursed through withdrawal before they are sold. Some of them die, and we're out the money, if we paid for them. Your boy was perfect. He was an easy sell and a profitable one. You made the boss happy."

The gunman shifted his weight from foot to foot as his partner spoke. His forehead was beaded with sweat. So, he wasn't so calm and collected after all. Maybe he didn't want to do this, Carla thought. Maybe he would let her go. She stared at him, hoping he would stare back, that maybe he would look into her eyes and feel something, but he didn't even seem to see her. His eyes caught hers and dismissed her. This was just a job.

"We have to get moving," he said. "Somebody might come nosing around. Do your thing, and let's get her out of here."

The first man pulled a case of some kind from his pocket, opened it, and removed what looked like a hypodermic needle. She fought to rise up from the bed, but he shoved her back down easily with one hand and laughed. She tried to scream again, but before she could make another sound, he forced the needle into her arm. The second man approached her with the gun and pointed it at her head.

"Shut up, or you die right here, right now." His eyes shifted from her to the door and back again. "How long will this take? I don't like this. What if they come looking for her? To hell with this. Just throw her in the trunk."

"Relax," the first man said. He pulled the desk chair up next to the bed and sat down, popping his feet up close to her head. "Ten or fifteen minutes at the most. We can't lug her out of here fighting us. It'll attract attention. If we're quiet, nobody will see us. I checked it. No cameras on the rooms. Just the office. A place like this doesn't want any evidence to give the cops. It's bad for business. The boss wants this clean. No evidence. No body left behind."

He tapped his foot against Carla's head to get her attention.

"You've been sunburned before, right?" He took his feet down and leaned forward, his face only inches from hers. " With that pale skin of yours? This will be just like that, except you won't need any aloe when we're done with you. There won't be anything left to rub it on. No skin, no muscle, no brains even. Nothing but a few bone chips."

Carla threw her head up and smashed her forehead against his. He reared back, holding his hand to his head, and she thought he might punch her. In her mind, she begged him to hit her. She begged him to kill her with his fist. She begged her heart to explode or her brain to give up, or the second man to shoot her in the chest or the head. Anything but what he was planning. Instead, he laughed.

"Go to sleep," he said, relaxing into the chair again.

She writhed and struggled to free her hands while they watched. Then, suddenly, she was tired. So tired. Her legs and arms were getting heavy, and so were her eyelids. She couldn't fight it any longer. She heard the first man telling the second to bring the car around. The last thing she saw was that smile again.

Chapter Thirty-Seven

Nick called Sawyer the second the text appeared on his phone, and within half an hour, FBI agents were in the house, confiscating his phone, making calls from their cell phones, and scouring Carla's office for who-knows-what. In a matter of minutes, they had access to her fake Facebook profile, which she had created from their home IP address. He was floored at their efficiency. But the air in the room had changed in the last few minutes. Something was wrong. People were talking in hush voices outside and around corners. Nick was no longer included. He grabbed Sawyer and pulled him aside.

"What's going on? What's happened? You have to tell me, Sawyer. I lost her once. I can't lose her again."

Something must have happened to Carla or to Christopher or both. They couldn't do this to him. They couldn't leave him in the dark. Was Christopher dead or gone? Were they too late? Nick tightened his grip around Sawyer's arm, and Sawyer cast him a warning with his eyes. He released his arm and took a step back. Sometimes, he forgot Sawyer was a cop.

"Come on, Sawyer. I have a right to know. This is my wife and son we're talking about."

Sawyer's voice was cautious and reluctant.

"Apparently, they found a Facebook message that doesn't make sense, like it came from someone other than Carla. Whoever wrote it said Carla was mistaken, that the baby was tested at birth and didn't inherit the health problem. But the adoptive mother confirmed the boy in the photo is Christopher, so she had the right kid. It doesn't make sense for Carla to say that. If the woman gets the message, she might cancel the doctor's appointment, and Carla won't be able to locate her. Maybe Carla had a good reason, but there is concern that someone else sent the message and that Carla might be in danger. The text she sent you is helpful. It left a digital trail. The FBI has already used triangulation to trace the burner phone to a general vicinity in Phoenix, and agents are waiting for the call to zero in on the location. You and I can't trace burner phones, but the FBI can. They will find her, and they'll find her fast."

Nick felt the heat rise up through his body and into his cheeks. He wasn't going to stay put and do nothing. If his wife was in danger, he needed to be there. He needed to get on the next flight to Phoenix. He grabbed his car keys and started for the door, trying to keep his back to Sawyer so he wouldn't see the pain he knew was evident on his face. The knife wound was healing, but certain moments triggered nerve pain.

"Where are you going, Nick?

"I'm going to Phoenix. What good am I here when she and Christopher are there? What if they find her? What if they find my son? I'm not going to make my wife and son wait however many hours it takes for me to get there and be with them. I want to be there when they are found."

An FBI agent, the man who seemed to be in charge of the investigation, stepped between Nick and the door and put a hand out to stop him. "Hold on. If you wait just a minute, I'll have one of our agents take you to the airport, walk you through security and get you on the next flight. You're right. You don't need to be here. We have your cell phone if she calls or texts, and the home phone is tapped. We're also monitoring her Facebook account, her fake profile, and your account. We'll have someone meet you when you land. If you stay with the agents, you'll always know what's happening. Now, why don't you grab a toothbrush and fresh pair of underwear or two while I find an agent to take you?"

Nick was prepared for a fight, not assistance. He couldn't seem to find his voice, so he simply nodded and started up the stairs. The agent called after him. "Nick. We have enough information to find your son. That's one piece of this you can stop worrying about. She did good work," he said.

Nick stopped on the stairs and dropped his head to his chest.

"Thank you," he said softly without turning around. "Thank you."

The next flight departed from Rochester in an hour and thirty minutes. They would barely make it. But the agent flew on the rural roads and took the highway at ninety miles an hour. He passed a state police car once, and the cop followed them with flashing lights. But then the cop backed off. Maybe it was the license plates. Maybe somebody radioed the driver. Nick didn't know, and he didn't care. He was grateful. He didn't need to know anything more. They came to a stop in the semi-circle in front of the main doors. A man in a suit was waiting. He led Nick to the pre-cleared security line, where he flashed a badge, and they were allowed to pass. Thankfully, the Rochester airport is small. They were at the gate within two minutes, and a flight attendant escorted him on board without ever asking for a ticket or a boarding pass. Then she slammed the door shut, and the pilot fired up the engine. They had held the flight for him an extra ten minutes. He never would have made it without the FBI's help.

Nick had stowed his backpack under the seat in front of him for take-off, but now he pulled it out and unzipped it, allowing his fingers to feel its contents. The agent said they had enough information to find Christopher, maybe even tonight. He had packed Christopher's favorite blanket and a t-shirt Carla often wore to bed that still smelled of her, along with diapers one size bigger than he wore when he disappeared, two spare outfits, an empty bottle, and some powered formula they had been given as a sample when he was born. Would Christopher remember him, or would he cry for his adoptive parents when they took him away? How big was he now? Was he crawling, starting to walk? He closed his eyes and tried to rest, but rest wouldn't come. The anticipation of finding Christopher, and the mood in the house, the sense that Carla was in danger, overwhelmed him. Nick was scared, but he couldn't deny that he was angry, too. He'd almost lost her once. He thought she was dead and that he was going to die. But that didn't happen. They were both alive and healthy, and Rachel was dead. The FBI was looking for their son. They were confident, and Nick was hopeful. Then she pulled this. She could have filled him in. She could have shared her plan with the FBI. She could have taken him along. But she didn't trust anyone, and now she was in danger again. He couldn't do this again. He couldn't lose her twice. He opened his eyes and tried to focus on the people around him. Distraction was safer. Distraction kept the pain and anger at bay.

Chapter Thirty-Eight

For a moment, Carla thought she was a little girl again, that she'd fallen asleep in the car on the way to Virginia Beach for summer vacation. It was hot and dark, but the movement of the vehicle beneath her body was comforting. But as the grogginess faded and her eyes opened fully, and she struggled to move, she realized she was in the trunk of a car with her hands still tied behind her back and the duct tape still on her mouth. Her breath came hard and fast as she remembered the men and the gun and the tape and the first man's words. He was planning to burn her, to leave nothing behind. She needed air. She had to get out. She couldn't breathe. She tried to sit up, but her head met the top of the trunk with a thud when the car passed over a bump. This wasn't helping. She forced herself to calm down and assess the situation. They were moving fast, probably down a highway. The trunk was roomy. She felt a slight cross breeze, so she knew it wasn't completely airtight. As long as the heat didn't kill her, she wouldn't die in here.

The man had tied her hands quickly. She had struggled to get free, but she might have better luck if she thought it through and worked with the rope. The rope was slightly loose, but only slightly. They were not very smart. She knew that when they failed to check the texts on the cell phone. She squeezed her palms together, flattened her fingers against each other, and rubbed them up and down until one hand came free. Her arms ached, and the rope had burned into her hands from the rubbing, but everything worked—wrists, fingers, and all. With her hands free, she ripped the duct tape off her mouth, thankful that it hadn't adhered to her lips. She felt along the trunk. There had to be an emergency release somewhere. She had done her research when she got pregnant. They were required in all cars made after 2002. But they were usually made of glow-in-the-dark material, and nothing stood out in the darkness. She didn't feel anything where it should be either. These guys had probably done this before. They would have known better than to leave the release intact. She felt along the wall that separated the trunk from the back seat of the car. It was metal. There was no way she could push down the seats and slip into the vehicle. They would catch her anyway and either kill her on the spot or drug her and tie her up again. There had to be another way.

That feeling washed over her again, the same crushing feeling she had when she was trapped in Rachel's basement and couldn't imagine any way out. She wanted to die, to get it over with. She wanted to give in to the helplessness and exhaustion and make it all stop. She wanted freedom from all of it, whatever the cost. For what felt like an eternity, she lay there, curled up like a baby, rocking her own body and soothing herself with soft moans, trying to push thoughts of flames eating her flesh from her mind. But then the car slowed down and startled her. The slow-down was brief, maybe a bit of a traffic jam, but it was enough to shake Carla out of it. The men might succeed. They might kill her, but she didn't have to make it easy for them. She picked a starting point along the wall and floor of the trunk and felt carefully, methodically, moving along the perimeter. She could feel wires under the floor. That might come in handy. Maybe she could disable the brake lights and get them pulled over. Then again, maybe someone would crash into the car from behind because she had disabled the lights, and she'd be killed or severely mangled. That didn't sound pleasant. Still, it was a possibility. It was a better way to die.

Her hands reached the sidewall, and her fingers tripped over something. A latch. She turned the latch, removed the cover, and felt inside. It was a tire kit—a lug wrench, a lever, and a jack. A jack. This could work, but only if they didn't drive off into some isolated patch of desert, where they'd shoot her and burn her before she could get help. Her hands trembled as she pulled it from the compartment and slid over to make room for it on the trunk floor. She prayed that it would extend far enough. Carla reached around in the compartment again until her hand rested on the jack arm and then ran her fingers along the jack, searching for the hole to insert it in. There it was. She inserted the arm into the hole and rotated the arm to the right, like she'd been taught so many years ago in driver's ed. The jack began to rise.

Carla turned and turned and turned the arm until it wouldn't rotate any further. This wasn't going to work. There was still a space of about six inches between the flat top of the jack and the roof of the trunk, and then she would need a few inches more lift to do any serious damage. She felt around the floor, looking for protrusions, but the only differences in floor height were in areas that were to the side of the trunk hatch. She reached into the compartment again and pulled out the lug wrench. It was the cross type. Good and solid. If she rested it in a standing position on top of the jack, it might give her enough height. But she would have to balance it perfectly. Otherwise, the pressure might send the wrench flying right at her.

She lowered the jack slightly and balanced the lug wrench. It was a struggle to keep the wrench steady while lying on her side and rotating the arm. Her muscles still ached from the ropes, and her arms were tiring easily. Twice, she had to lower the jack again and reposition the wrench, but finally, it caught. She rotated a little more and pulled on the wrench. It wasn't going anywhere. This part was crucial. The trunk might just bend and never break, or it might break with such force that it caught the attention of the two men. She kept working, checking the wrench now and then to make sure it remained in place. Her arms and shoulders burned, but she pushed through it. Then, without warning, the wrench tumbled down and struck her on her wrist. She let go of the jack arm and felt a tug on the trunk hatch. It was air. She was holding the trunk shut with her right hand. She did it.

Carla ignored the pain in her wrist and grabbed the trunk frame with her left hand as well. She allowed it to open slightly and lifted the hatch just enough to peer out. They were traveling on a four-lane highway, but there were no other vehicles in sight and only a few scattered buildings. If she jumped out now, there would be no one to rescue her or to call the police. They could easily chase her down. Or she might be badly hurt and unable to run. She would have to wait and hope they still had a way to go before they reached their destination or that they would need to stop for gas or a bathroom or food. But if the car slowed down, even for a minute, she would have to take the chance. There might not be another.

Chapter Thirty-Nine

The FBI agents barely knew Carla, and Nick was already gone, so when they decided to reply to Carla's text, they handed Nick's phone to Sawyer. He could feel the excitement in her words as he read them. She had found their baby. Christopher was within reach. The phone was their best hope for communicating with her kidnappers, and by now, they knew she was kidnapped. Whoever replied as Carla on Facebook had deleted her account, the post, and the message, but deleted accounts never really go away. They also used her laptop to message the adoptive mother, which allowed the FBI to obtain a location on the IP address. The account had been accessed through the WiFi of a small motel in downtown Phoenix.

The manager said he considered calling the police. He thought he recognized Carla from a recent missing persons site, but she was supposed to have a baby with her, and he didn't see a baby. She also didn't seem distressed in any way, not any more so than his usual customers. He was still mulling it over when he saw a light blue sedan park outside her room and watched two men get out. They knocked on her door and went in. He kept checking now and then until they left about twenty minutes later. The last time he looked, one of the men was shutting the trunk. He swore he saw a figure inside it, and when he knocked on Carla's door moments later, no one answered. He didn't dare go in, he said. It was always possible he was wrong—that she was a prostitute or was dealing drugs and that he might get himself killed. But he did get a partial plate. An FBI agent found Carla's purse and laptop in the room, but the burner phone was gone. The FBI was pinging the burner to get a location, but it could take up to a dozen tries and, even then, it might not be accurate.

An agent by the last name of Chen held the phone out to Sawyer.

"If they saw her message, they are going to expect a response. And, if they don't get one, they might know we're onto them," he said. "Just write what you think Nick would write. If she sees the text, we need her to believe it, too."

Nick would be excited, but worried. He wouldn't want Carla to take matters into her own hands, and he wouldn't be thrilled that she wanted to make this decision without him. He was Christopher's father. He had a right to be part of it. He was overthinking it. He needed to react like he would if he didn't know something had already happened to her. Sawyer drew a deep breath and started writing.

Carla, please don't do anything rash. Call the police. Let them help. What if something happens to you or to Christopher? What if it's the wrong baby, and you get yourself arrested? Please call me. Tell me where you are and what you know. I'd do anything to get our baby back. You know that. But we have to be careful. We have to do this right.

Sawyer showed the message to Agent Chen, who nodded. Then he pressed "send." It was a waiting game now—waiting for the cell phone geolocations, waiting for a reply to the text, waiting for someone to recognize the car and the partial plate, waiting for an emergency subpoena for the pediatrician's records, waiting for the pediatrician to cooperate without further legal action, waiting for their analysts to find "Belinda Ann" based on her posts and her Facebook friends, waiting for the feds to find the baby. Waiting. The longer they waited, the more likely Carla was already dead, and the more likely the parents would flee with Christopher.

Sawyer texted Heather and told her he would be home late. He hoped tonight was a good night, that she would feed the kids something healthy and get them to bed at a decent hour. He shouldn't have to worry like this, worry that his kids were safe with their own mother. She'd been better since they had talked, but it wasn't enough. She was there, but she wasn't there. It was time for a serious talk and time for her to see a therapist. If she refused, he would have to move into his parents' house with the kids. They didn't know what was going on. They'd been on vacation for two weeks and had only been back for a few days. When they asked to come over with their photos and with souvenirs for the kids, he told them a stomach bug was making its way around the house and that he didn't want them to catch it. He didn't want to take the kids away from Heather. He loved her. But he couldn't force her to get help either. He needed to feel confident that his kids were safe with her. Maybe the thought of losing him, of losing the kids, would be the incentive she needed.

He reached his hand into his pocket and pulled out the copy of the note found on Leland. There was nothing he could do right now for Carla and Christopher, but he could focus on Leland's case. He thought about what the doctor, Dean Mills, had said about leaving things alone. The way he said it, something about his tone and the look in his eyes, bothered Sawyer. He knew something, and he was warning him to back off. Sawyer had thought Dr. Mills was different from the other men who gathered for coffee each morning on Main Street. Maybe it was because of his profession or his education, or maybe it was because he lived in a community that was only ten miles away but might as well be located in a different universe. Maplewood Falls was old, established, and tight-knit. Children were born here and died here, just like their parents and their grandparents before them. Strangers who relocated here didn't bring new life into the community. They were sucked into the politics and the culture, lulled into conforming. He had always thought of Dr. Mills as an outsider, not someone who would feel compelled to conform, to be loyal beyond reason, and protect the community as a whole. But he'd forgotten that Dr. Mills was born and raised here. His loyalty was with Maplewood Falls from birth. He was just like the rest of the morning coffee crew, brushing off crimes as family embarrassments or mishaps that should be swept under the rug for the sake of reputation.

But this wasn't a barn break-in or slashed tires or teenagers drinking under the railroad bridge. This was a murder, brutal and intentional. If someone could do this to a harmless, wiry teenager, what else could they do? Who else might they kill? Maybe the suspect has killed again already. He tucked the note back in his pocket. It was time he and Dr. Mills had another conversation. Sawyer drew himself a cup of coffee from the Dunkin Donuts boxful someone had left on the kitchen counter. The mug was Carla's, a gift from the magazine where she worked. He was stirring in some cream when he heard a shout from the living room.

"We've got a sighting of the vehicle," one of the agents hollered.

Sawyer left his coffee behind and moved into the living room.

"It was spotted about an hour east of Phoenix, along the same route that the cell phone signals were leading us. The driver said he noticed the trunk lid was bobbing up and down a bit, and he was going to pull alongside the driver, but then he saw what looked like a hand holding it from inside the trunk. So he pulled over and called the police instead. He got the plate. It matches the partial, and so does the make, model, and color," the agent said. "That was half an hour ago. Local police haven't found it yet, but the sheriff's department has a helicopter in the air."

A hand holding it from inside the trunk. If that was Carla, she was still alive. But how much longer? Where were they taking her, and how close were they to their destination? Sawyer leaned against the wall and took a deep breath. Nick didn't need this kind of play-by-play action. He'd been through enough. Maybe it would be over before he even landed, but would he be happy with the ending?

Chapter Forty

Carla's arm ached from holding the trunk shut. She was terrified she would lose her grip, and they would see it flopping up and down behind them. She could hear music coming from inside the car. She hoped it was loud enough to cover any noises she made. Where were they going? She wished she'd done a little more research or even looked at a map before she arrived in Phoenix. Carla had no idea which suburbs were where and whether it was possible to drive for hours without passing through another well-populated community. Her muscles had not yet fully recovered from whatever drug they had given her, and her leg still burned where the bullet grazed her skin. Would she even be able to run if she got out?

She didn't have much time to think about it. The car slowed suddenly and made a sharp right turn, throwing her off balance. So, this wasn't an interstate. There were at-grade intersections. That could be a good thing. That might mean that roadside houses and businesses would eventually be within reach. By the time Carla regained her balance, the car had picked up speed, but it was still moving more slowly than it was on the highway. She peeked out and saw what appeared to be a complex of empty office buildings and warehouses. They were fairly new, like someone gambled that the population would creep in this direction but lost the bet. She saw no signs of life or activity. This must be where they planned to kill her, where they planned to shoot her and then burn her body. Or maybe they planned to burn her alive so they wouldn't leave any blood behind. No one would hear her screams way out here. Her stomach wrenched, and she nearly vomited.

She couldn't let this happen. She needed to keep it together. She could jump out, but then where would she go? No more thinking. If she didn't jump out, she would be dead anyway. She had to take that chance.

She guessed the car was going about twenty miles an hour now. Still not slow enough to avoid injuries, but she couldn't wait any longer. They would probably be stopping soon, and if they pulled into one of the warehouses or a garage, she would become trapped. Her chance would be gone. She figured her best option would be to roll out, cradling her head in her arms. That would help prevent a head injury and save her from the instinct to reach out and break her fall with her arms, which would probably also break a bone or two. She closed her eyes for a moment and took a deep breath. In one awkward movement, she let go of the trunk, slid one leg over the edge, and then heaved herself out of the car, hitting the pavement with her shoulder first. In the moment it took to stop rolling and recover her senses, the car disappeared. It must have turned a corner, but which way? She stood and forced herself to run to the nearest building, despite the blood trickling down the side of her face, her shoulder, and her leg, and the searing pain that came with it. She leaned against a wall and took a quick inventory. Her blouse was shredded and soaked in blood on her right side, and she didn't even want to touch her cheek and ear. The pavement had burned her leg, too, right through her capris, and her knee throbbed. But the rest of her body seemed to be intact. Nothing broken. Nothing that would kill her any time soon. Her heart was beating so loudly, she could hear nothing else, but her senses were working in overdrive. She took in her surroundings and did a quick evaluation. On the opposite side of the road, she saw several large, one- and two-story buildings. Maybe old factories or warehouses. The buildings on her side were smaller—sprawling with narrow, winding two-lane roads connecting them and landscaped with cacti and desert shrubbery. This side appeared to be an office park, and its configuration and landscaping offered more places to hide.

Her kidnappers had probably figured out she was gone by now, and they were clearly in good physical shape. They must also be familiar with the complex, or they wouldn't have brought her here. She had to get moving fast. Carla decided to go deep and then hide, hoping they would assume she would take the first hiding space. Then again, they might not know exactly where she jumped out, and she had no idea where they had planned to stop. For all she knew, she could be running toward them. But wouldn't it be more practical to kill a person in a warehouse rather than in an office park? She guessed they had turned in that direction.

She couldn't let fear rule her now. She needed confidence that this was the right direction. She had no choice. So, she pushed her doubts deeper into her gut and kept moving, slipping among the buildings, behind dumpsters, and around overgrown bushes and cacti, and pausing every now and then to listen for footfalls or a car engine. It was so quiet here. Every sound was amplified. The false alarms were wearing on her—a road runner darting across the gravel, a hawk swooping in for its prey, a rattler warning her to stay away. All of these creatures and their noises stopped her heart until she discovered their sources. Between structures, she caught a glimpse of the highway, but it had to be at least a mile away, and the stretch between the highway and the buildings was wide open. That direction was a death trap, at least during the day.

The sun was lowering in the sky, and the air was beginning to cool. She was thirsty, tired, sore, and exhausted by the surges of adrenaline. She would have to try to remain hidden until nightfall, conserving her strength and her fluids, and pray there was no moonlight, a wish that was unlikely to be granted given the undisrupted swath of deep blue above her. She sank down into a gap between a wall and a short staircase leading into a building, where she was shielded by a couple of low shrubs, knowing this was the kind of place where they would look. But what could she do? The desert didn't lend itself to games of hide-and-seek. She had been so close to Christopher, so close she could almost smell him again. Maybe this wasn't the life she had envisioned ten years ago, but she and Nick had made Christopher together, this gorgeous creature who had her hair and his eyes, and Christopher was worth fighting for.

Carla closed her eyes to picture her son and found it hard to open them again. She was running out of adrenaline, and it left exhaustion in its wake.

She couldn't do this. She couldn't let herself fall asleep. She would have to move again, to someplace where she could stand and stretch and maybe pace. She stepped out from the shrubs slowly and in a crouch, taking in her surroundings from this new perspective. The landscape was more barren than she realized, and the setting sun cast shadows on the dirt, gravel, and concrete. A full moon was already visible and rising. She might be easier to find in the dark than she was in the daylight. Every time her eyes located potential hiding places, she thought of the men and realized they would also see those places and see the potential in them. The anxiety was crippling. She needed to hide, but she was afraid to hide. She needed to make a decision. Now. She turned to evaluate the spot she'd crawled out of once again, and that's when she saw it. A slight crack at the base of the window she'd crouched beneath. She had tried several doors and windows throughout the complex, but they were all locked. If this window wasn't fully closed, there was a chance the lock had not engaged.

The window was only a few feet off the ground. Carla reached for it and pushed, hoping and praying no one would see her stretched-out body against the building. The window started to give, but it was slightly cockeyed, which was probably why it didn't close all the way. She jiggled and forced it and gained another inch or so in the opening, cringing and stopping to look around every time it made a noise. She could do this. Maybe there would even be a working phone inside. She could call the police. Carla threw all her force into it this time, pushing up on the top of the lower pane's frame, and being careful not to grunt or groan. It gave a little more. Now, she could put her hands underneath it and pull up a bit. She got into position, squatting to give herself more leverage, and rose up, pushing with everything she had. The window opened so fast she nearly stumbled backward. She regained her balance and moved toward it, ready to climb in headfirst, but her celebration was cut short. A hand clamped over her mouth and a strong arm wrapped around her arms and chest. She tried to scream, but nothing came out.

Chapter Forty-One

It was newly dark when the plane landed at Sky Harbor International Airport in Phoenix. Nick couldn't get off the plane fast enough, and he was grateful to find another FBI agent waiting for him at the gate. These guys were efficient, and they were the only people with information. Without his cell phone, Nick had no way to communicate with Sawyer or anyone else to find out what was going on. The distance from the gate to the airport exit seemed endless, and the airport was a sea of business travelers with rolling carry-ons and cell phones going to their ears, athletes arriving for matches, families on vacation. The FBI agent, who introduced himself as Scott Dunham, led him through the crowd to a sedan parked illegally along the curb. He talked while they buckled in.

"We have an approximate location on the car," Dunham said, "and we are closing in. We are also getting records from the pediatrician's offices. We should have names and an address for your son's adoptive parents shortly. Is there anything you need? I've got protein bars and water on the back seat."

"I can't even think about food right now," Nick said, though he reached for one of the waters. "Where are we going? Are we going to where you found the car? I want to see Carla. Is she okay?"

"We can't do that. The cell phone signal shows that the car stopped in an area of about three square miles at a location pretty far east of here, and we know there were two men with her. We don't want to jeopardize the search. My hope is that they will find her long before we can even get there. I thought I would take you to Scottsdale, where we believe your baby is, so you can take custody of him as soon we find him and confirm that it's

197

Christopher. We're hoping to get him tonight. Very soon, in fact. We'll still have to do DNA testing, but I am guessing you will know your baby when you see him."

For a moment, Nick couldn't catch his breath. This was real. This was happening. He was going to get Christopher back. When Christopher and Carla first disappeared, the whole situation felt surreal. It overwhelmed him to a point where he couldn't imagine ever having a normal life with his wife and child again. But his son was alive and well. Christopher was here in Arizona and might even be in his arms within a few hours. When Nick spoke again, he could feel the tremor in his voice.

"How far is it?"

The agent navigated the airport traffic with ease. Nick was glad he didn't have to think about any of that. He could not possibly have focused on driving with his head this messed up. He would have wrecked or been pulled over by now.

"It's about forty minutes more or less in this kind of traffic. We're heading to the Scottsdale police department. They are working with us to end this as peacefully and as quickly as possible. The adoptive parents will be questioned and possibly arrested. We don't know whether they fully understood the adoption was illegal, but they must have known something was up. We're still trying to get more information, but their bank records show they paid twice what they would for a legal adoption, and according to the mother's Facebook posts, they got the baby within a month. Most people wait years for a private adoption of a white infant. That's probably what attracted them to this operation."

Before Nick and Carla started trying to get pregnant, they discussed how far they would go if they ran into medical problems along the way. Carla wanted to be sure they thought everything out before they even got started. They agreed that the first level of drugs was the limit. There were too many babies out there in need of homes, especially in foster care, and they didn't want to risk having multiples with other, more invasive methods. They also didn't want to drive themselves bankrupt, paying for the costs of fertility treatments insurance might not cover. Carla suggested going through Social

Services should they have to adopt. Nick was reluctant at first. He worried about the legal mess and about the possibility that they would come close to adopting a foster child they had become emotionally attached to only to lose the child to a parent who suddenly turned her life around. What if a grandparent or an aunt or uncle surfaced who wanted custody? But then Carla showed him articles about the process, how Social Services only placed children whose parents were likely to lose or waive custody with people looking to adopt. She showed him how much less expensive it was than private adoption and how unlikely the parents were to step back into their children's lives. When he expressed concern about alcohol and drug use during pregnancy, she reminded him of her own college friend who lied to Catholic Charities about smoking pot during her pregnancy and the three times she got so drunk, she thought she might have killed her baby.

"There are no guarantees either way," Carla said.

And just like that, he was convinced. Having a backup plan took the stress off both of them while they tried. It took only three months for Carla to get pregnant, and Nick had to admit that his excitement was tinged with disappointment when he saw the plus sign on the test. The idea of adoption had grown on him, and it was hard to let go of. What if these people had explored their options more? Would Carla and Christopher have been spared, or would someone else have paid the same amount or more to take him? Then Nick remembered Rachel. Maybe he should be grateful to these people. Rachel wanted Christopher out of the way. If she couldn't sell him, she might have killed him. They offered her money, and she was greedy. If not for this organization, Christopher might be dead.

The thought made Nick nauseous. He rolled down the car window and breathed in the dry desert air. He had always wanted to visit Arizona, maybe do some hiking in Sedona or Flagstaff and take in a few spring training games for the Majors. See the Grand Canyon and check out the Native American historical sites. But this was not how he imagined his visit. He wasn't sure whether he would ever want to return after this. As they drove, he stared at the saguaro cacti that lined the highway, standing guard with their prickly, green arms held high, reaching for the stars. Carla was out there somewhere, breathing in this same air. Was she scared? Was she safe? Was she hurt? He was still angry with her. She put herself in this position. She could have confided in him and asked for help. But he still loved her, and he wanted her back.

Finally, Dunham turned off the highway and onto a four-lane road lined with stucco-covered houses that all seemed to look the same. It was hard to imagine Christopher growing up here in such a different environment. What would he have been like? Would he be different from a boy raised in Western New York? After a few blocks, the buildings became more commercial, and they turned into the parking lot of the Scottsdale Police Department. More waiting, Nick thought as they stepped out of the car and headed toward the doors. He wasn't sure he could take anymore. They were almost to the entrance when he was distracted by a commotion around the corner of the parking lot. He pulled away from Dunham, drawn by sounds of wailing and distress. As he rounded the corner, he heard Dunham call to him, but he couldn't answer. Four officers and a couple of plain-clothes men, FBI agents or local police, were escorting two handcuffed people into the building, a man and a woman in their late forties or early fifties. They were yelling at the officers and yelling at each other. The woman was wailing and threatening to sue.

"He's ours. We have the papers. You can't do this."

The air was thick with desperation. Nick couldn't take his eyes off them. He was confused, torn between beating them both to a pulp and wrapping them in his arms, assuring them it would all be alright. He knew what it was like to lose a baby. But his feet wouldn't move. Then he felt a hand on his shoulder, urging him to move toward the police station's front doors.

"You don't need to see this," Agent Dunham said. "Come with me."

Chapter Forty-Two

Carla tried to bite the hand that covered her mouth, but it was useless. She couldn't sink her teeth into him. She kicked at his shins, but he bent backward and lifted her in the air. She twisted and turned but couldn't get enough force to do any harm. This was it. It was time to die. She would be a pile of ash, easily swept away. No one would even find her.

"Carla, you have to calm down," the man whispered in her ear. "I'm with the FBI. I'll take my hand off your mouth, but you absolutely must be quiet. We are still looking for your kidnappers. They are here in the complex, and we'll find them the same way we found you, with infrared technology. But we can't have you scaring them away. Do you promise you will be quiet?"

Carla stopped kicking and nodded her head as he released his hand. She sucked in the air and struggled to breathe normally. He still had an arm around her, which was good, because she felt her knees go out from under her. She wasn't going to die. He was an FBI agent. She was safe. She was really and finally safe. The tears came without sound and without warning.

"My baby?" she asked as quietly as she could manage.

"He's at the Scottsdale Police Station with your husband. The couple is in custody. I need some information from you, though. This is important, so I need you to focus. The motel clerk and a person who spotted the car on the highway said there were two men in the vehicle. Is that right? Were there more?"

Nick and Christopher together. It was over. It was done. She wanted to close her eyes and collapse right there. She had nothing left. No energy. No emotions. She needed to see them. She needed to see Christopher in Nick's arms, but the agent was waiting, and the men were out there. She wasn't free yet.

"Carla?"

"I'm sorry. There were two men at the motel, but I was unconscious when they put me in the trunk of their car. That's where they put me, in the trunk with my hands tied behind my back. I got out of the ropes. Then I broke the latch and rolled out when they slowed down in this complex. As soon as I hit the ground, I got up and ran. I never saw them after the motel. Not even a glance."

She rubbed her wrists, which were raw and burning.

"They killed him," she said. "They killed the man who bought the baby."

"Okay. We're going to stay right here until I receive word that the men have been captured or at least cornered. We don't want them to know we are looking for them, so we can't attract any attention. You were smart to run in this direction. They are on this side of the complex, but we believe they are closer to the north end. They might have found you eventually, but it would have taken a while. We've got about twenty people—FBI and sheriff's deputies—combing the place. They won't get away."

The agent moved with Carla over to the steps of the building and helped her sit down. Twenty people were here in this complex searching, and she didn't even know it. How could she possibly have protected herself from the kidnappers? But Christopher. He said they had Christopher. Her baby and husband were together right now. The relief that washed over her drained her completely. She rested her head against the agent's shoulder and, right there in the complex with FBI agents and sheriff's deputies hunting down the two men who were hunting for her, she nearly fell asleep.

But she sat up straight when she heard gunshots in the distance.

"Take cover," she heard over the agent's radio. "We've got one in custody, but the other is headed in your direction, and he is armed. Repeat. He is armed."

Carla was wide awake now and terrified. She had let herself feel safe. That was a mistake. She and the agent stood at the same time, and he pushed her toward the open window. "Get inside and lie down on the floor away from any windows. We'll get him, but you need to stay out of the line of fire."

They heard a shot again, and this time, it was closer.

"Forget it. There's no time. Lie down in those bushes."

She did as she was told while he crouched in front of her, partially hidden by the stairs. The lull of silence was as frightening as the gunshots. What if he came from around the corner from the opposite direction? Would the agent see him on time? What if he shot them both dead? The sun had set by now, and the moon had fully risen. It was like a nightlight in the sky. They would be able to see him, but he would be able to see them as well.

Then they heard it, footsteps falling hard and fast on the pavement. They grew louder and louder, and they didn't hesitate, not even for a moment. Another set of footsteps followed behind him, but more steadily, more carefully. The movements echoed among the empty buildings. Carla lifted her body slightly and peered out around the agent to see a man running in their direction, silhouetted by the moonlight with what looked like a gun in his hand. The man twisted his upper body, slowed down a bit, and fired behind him. Carla watched in horror as the agent rose from his position, lifted his gun, and pulled the trigger. The silhouetted figure crashed to the ground with a sound Carla would never forget. Everything was quiet for a moment. Then another man appeared out of nowhere with his gun drawn and began walking slowly toward the crumpled figure. The man on the ground didn't move.

"Put your hands where I can see them," the approaching agent hollered. "Do not reach for your gun, your cell phone, or anything. If I see you with anything in your hands, I will shoot." But the man still did not move. He was either unconscious or dead.

The agent who found Carla motioned for her to stay back and walked forward in the same manner with his gun drawn. It wasn't long before the complex was lit by flashlights and the headlights of squad cars. A few of the cars turned on their flashing blue lights, casting an eerie glow about the buildings and the desert landscape. An ambulance had been waiting nearby and was already on the way. Carla moved back to the stairs, where she put her head in her hands and tried to process all that had happened. They had found a pulse on the man, who had been shot in the abdomen. He apparently lost consciousness when his head hit the pavement, but he was beginning to stir. No one made any attempt to comfort him or tend to his wounds while they waited for the ambulance crew.

Finally, they carried him away on a gurney while sheriff's investigators marked the spot where he fell and took photos of the scene. One of the medics came to Carla with water and a space blanket and asked whether she was hurt.

"I'm fine," she lied. "I just want to see my baby."

Her injuries could wait.

Chapter Forty-Three

Only three agents were in the house when the call came that Carla was found alive and well and that her kidnappers had been apprehended, but the eruption of hoots and hollers that followed made it sound like a crowd. Sawyer sank into Nick's recliner and breathed deeply. The baby was with Nick at a Scottsdale hotel, and he appeared to be healthy as well. It was finally over. Sawyer decided he would stay at the house for a while and make sure the agents cleaned up after themselves and then go home. Maybe he would even get some sleep.

But as he prepared to leave, Sawyer felt a rush of adrenaline. The sun was up, and the day was warm. From Nick's stoop, he watched people pass by—a teenage boy walking a dog, an older couple power walking side-by-side, a woman running while pushing a stroller. He doubted word had gotten out yet about the night's events, but it felt like a celebration, and he wasn't ready to return to the darkness of his own home. He reached into his pocket and pulled out the grocery list Heather had left on the dining table the morning before. Her list was short, just the bare necessities. He would go to the store and get some pancake mix, bacon, and fruit and whip it up for dinner. The kids loved having breakfast for dinner, and he would make it tonight after a good, long nap. He had waited long enough for Heather to recover from her funk, and the kids were suffering because of it. He needed to make some changes in their lives, and he needed to start now.

It was eight o'clock when he pulled into the Tops plaza parking lot, but he noticed that the neon "open" sign at Zane Williams' jewelry shop was brightly lit. There were no cars parked in front of the store, so he decided to stop in. It would take only a few minutes, and his family was not expecting him at any particular time. He would sleep better today knowing he had at least done something on Leland's case. He still wanted to talk with Dean Mills again, but that could wait one more day.

Zane's father was known throughout the area for his custom-made jewelry, but his steady income came from repairing watches and changing their batteries. Zane joined his father twenty-five years ago, right out of high school, and apprenticed with him. He repaired everything from watches to grandfather clocks and was as much an artist as his father. But by the time Zane's father died, that part of the business had been reduced to a drizzle. Watches were no longer necessary pieces of jewelry that were made to last a lifetime. We had become a culture of time-telling cell phones, smartwatches, and Fitbits, devices that require more technical knowledge than mechanical expertise. And more and more people were buying custom-made jewelry from websites like Etsy, where Zane also sold his art. So Zane evolved his business, slowly at first, and then more rapidly over the past seven years. He still carried custom-made jewelry, but he also sold fitness watches, smart watches, purses, and wallets. He had been talking about moving his business to Main Street, where it might attract passing tourists. Many of the purses and wallets he carried were handmade by a local artisan. He was thinking about adding locally made soaps, honey and syrup as well.

"Good morning," Sawyer said as he pushed open the door and stepped inside. Zane was behind the counter, arranging silver rings in a small glass case. The shop was cramped. It was definitely time for Zane to move.

"Morning, Chief. What can I do for you?" Zane asked, looking up. "No pawns or suspicious appraisals lately, if that's what you're after. You look a bit like hell, by the way. Long night?"

"A long night, but a good one," Sawyer said. "Carla Murphy and her baby are safe and will be heading home soon, and the bad guys are in custody. We've got some good leads on the whole organization, too. It doesn't get much better than that."

Zane gently closed the glass case and came around the counter to shake Sawyer's hand. He clapped him on the back hard enough to make Sawyer cough. "Well done, Sawyer. That's some great news, alright. Can I get you some coffee? I brewed a fresh pot half an hour ago. I'm thinking about getting one of those machines that make lattes and all that stuff. People will pay a lot for a good latte."

"No, thank you," Sawyer said. "I have a question for you, and I know this is a long shot. About fifteen years ago, just before he died, Leland Boise bought a necklace as a gift. Nothing super expensive. An amber heart framed in silver. I'm asking around, trying to find out where he got it and whether anyone knows who it was intended for. I know chances are slim that you'll remember anything, but do you? Could he have bought it here?"

Zane laughed.

"How could I forget? The kid paid in pennies, dimes, and wrinkled dollar bills. It was probably the sweetest thing I'd ever seen. He wasn't sure what he wanted when he came in, but then he laid eyes on the necklace, and he was determined to buy it. My father even gave him five dollars off because he was short, and he never gave discounts. The kid said the amber matched his girlfriend's eyes. He said they were super dark, but they had these bright flecks of amber that he couldn't help staring at. We both figured he ran off with the girl when he disappeared. My dad would be heartbroken if he knew he was dead. Kind of ruins a good story."

Sawyer felt the blood drain from his face. Slowly, he pulled the grocery list from his pocket again. Then he called up an image of the note found in Leland's pocket on his cell phone. There was no doubt. No wonder the writing looked so familiar. His hand shook as he returned the grocery list to his pocket.

"Hey, man. You okay?" Zane asked.

"Yeah." Sawyer closed his eyes and struggled to recover. "I haven't slept in thirty-six hours. It's getting to me. This wasn't the best time to have this conversation. How about I come back tomorrow?"

"Anytime. Are you going to be okay driving home? You look kind of pale."

"Thanks. I'll be fine. It's just a short drive." Sawyer tried to keep his voice level and light. "I can't believe you remember that from so long ago. Did he tell you who his girlfriend was, or did you figure it out?"

207

"Nope." Zane picked up a leather purse and blew the dust off it, returning it to the display. "He was awfully coy about it. With a kid like him, it could have been a crush he'd never even spoken to. He was quiet, you know? I guess now we'll never know who she was."

"It's too bad, Sawyer said. "He was so young. Thanks for the help. Enjoy the day if you can. It looks like it's going to be a good one."

Sawyer wasn't sure how he got from the shop back to his car or how long he had been sitting behind the wheel. The nausea was overwhelming, and his eyes seemed incapable of comprehending anything he saw. Heather's funk wasn't triggered by Carla's disappearance. It was the discovery of Leland's body that threw her off-balance. But his skull. It was crushed with so much violence. So much hate and anger. Was she capable of that? His own wife? The mother of his three children? Why would she do something like that? Did she kill him, or was someone else involved? Were there any other bodies that might surface soon? Who was this woman he married?

He had to pull himself together and get home. He was hyperventilating, and the lack of oxygen was affecting his alertness. He forced himself to breathe and to see his surroundings. Then he started the car and drove slowly, aware that he might not react as quickly as he should to any obstacles in his way. He ignored the people who waved from the street or from passing cars and focused on the most important thing: getting home.

Heather's car was in the driveway when he arrived, but no other vehicles were there. The two older kids would be at the YMCA program, thanks to the sitter who had been picking them up for the past week. Only Heather and their youngest should be home. He had no plan, no idea what he would say to her. It occurred to him as he walked up the front steps that he could keep this to himself. State police didn't know about the necklace, and he hadn't written a report yet about his interview with the Ellises. There was no record of it. No one would have to know. But then he pulled open the front door, and there she was, in shorts and a baggy t-shirt, balancing a laundry basket on her hip. He couldn't hide it. She looked into his eyes and dropped the basket, sending the clothes tumbling about the floor. The sound that came from her throat was not human. She looked so helpless, so defeated.

He pulled her into his arms and held her shaking body, and they stood like that for what seemed like an eternity.

Chapter Forty-Four

The police had brought Carla's belongings from her downtown room to the Scottsdale hotel, where she had been holding Christopher for hours on end, relinquishing him to Nick only when she needed a bathroom break or when he demanded a moment with his son. They told her to sleep—Nick, the FBI agents, the woman from Social Services—but she couldn't bear to put him down or let him out of her sight. He was heavier and more alert than he was when Rachel took him away, more aware of his surroundings than she remembered. He smiled more readily, and his giggle was addicting. He loved Cheerios and applesauce, and he no longer reached for her breast. He had been exclusively bottle-fed for too long, but he knew her instantly. There was no denying that. Christopher had not forgotten that she was his mother and Nick was his father. He buried his face in her neck when she held him that first time, and he didn't seem any more willing to let go than she did. The bond was still there, probably stronger than ever.

She had cried all that she could, so there were no more tears. Carla had refused medical attention. It didn't seem like anything was broken, and her cuts, bruises, and sore muscles would heal. She just wanted to go home. FBI agents, local police, and sheriff's deputies had been in and out of the room the entire time, all wanting to get their own portions of the paperwork done and filed as long as she insisted on staying awake. Carla identified the kidnappers from photos. but she didn't have to. The man who was arrested first, the one who was not injured, confessed to police immediately, giving up names, locations, and contact information for his employer, including a physical address. He eventually gave the FBI details on the whole operation, explaining that regional cells operated throughout the country, reporting to headquarters in Colorado, where his boss lived in a ten thousand square-foot house with two pools, a personal chef, and not as much security as they would expect. They had been operating successfully for at least a decade. His boss wasn't worried about getting caught.

The kidnapper's name was Sam. He was the one holding the gun, the one who was sweating because her kidnapping was taking too long. Sam was inspired to confess more fully by the fact that his partner was also in custody and might rat him out. The investigators made it clear that the person who gave them the most information would get the better deal, but they neglected to tell him his partner died in surgery two hours after he arrived at the hospital. The FBI planned to move in on the head of the organization quickly for fear he would flee the country, but they had a lot of work ahead of them even after they captured him. Who knew how many babies had been sold or snatched and illegally adopted? How would they ever find their biological parents? Should they even be returned to their biological parents? Many of the mothers apparently gave their children up willingly in exchange for cash.

Sam told the FBI their operation routinely took babies from homeless women, especially those who were mentally ill or drug addicted. They looked for women who were unlikely to report it for fear that they were somehow at fault or would get busted. Sometimes they bought the babies for a few hundred dollars from desperate addicts. One father sold his daughter for ninety dollars. Some cost ten or twenty thousand, but they could sell them for a hundred thousand or more, especially the youngest ones. Babies could not be sold within the region they came from. They tried to place them as far away as possible to avoid recognition in the future. The deal with Rachel was negotiated by the boss' cousin, who had been a thorn in the organization's side for years. He thought his status as a relative gave him free rein. He bought the baby without approval and then set up the adoption on his own. They had planned to kill him even before the FBI became involved just to teach others who might go rogue a lesson. He gave them details of the killing, claiming his partner pulled the trigger.

"He didn't see anything wrong with their operation," Dunham said. "They took babies away from unfit parents and put them in good homes. In his mind, the kidnappings were justified and honorable. He figured they weren't hurting anybody if they made money off the deals. The fact that they killed the boss' cousin and tried to kill you, well, that's just part of doing business. We are still trying to decide whether the adoptive parents broke any laws when they adopted Christopher. These guys set it up to look pretty legitimate. They explained to their clients that the exorbitant cost was due to higher fees for faster processing. The couple had been rejected by two other agencies because of their ages, and then they found this agency online. They are both nearly fifty. It is quite possible that they had no idea."

Carla shuddered to think how close she had come to losing Christopher forever. What if no one had responded to her Facebook post? Would they ever have found him? The police or the FBI might have gotten a tip that led them to Christopher years later, but would he even want to come home at that point? The older he grew, the more attached he would have become to his adoptive parents. It was easy to take him back now, to shut those people and their emotions out of her mind, but could she have done that if Christopher was nine or ten or eleven? Even a few months more, and he wouldn't have remembered Carla and Nick as well. She pulled him a little closer and kissed his feathery baby hair, taking in his scent once more. She couldn't get enough of him. She never would.

Carla could not bring herself to have any sympathy for the couple. She wasn't ready for that. She was grateful they had cared for him so well, but she wanted nothing further to do with them, and she couldn't bear the thought of them ever touching Christopher again. She wanted to leave Arizona and go back home, where they couldn't reach her. She wanted to put Christopher in a blow-up kiddie pool and watch him splash in the water in the backyard. She wanted to watch him crawl and hold his hands as he practiced walking on his tiptoes. She wanted to name everything for him and listen closely to every bit of babble, waiting for that day when the sounds formed a word. She wanted to put the past behind her and move forward, but she couldn't help noticing her visions for the future did not always include Nick. She loved him, but she was no longer sure she loved him enough.

She looked at Nick, who was curled up on the bed, fast asleep for probably the first time in more than a month. When he was asleep, the resemblance to Christopher was even stronger. If they ever separated or divorced, Christopher would have to bounce between two households. The courts would force her to give him up, at least some of the time. She couldn't do that. She couldn't stand to be apart from Christopher, and she couldn't bear to take him away from Nick, not even just for a day or two at a time. She remembered what Nick had said about the conversation he'd had with that reporter. The reporter told him these situations often ruined marriages because spouses blamed each other. He told Nick that he and Carla needed to talk, to communicate their feelings to each other. That was good advice. She needed to change her mindset. She needed to remember what she loved about Nick and their life together and work to get that back. She would not let Rachel victimize her again.

Carla stretched out on the bed, facing Nick, with Christopher between them. Christopher was tired, too. He was restless for a moment, struggling to sit up and roll over, but then his movements slowed, and he curled into Nick. She watched his flushed face as his eyelids fluttered, the final fight to stay awake and experience every moment of life. She caressed his cheek as his eyelids closed and stayed that way. His body relaxed into sleep. Despite all that she'd been through, Carla couldn't help thinking about how lucky she was. She smiled and fell into a restless sleep.

Chapter Forty-Five

The air was cold by Orlando standards, but Sawyer wore short sleeves anyway. He was still new to the southern climate, and he wanted to enjoy it. Never in his life had he imagined living in Florida, but Orlando was a big city with plenty of transplants. That meant fewer questions and the ability to live in relative obscurity. The kids were adjusting well to their new school and daycare, and Heather seemed happy for the first time in months. Their new house came with a pool and a hot tub. She had taken to swimming laps each morning and evening, and the exercise seemed to help. Therapy would have been ideal, but that was not an option. Patient/client privilege does not apply to murder.

His new job paid far more than the police chief position, though it was nowhere near as fulfilling or exciting. He was a senior supervisor for a security service that employed more than five hundred people. The higher-level position allowed him to work days with only the occasional late-night or weekend emergencies, and the benefits were excellent, but he spent most of his time in an eighth-floor office on International Drive, sitting behind a desk. The height of his office gave him an advantage, though. He had a clear view of the parking lot and would see the men in suits coming to whisk him away before they entered the building. He was always looking for them, always on edge. It was only a matter of time before someone figured out that Heather had killed Leland and that he had helped cover it up.

A knock on his open office door made Sawyer's heart jump, forcing him to turn his attention from the parking lot. It was his assistant, Jay, a criminal justice student who attended night school.

"Hey. I'm going to Starbucks. Want anything?"

"I'm good. Thanks."

"You sure?"

"Yeah," Sawyer said. "Too much caffeine already today."

Jay shrugged his shoulders and walked away. Sawyer did want coffee, but he was careful not to become too close to anyone in his office. Too many ex-cops on staff. Coffee could easily lead to drinks after work, and drinks could lead to invitations that included Heather. She wasn't ready for that. Not yet. When he first put it all together, that morning when he confronted her, she didn't speak at all. She simply shut down. Over the next few days, she offered bits and pieces but nothing more and only on her own terms. A week went by before she finally told him the whole story, and that had given him time to think.

Heather told Sawyer she had been seeing Leland before she killed him, but she didn't love him or even like him that much. She was a virgin, and she didn't want to be. She was working at the ice cream stand on the outskirts of town that summer, and the owner was too cheap to double up on staff, even in the evenings, even after the stand was robbed at closing time the previous summer. Leland was her last customer one night. He offered to stay while she closed and walk her home. He was cute in his own way, she said, and he wasn't the type to brag. She decided then and there that he would be the one, but she knew she would have to take it slowly. She didn't want to scare him away.

So, she lied. She told Leland her parents would not let her date and that her father was abusive. He would beat them both if he caught them, she said. That's how she convinced him to keep their liaisons secret. She hadn't intended to keep it up so long. She had planned to break it off with him as soon as she got some experience, but he became attached, and he was less timid than she thought. He started suggesting ways to talk to her father, to win him over. And then came Sawyer. Heather said she fell in love with Sawyer the moment she met him, and that gave her the courage to break up with Leland. He didn't take it well, but who was he going to talk to? He had no close friends, at least none at school. She wasn't worried that he would go public about their relationship, but then she missed a period. After she missed a second one, she took a pregnancy test, and it came back positive.

Heather didn't want to tell Leland about the pregnancy, but she had no choice. She couldn't afford an abortion on her own. She had already spent all her earnings from the summer, and if she waited until she saved more from her babysitting jobs, she would be too late. And she wasn't about to tell anyone else. So, Heather told him, expecting him to pay for the procedure, but he didn't offer. Instead, he got excited, insisting he would keep the baby with or without her help. She didn't know what to do. She told him neither of them could afford a kid, but he said he would drop out of high school and get a job.

"Then he told me about his grandmother's money, how she hoarded it and would keep hoarding it until the day she died. You should have seen him, Sawyer. You would have thought it was millions. He said he would inherit it all when she died and that it probably wouldn't be taxed because it was cash. He thought we would be rich," Heather said. "He really believed it. I couldn't convince him I didn't love him, that this was never going to happen, no matter how much money he had."

That was when Heather came up with a plan. She told Leland her father would beat her if he knew about the baby and kill it, and maybe kill her, too. She suggested they take his grandmother's money and run away the next night when everyone was asleep. She told Leland she knew of someone who would sell them a car for a couple thousand and that they could probably live in Buffalo or Cleveland or somewhere like that on the rest of his grandmother's money while they looked for jobs. The idea was to take enough money for the abortion and leave him standing there, brokenhearted. He bought it, but things didn't go as planned.

"Sawyer, he wouldn't let go of me," she said. They were sitting on the back porch after the kids had gone to sleep. She had been silent for a long time, so her words startled him. He wanted to look into her eyes, but she was staring at something far away, and she was so still he didn't dare disturb her.

"I told him the truth. I told him I had used him for sex and that I wanted four hundred dollars for an abortion. If he didn't give me the money, I was going to tell his grandmother about the pregnancy and make her pay for it. He grabbed me by both arms and called me a liar. I'd never seen him so angry. He said it was the hormones, that I was just scared, and that I needed to come with him. I didn't mean it. I pushed him, and he hit his head on a rock or something. I didn't mean it. I didn't mean to kill him, and I didn't know what to do once I realized he wasn't breathing. I panicked."

She said she ran back home and got a shovel afterward, that it was almost dawn before she finished. She covered the freshly tilled ground with a few boards and other scraps, so it wouldn't be so obvious. It rained hard that morning, helping to level the mud and smooth the area. She sneaked back into her house, showered, and went to school like nothing had happened. The police never would have thought to look there. They had no reason to suspect he was buried near the warehouse. She had an abortion the next day. Dean Mills was the doctor, but he assured her the procedure was confidential and that he couldn't tell anyone. So, she felt safe.

"As long as his body was hidden, I could pretend it was a dream," she said. "So that's how I got through it. I pretended it never happened."

But she didn't know what Sawyer knew. She didn't know the first thing about forensic science, that even an untrained eye could tell the difference between a skull that was fractured during a fall and a skull that had been bashed in repeatedly. She didn't know that he knew the ground where she buried him was hardened with clay and that it was obvious she would have had to work for several nights in a row to dig a hole deep enough. She didn't know a lot of things, but by then, he had made his decision.

Sawyer had gone over and over the options in his head. If he turned her in, the kids would lose their mother to a prison sentence of twenty years or more. The evidence would show that the murder was intentional and well-planned, not an accident. His own career would be over because who wants a police chief or even a cop whose wife is a killer? Raising the kids with no money, no mother, and the stigma of their mother's crime would be a struggle. They would always be worried that they had inherited that gene, a gene that allowed them to kill. He loved his kids too much for that.

He could keep her crimes to himself and divorce her, but he wouldn't be able to tell the judge the truth, the real reason he was divorcing her. She would win at least partial custody, and he wouldn't be able to keep an eye on her to make sure she never killed again. What if she hurt the kids? What if she became violent with someone else and put the kids in danger? She could also blackmail him with the fact that he didn't turn her in if she wanted anything from him or, worse, she could kill him to get him out of the way. Divorce wasn't a feasible solution either. She had already proven what she is capable of.

So, he did what he thought was best. He told his own lies. He assured Heather that he believed her and that he still loved her, and in his own way, he did still love her. She gave him their children, and he would be forever grateful for that. He told her they would move far away and never have contact with anyone from Maplewood Falls again, with the exception of their families. He left public service to get out of the public eye. Both sets of parents were upset. The kids are young, and their grandparents looked forward to being involved in their upbringing. But both her parents and his were already looking at winter living options in Florida. They would be around for the most important family holidays—Thanksgiving and Christmas. They might not ever have to go back to Maplewood Falls at all.

His relationship with Heather was not the same. The revelation of guilt seemed to affect Heather deeply, despite her lies. Unless she was faking that, too. He couldn't imagine ever making love to her again or sleeping at night without the help of medication. But the plan was working, and that was the important thing. They were a family, and the kids were healthy, physically and emotionally. He could support them better than he had before, even saving for college and retirement. They were fortunate, but he hadn't counted on this, the constant burden of fear, the paranoia. Whenever he was tempted to let down his guard, he remembered those who did. The Nazi war criminal who was arrested in his eighties in a comfortable suburb. The Russian spies who hid from the law long enough to have children and grandchildren who were American citizens. The killers and rapists who were identified by DNA tests decades after their crimes when newer, more sensitive tests were developed. Letting down his guard was not an option. Paranoia was the side effect of his new reality, but it was not entirely unwarranted. Dean Mills was still out there. Dean Mills performed the abortion. Under doctor-patient confidentiality laws, he could not divulge the fact that he aborted Heather's pregnancy, but there were ways to leak that information. And there were other staff members who might suddenly remember Heather's procedure—the nurse, the receptionist.

Sawyer's cell phone buzzed. The video cameras were down in a hotel in Miami, and the chief of security could not get a response from the vendor. Did he have permission to contact an outside technician? Distraction was how Sawyer got through each day. He would find that vendor if he had to drive to Miami himself, and he would get one of their technicians there if he had to escort him at gunpoint. He was not in a mood to be messed with. Not today.

Chapter Forty-Six

The sidewalks were wet with melt from the icy, condensed snow along their borders. The trees were barren of both snow and leaves, but the exposed grass below had started to evolve from dull brown to the green of spring. Carla walked the familiar streets with only a sweater protecting her from the early April air, but Christopher toddled beside her in a jacket, fleece pants, a hat, and mittens. She didn't trust the weather enough just yet to peel his layers off and set him free.

The car was packed, and the movers had already left for Queens. Nick was at the house, doing a walk-through with the tenants and giving them the keys. They were a nice couple, young and newly married with no children. She hoped they would be happy there. She hoped they would spend summer evenings on the porch, talking about their pasts and their futures, their hopes and their dreams, their individual wants and needs. She hoped they would keep talking and listening through the fall, winter, and spring and for the rest of their years together, like she and Nick should have done. She hoped they would always be happy.

They were doing better, she and Nick. Therapy helped at first, but time helped even more. With some distance, Carla could understand the pressure and confusion Nick had endured, and she could see her own role in it. Rachel had manipulated them both, preying on their weaknesses. If Carla wanted to harbor anger, her anger should be directed at Rachel, not Nick. But she didn't want to be angry anymore. Anger was exhausting and so she had made a conscious decision to let it go. But the whole experience had awakened her. She had not been herself for the past decade. She had slipped into Nick's dreams and become a character in them, shelving her own. It wasn't his fault. She had been complacent. They had a shared dream once, but they were still children when they started dating, and children change as they mature. Carla saw that evolution in Nick. The more he experienced life, the farther he drifted away from Carla. So she compromised again and again and again to stay close to him, leading him to believe that she wanted the same things he wanted. He had no idea she was unhappy with the trajectory of their lives, and neither did she. She had pushed that discontent so far down that she'd become numb to it. But that was about to change.

"Hey, Carla!"

From the porch across the street, Carla saw a hand wave and a figure make its way down the steps. She had barely known the neighbors who lived this far down the street before the kidnapping, but she and Christopher were local celebrities now. It seemed everyone wanted to forge a connection of some sort with them, mostly for the sake of gossip rights. That was another reason to move. Western New York was foreign territory to most city dwellers. Chances were slim her new neighbors in Queens would know of her. The figure, Susan Maher, stepped into the sunlight and rushed across the street. She was breathless when she reached her.

"I hear you're moving, and just when I was getting to know you better."

Susan was among the few people who did seem to genuinely want to become part of Carla's life. They just hadn't been aware of each other before the kidnapping. So many others reached out but pulled away if they sensed Carla and Nick might take them up on that offer of coffee or playdates or "dinner sometime." They wanted to know them, but they didn't want the baggage that came with friendship. Not their kind of baggage, anyway. Susan wasn't like that.

"Yes, we're leaving in a few minutes, actually," Carla said, guiding Christopher from the curb across the sidewalk and onto a lawn where the sun had dried the greening grass. "But we're not selling the house. We are renting out our house and renting a house for ourselves in Queens. If it doesn't work out, we'll be back."

"Queens?" Susan stood, hands on wide hips, ignoring the wisps of dark hair that brushed across her face. "Why Queens? You're both from here, aren't you? I would think you'd want to be around family at a time like this."

Carla had learned to avoid the full answer to that question, so she gave the abbreviated one she had practiced. "I got an offer we couldn't refuse, a full-time senior editor job at a magazine for working moms. Nick made Tony manager of the store. Nick will oversee it from afar and come up once a month or so to check on things. He's thinking about going back to school, too. The sciences, maybe."

Susan winced, and then smiled. A sad, slow smile.

"I don't talk about it much, but I had a bit of trauma of my own in my life."

She sighed and shifted her focus to something far beyond Carla. Carla turned her attention to Christopher, who had discovered the joy of crunching the remaining snow mounds with his tiny boots. He crunched and giggled. Crunched and giggled. If only life could always be so simple.

"When this stuff happens, and you start to emerge, everything looks different," Susan said. "You examine your life from a new perspective, and you believe deep in your soul that you were blind before, that this is the real thing, that you are finally seeing life clearly. You make decisions you think are sound based on this new vision of reality, but reality is not stable. There is no one real vision. Life is always colored by perspective and perspective changes with experience. You can't really know your decisions are sound until the shock wears off, and it takes years for the shock to wear off."

She drew in a deep breath and focused on Carla again.

"So, I'm glad you're keeping the house. I'm happy you're leaving, that you're giving the city a try, and I honestly hope it works out. But keeping the house, that's a good idea. Let me know if you need anything."

She reached out and pulled Carla into a hug.

"Thanks, Susan. I wish I'd gotten to know you sooner. I'll send you my contact information as soon as we get settled. If ever you are down in the city, you have a tour guide and a place to stay."

She slipped from Susan's embrace and offered a warm smile. A car horn sounded from far behind her, Nick's signal that it was time to go. Carla scooped Christopher into her arms and said one final goodbye to Susan. The air was fresh and clear. The sky was a perfect blue. She would miss this place, no doubt, but she had a good feeling, and as she walked along the sidewalk toward Nick and the waiting car, that feeling grew stronger. Maybe they would regret this move. That was always a possibility. Maybe Nick would regret it and return on his own. But Carla doubted she would. She felt solid, strong, and sure for the first time in more than a decade, stronger even than before the kidnapping. The kidnapping changed her in ways she couldn't explain. She couldn't imagine she would ever truly feel safe again, and she still had a hard time trusting anyone else with Christopher, even for just a few minutes. Nick would stay home with Christopher for the first few months and take online classes, but he couldn't stay home forever. That wouldn't be fair to him. She would have to learn to cope, but she knew now that she would learn to cope. She knew she was doing the right thing for Christopher and for herself, and probably for Nick, too.

Carla took one last look at the house with its broad porch and well-tended lawn. The memories there were good ones for the most part. She didn't regret the past, but she was anxious to face the future. She opened the car door and buckled Christopher into his car seat. She'd kept him up past his nap time. He would sleep a good two hours at least. She closed the car door, and then slipped into the front seat next to Nick, buckling herself in. He smiled at her, and she closed her eyes as they pulled away from the curb. She had no desire to look back.

A Note from the Author

I hope you enjoyed *Never Let Go*. Feel free to contact me at lori@loriduffy-foster.com with any questions. Reviews are greatly appreciated it you have a few minutes to spare.

Acknowledgements

There are two kinds of people I lean on when I am writing a novel: those who offer direct input, sometimes reading multiple versions of a novel, and always giving concrete feedback; and those who support me as an author, always asking about the next book or the status of my career. Many people do both. I am lucky in that way.

My husband, Tom, has read *Never Let Go* so many times, he can probably recite it by heart. If it exhausts him, he never lets on. Our family would benefit financially if I gave up on writing and took a full-time, salaried job, but he doesn't push me in that direction. He has always lifted me up when I have wanted to give up. I couldn't do this without him, and I can't thank him enough.

My sister Angela Bader, to whom this book is dedicated, and my brother Andy Duffy have both read all my first drafts and have provided great feedback. Their critiques are invaluable as is their support. I am fortunate to have support from all my siblings—Dave, Jim and Ed Duffy, and Patricia Bardua—and from my sister-in-law, Karen Zinck. My sister Kathy Riley left us before I finished this novel, but I know she would have been happy for me. I miss her always.

Special thanks to my stepdaughter Kelly Foster, my aunts Kathleen Lahue and Dolores Martin, my cousin Kelly O'Leary and my dear friend Georganna Doran. I appreciate you all more than you will ever know. Then, of course, there are my kids—Riley, Kiersten, Matthew and Jonathan. They are all I could ever ask for. Their unconditional love and support fuels me every day. I am proud to say that all four are fantastic writers. I hope they never lose that passion for the written word.

I owe a huge debt of gratitude to the Dames of Detection—Verena Rose,

Shawn Reilly Simmons and Harriette Sackler, co-owners and editors of Level Best Books. You believed in this book and gave it life. Thank you. The authors of Level Best are a cohesive and selfless group, always reaching out to support and promote each other. I am fortunate to have that connection with them.

Every author needs a tribe. I have found that sense of community in my fellow Level Best authors, but also in Sisters in Crime, Pennwriters, Mystery Writers of America, International Thriller Writers and Private Eye Writers of America. If you are a writer, I encourage you to seek out a similar group and join. You will not regret it.

Finally, I want to thank all the readers, reviewers, librarians and booksellers who have supported me since my first book was released. My books have connected me with some awesome people I might never have met otherwise. You are the heart and soul of this industry, and you have made me feel welcome and at home in this world. Your passion inspires me.

With so many people to thank, I am sure I have left someone out. For that, I apologize, but know that you are in my heart.

About the Author

Lori Duffy Foster is a former crime reporter who writes from the hills of Northern Pennsylvania. *Never Let Go* is her first standalone novel. *A Dead Man's Eyes,* the first in her Lisa Jamison Mysteries Series, was a Shamus Award finalist and an Agatha Award nominee. *Never Broken*, book 2, is now available and *No Time to Breathe*, book 3, releases in April of 2023. Lori is a member of Mystery Writers of America, Sisters in Crime, The Historical Novel Society, International Thriller Writers, Private Eyes Writers of America and Pennwriters.

SOCIAL MEDIA HANDLES:
  Facebook @loriduffyfosterauthor
  Instagram @lori.duffy.foster
  Twitter @loriduffyfoster.

AUTHOR WEBSITE:
  www.loriduffyfoster.com

Also by Lori Duffy Foster

A Dead Man's Eyes: A Lisa Jamison Mystery, #1

Never Broken, A Lisa Jamison Mystery, #2

CPSIA information can be obtained
at www.ICGtesting.com
Printed in the USA
BVHW081906231222
654914BV00002B/207